THE MAGIC FORM OF THE EXPRESSIONLESS

THE MAGIC FORM OF THE EXPRESSIONLESS

E O'SULLIVAN

Emmet O'Sullivan

ONE DAY, IN A WARM MUSTY ATTIC, A BIG RAT SCURRIED ALONG A WOODEN BEAM AND FELL PLOP INTO THE WATER TANK UNDERNEATH.

*

The shifting, morphing light of a world not here washed over the face of Keehan Dang. It was a grey evening in late August and the streets outside had seen the day's work and now lay sleeping lonely and desolate. Keehan sat in his favourite pair of knock-off Ray-Bans. Partly there, but mostly in that other world; watching himself on the screen as photographers called his name. "Keehan..." "Keehan..." "Over here Mr Dang..." He felt the buzz of admiration and the flicker of camera flashes all around him. Flash, flicker, flicker, flash. Flash? Flash?... Flash? He turned his head to look behind him. A blonde girl in a fake fur lined duffle coat had entered the room and was banging her open palm on a broken torch, sending momentary beams across the room before the light finally held. "What're you at?" Keehan asked, trying to regain his composure and come back to the world that surrounded him. "I think there's a rat or somethin' in the water tank," muttered Lisa still fiddling with the torch in an attempt to liven it up a bit. "James is tryin' to fish it out."

She switched the torch off and looked up towards the flickering screen in the corner of the living room, on which a host of glamorous Hollywood stars were parading gracefully down a red carpet. "What're ya watchin'?" she asked. Keehan had already grabbed the remote and quickly switched on to the next channel, and then the next, after a micro-second pause to affect an air of nonchalant browsing. "Ah I'm just flickin' through the channels," he muttered. Lisa smiled and eyed him quizzically, then turned to jog back upstairs.

Keehan, feeling the softness of dreams return to infiltrate his awareness once more, sank down in his chair and looked through the listings for something unchallenging to keep his senses occupied.

He came upon a late-night panel comedy show that he had seen before and had found pretty entertaining, so he clicked it on and settled back into his reverie.

About twenty minutes later Lisa came rushing back down the stairs, and Keehan, awoken once again; looked up to see James come bounding down behind her holding a Tesco bag at arm's length in front of him. Keehan watched the bag closely as though he'd read a glint in James' eye and sat tense and poised, ready to duck. Suddenly he felt something wet and furry on the back of his neck. He jumped up with a panicked gasp, arching his back, as he simultaneously brushed the back of his neck with the sleeve of his jumper and tried not to retch. As he vigorously swiped at the moist patch on the back of his neck while vainly trying to turn his head far enough around to see what was on it; one of Lisa's woollen gloves, now soaking, fell to the floor behind him with a wet slap. Keehan whirled around to look at the drowned rat carcass, still rubbing his neck clean, and immediately realised what it was. His panic and nausea ebbed away to be replaced by a mixture of relief and growing embarrassment as the reality of what had just happened became more achingly obvious. "Fuckin' pricks," he muttered as he kicked the glove across the room sending a light spray whizzing into the air and turned to slump back down indignantly in his chair and scowl at the TV.

Seeing the fun was over, James took the bag containing the rat to the front door and tossed it deftly into the neighbour's wheelie-bin outside which had been wedged open with the weeks refuse. He went back in to wash his hands in the kitchen sink before re-joining Lisa and Keehan in the living room. Lisa was leaning on the back of Keehan's chair, trying to entice a laugh out of him by sporadically tickling the top of his head whilst making a squeaking noise in his ear. Seeing that she was getting nowhere she eventually gave up and moved around to settle down on the couch beside James. He was leaning on his elbow, face in palm, with his legs dangling over the armrest and was flicking through the music channels with a growing sense of disillusionment. After traversing the whole section three times he finally dropped the remote and leaned his head back to relax for a moment as the black and white waves introducing Pearl Jam's Alive video washed across the screen.

The three sat and listened contentedly for the duration of the song, humming along to the words that had been indelibly printed in their minds, whether correct or not, and tapping their feet and fingers until the waves washed up again to signal the end of the video. The waves were replaced by the spiky, jarring guitar riff of some mediocre, soon to be forgotten band; their punk style outfits and black spiky hair cartoonish and vapid.

"I've been listenin' to Rearviewmirror a lot the last while," Lisa turned to James as he began to flick through the channels again. Keehan had gone into the kitchen to get another drink. "I remember coming across it once when I was a kid," she continued, turning back towards the TV and gazing at it with disinterest. "This one clip, I think it was off Saturday Night Live or something. Eddie Vedder was playin' guitar so there was like three guitarists and the bassist standin' there. It looked so cool." She tilted her head up slightly and squinted, as though if she tried hard enough, she could follow the track into her own memory. Looking to an invisible screen hovering somewhere between her and the wall in front of her, showing the clarified version of what was now just a cloudy mirage accompanying a vivid and beautiful feeling. "Don't think I ever saw it," James muttered, still looking at the TV. Lisa picked up a pencil sharpener that was laying on the table in front of her and began to play with it, turning it over in her fingers absent-mindedly as she continued to reminisce. "That was the days before YouTube as well," she continued. "Where like you'd come across a clip somewhere and you knew unless you taped it you'd probably never ever see it again."

The pencil sharpener dropped from her hands and bounced away with a click on the wooden floor. Hauling herself up slightly she pushed her feet against the coffee table in front of her and leaned back and down over the arm of the couch to grapple at it with her fingertips before picking it back up and turning back to the television. "I can still see it in my mind," she continued, "even though I only saw it once and I was like ten or eleven or something."

She reached over to place the sharpener back on the table in front of her. James emerging gradually from his stupor now twisted around to wrench his torso from its stasis, something in his body making a satisfying crack as he stretched his feet up onto the coffee table. "Yeah it's cool those little memories ya have," he replied in a continuation of Lisa's musing. "When I was at home, when we had no internet and no satellite..." He turned to her. "Remember I had that little telly in my room that could only get Network Two?" Lisa nodded, smiling with fond nostalgia at the quaintness of the times. James began to wriggle awkwardly as he tried to adjust the cushion beneath him, the corner of which was sticking jarringly into his ribcage. After a couple of attempts at readjusting; finally admitting defeat, he pulled the cushion out and threw it across the floor, as Lisa waited patiently to hear the rest of his memory. After a moment's pause to regain his train of thought, he continued, "Yeah, like so if ya wanted to see a film you pretty much had to just hope there was a decent one on that channel. Well, one night when I was like ten or something and was up really late I flicked it on and Before Sunset was on. I remember I thought it was so cool seein' this amazing foreign city and these two sophisticated people walking around talking about life and philosophy and stuff, even though I probably didn't know half of what they were talkin' about at the time." Lisa smiled. "I never knew what the film was," James continued. "Couldn't have told you who was in it, or what it was about, until a couple of years ago I came across the DVD in a shop; and for some reason, before I even watched it, I knew this was the film I'd seen. Even though I never knew the name of it and could only vaguely picture it in my mind anymore. I couldn't even picture it really; it was more like an impression." He ran his hand absent mindedly across the top of his head leaving a great tuft of hair sticking straight up that drooped straight back down under its own weight. "I wasn't even sure if I'd just dreamed it or something," he continued. "But once I watched it again I knew straight away. Without a doubt."

Lisa smiled to herself, basking in the fuzzy glowing and bittersweet comfort of reminiscence. "I love those little weird memories," she agreed dreamily. The room around her that had previously been so dull and suffocating was now shining into her with a precious and muted brilliance. "They make you feel kinda solid or something," she continued. "Like you're a part of everything."

Keehan was half-listening to them from the kitchen where he was attempting to cut an opening in a carton of orange juice and having great difficulty. The scissors, like most human designed implements of convenience in the world; had not been designed for lefties. He was taking a kind of morbid pleasure from this struggle though, as he always did. It was only more evidence to him that he was special, different from everyone else. *More creative and intelligent*, he had read one time in an article somewhere. Like Da Vinci, Alexander the Great, Kurt Cobain, Einstein.

He listened with a vague, intellectual curiosity to the others and wondered why anyone would *want* to be part of everything? Everything, for the most part, seemed like a pile of shit as far as he was concerned. Finding a way out of all the crap seemed like a more pressing concern. "You doin' anything tomorrow lad?" His drifting thoughts were interrupted by James calling in from the living room.

He finally managed to gnaw the corner off the carton, feeling the sharp tingle of aluminium on his teeth as he reeled away; just managing to loosen his grip on the container enough and in time so as not to squeeze a jet of juice all over himself. He spit out the stubborn piece of cardboard, picked up his glass and the carton and went in to join the others in the living room. "No, I don't think so," he replied as he sat down on the armchair opposite them and began pouring the juice into the glass. "I'm probably gonna head to my parents for a while in the morning." He reached underneath the coffee table and produced a clear glass bottle, and proceeded to pour a sizeable portion of vodka into the orange juice. He replaced the bottle on the floor and looked over at James to see if any elaboration on the previous question was forthcoming. "Why?" he enquired eventually, seeing that it wasn't. "Ah there's an openin' for the new library tomorrow," James replied, as he absent-mindedly leafed through an Irish Times newspaper that had been lying on the coffee table almost since they'd moved into the house three years ago. "We were thinkin' of headin' up and seein' is there any craic if ya wanna come." *A new library*, Keehan thought. *Well whoop-dee-frickin'-do.* "Naah yer alright..."

Shortly after eleven Lisa got up to go home. James, after seeing her to the door, said goodnight and headed upstairs to bed.

Keehan continued to sit drinking his vodka and watching

TV. He enjoyed the buzzing and the colours. As long as it didn't get quiet. When it got quiet then all he had for company were his memories and his aspirations. His memories which seemed to him to be becoming increasingly just a litany of misery, embarrassment and awkwardness; and a future that he knew deep down would most likely be nothing special, nothing really worth bothering about. And a bright, loud nothing seemed to him to be the preferable option to a quiet, defeated and productive contentment. So he kept his mind dancing, kept his heart alive in a world of abstraction, lost in spirals of re-interpretation. So far gone that it seemed like nothing awaited him in tangible reality now but fear and inadequacy and he had no other choice or no other aspiration than to keep spiralling. At one point he knew, he'd been looking for something definite. Trawling through the muck in the hope of finding the one thought, the one answer; that would make it all fall away and bring that feeling of living that had once come so naturally. Now he wasn't even looking any more. He was just chasing and playing with his own reflection, so accustomed to the world he had made that he was afraid to go outside, and wasn't even sure if he knew how to any more. He sat flicking flicking flicking through the channels as the night drew on, avoiding the moments before sleep when he must lay in the dark and quiet waiting for unconsciousness.

Finally unable to avoid it much longer, with the onset of test screens and TV marketing, he turned off the telly and threw the remote on the couch. He stood up and stretched and drained the remnants of his vodka and orange juice, leaving the empty glass on the coffee table to await him again tomorrow. He picked up his phone and slid it in his pocket and feeling stiff and muggy, began the slow climb up the stairs to bed.

As he approached his opened bedroom door he could see the contours of his bed picked out by the moonlight, which was streaking through the crack in the curtains: so he didn't bother turning on the light but half-stumbled, half-shuffled across the floor; hoping not to step on or fall over anything. Diving in under the covers he pulled the duvet up to his ears and writhed for a moment to adjust to the coldness of the cotton sheets.

His clock radio was on the locker beside his bed and he turned it on and turned the volume down low. Sufficiently warm and cosy now he allowed the muffled conversation on the radio to permeate his mind without really listening, and the words soon lost all importance as he gently drifted off, aided by the comforting sound of meaningless voices.

The next morning Keehan got up feeling groggy. He didn't seem to get hangovers like the way other people talked about them: no splitting headaches or churning stomach. Just a low-level and constant feeling of heaviness. A slight stupefaction accompanied by depression. He wasn't sure if that was just due to the fact that he drank nearly every day and his body had gotten used to dealing with it. Maybe it had become such a routine ordeal for his body that it was no longer necessary to produce anything so dramatic as a headache? He suddenly had to contend with the thought that popped into his head occasionally and with increasing frequency of late; that if his bodily organs were working at full capacity all the time to deal with this, then chances are they're going to exhaust themselves much earlier than they should in any normal, healthy, clean-living person. He began to feel a little sick.

He went down to the kitchen and poured himself a bowl of cereal and sat down at the table to eat it. As he ate, the morning sun and the increasing fullness of his belly combined to ease his grogginess and he began to feel a lot better. The clouds in his head began to dissipate as he slurped the remaining milk from the bottom of the bowl. After finishing his cereal and following it down with a small glass of juice, he got up to get changed and go catch the bus out to his parents house.

His parents -or rather his mother and his step-father; lived just outside the town, where the urban began to dissolve into the green expanses of the rural. There was a shuttle bus service that went twice a day and ran up the country from the town and back, that was used for the most part by old folks coming into town from the surrounding areas to do their weekly shopping. It stopped in town just on the other side of the road from Keehan's house and was just parking up as he pulled the door behind him and locked it.

After a half hour bus ride Keehan walked up to the house he grew up in and paused for a moment at the door as if about to knock, before pushing it open and stepping inside.

The house was quite old. Not lavish, but immaculately kept. The cabinets held rows of china plates lined up with the poised conformity of a fascist militia that looked down haughtily over the chipped pine table and its cheap cotton covering. He noticed there was a shiny new vase on the windowsill. On the wall opposite it was a framed painting of a vase. He looked around and felt like he came from nowhere. Like he'd just popped into existence and was now walking into a stranger's house without memory or purpose.

His mother Helen welcomed him cursorily before returning to busily searching through her handbag. His step-father Alan was in front of the living room mirror adjusting his tie and barely glanced sideways as Keehan walked in and sat down on the couch. "We're heading to mass at twelve if you want to come," his mother, still preoccupied, called in from the hallway. Keehan, already feeling awkward and out of place, was fiddling with a pen that had been lying on the couch on top of a half-finished crossword puzzle on the back page of the previous day's newspaper. "Mass, no, hardly," he replied, slowly and repeatedly clicking the nib of the pen out and back in again. Alan turned around to look at Keehan, his fingers still toying with the maladjusted Double Windsor. "Don't speak to your mother in that tone," he growled. Keehan felt he was talking more with the air of someone whose thunder had been stolen than out of any sort of genuine respect or consideration for his mother. "You should go to mass more often," Alan continued. "Might straighten you out a bit." Keehan was about to retort but the weight of the two of them and the whole environment held his spirit in place and he sighed and resorted to a feeble and disheartened "Yeah, maybe I will."

Alan turned back to the mirror to continue brushing the flecks off his lapels, and his lip curled up at the corner of one side in a satisfied smirk. Helen entered the room again, struggling to pull her massive fleece coat up over her shoulders.

"Well it's twenty to twelve, we'll have to be going soon. Are you staying here or...?"

Keehan pulled himself up off the seat. "Nah I'll head back," he replied, watching her button up her expensive looking jacket which for the mild weather they were currently experiencing seemed excessively heavy. He felt a slight up-swelling in his chest at the thought of his mother lugging this awful monstrosity of a jacket around for the admiration of people; most of whom would play no real role of any importance in her life beyond the occasional polite conversation.

Helen looked over at him, addressing him directly for the first time since he'd walked in. "Could you not have come another time, sure did ya not know we'd be going to mass?" Keehan was stabbing his toe sheepishly into the floor, just waiting now for them to finish getting ready so they could leave. "Yeah. I forgot," he mumbled, confused himself as to why that mainstay of his life; the constant weekly chore since the day he was born, had somehow not interjected into his mind at any point on the planning or execution of his journey. "I guess I forgot what day it was," he continued, realising the answer as he said it. "I'll drop back over tomorrow maybe." Helen rolled her eyes. "What are you going to do with your day?" she returned to fumbling with her buttons. Keehan pursed his lips and tilted his head to look thoughtfully into the distance, as if to demonstrate that he was in the process of scheduling some appointments but had yet to definitively rank them in order of importance. "Ah I've a few bits and pieces ya know, a few things to do," he replied finally, discovering nothing he could even pass off as a productive use of his time. Knowing that what he would most probably do was all he ever really did; namely drink vodka and watch TV.

Helen picked up her purse and checked to see if it contained some coins for the priest. "Have you looked into that job yet?" she asked, at this point not even vaguely expecting an affirmative answer. Keehan's job hunt had been undertaken with what could only be described as a listless indifference. He'd heard the sighing and complaining over the years; watched the continuing procession of zombified humanity trudging back and forth daily to sell their lives for savings accounts; and had even had some brief sporadic forays into working life himself until the economy had collapsed. Consequently he was less than eager to join the ranks of the full time employed. Helen had attempted to instigate some activity by contacting her friend Danielle, who had for some years been a neighbour of the Dangs' and had occasionally taken care of Keehan and his older brother Kevin as children. Danielle happened to work at Halton's department store in town, which was currently hiring cashiers, and she had gladly agreed to put in a word with the management for Keehan if he dropped in his CV. "Well…did ya?" Helen repeated.

Keehan winced with disgust. "Like fuck I did," he muttered to himself under his breath, before reeling back and adding more loudly, "Ahh yeah, I'm just finishin' off me CV now, I'll leave it in this week." He had neither a CV nor any intention of creating one. It infuriated him that he had to deal with all this crap and it infuriated him even more that everyone else seemed hell bent on arranging things for him. "Grand," Helen continued, realising that Alan was already in the car waiting to leave. "Sure drop over during the week and let us know how you get on." She opened the door and stepped outside. "You sure you don't want to come to mass?" she added, her attention already captured by Alan's face staring impatiently through the driver seat window of the car. Keehan grimaced. "No I'm grand thanks," he replied with such a controlled voice as he could muster. "I'll see ya's durin' the week."

He closed the door behind him and headed into the cool autumn afternoon. As the bus only passed twice a day and the next one wasn't until six, he set off walking.

No more than three cars passed by him in the space of an hour and it didn't take long for his mind to start running to fill in the gaps in entertainment. Drifting out onto the middle of the road and back again, he watched himself in states of privilege, striding around purposefully; awed gazes following wherever he went. He sat on the balcony of his opulent mansion, rich, famous and admired. Sunglasses on and sipping from a colourful drink as he watched Alan down below raking up the leaves in his dingy overalls; occasionally slipping in the dogshit –no not just slipping but falling into it. Maybe he'd slip in the dogshit then stumble into Keehan's huge swimming pool, splash around frantically for a while trying to regain his composure. Trying to avoid swallowing mouthfuls of water, before grabbing the side and hauling himself out, soaked to the skin. "I'm not paying you to act like a buffoon," Keehan would call out then and the four gorgeous women in bikinis sitting on the balcony with him would collapse into laughter. He walked along in a daze of furious dreaming, completely oblivious to the chestnut trees on either side of him which had scattered the road with conkers almost a full month earlier than usual. Lifted from the solidity of the earth and life he drifted into the clouds and back to the world of infinite possibility. Building towers of visions and ideas of shimmering whimsical complexity and absolute glory that real life would never touch. Keehan had been blessed with an active, agile -even impressively capable mind. But it had become prey to the follies of a broken spirit and the lack of any real hope in the benevolence of the universe: a private world created by loneliness and misunderstanding through which he dragged himself aimlessly, and used now merely to while away the hours and days; keeping himself entertained and sometimes soothed by the reality that fell to his whims.

CHAPTER 2

Monday morning. Keehan looked at his phone. Monday the first of September. Ten sixteen a.m. He lay back in bed and enjoyed the warmth of his cocoon. The weeks had no real end or beginning for him anymore. Not in a practical sense anyway. Every day was pretty much the same. Even so, Monday; for someone who no longer had to go to school and who didn't have a job, still held the same sense of beginning, for better or worse.

He lay for a while trying to think of a reason to get up. Starting something new was always fun; not knowing where it would lead. The vague sense of possibility swam in his mind for a short while without really catching as he auditioned prospects and novel ventures. Before long it had dissipated and faded back to the murky grey of responsibility. He knew where it would lead. It would soon be Tuesday, then Wednesday. And so on... He lay back in bed, pulled the covers up and returned to his dreams.

After an hour or so of contented dozing he woke again. The local church bell was chiming and he could hear the echoing fleshy rhythmic slapping of what sounded like people screwing in the house next door. Physically unable to sleep anymore he decided to get up.

He rolled himself out of the bed in increments, pausing for a break between rolls to enjoy the new position of his body and how his particular limbs and muscles were contorted into satisfying stretches; each one turning an unrecognised ache into a pleasing release of tension. He eventually reached the edge of the bed and with a final roll, dropped his feet down onto the floor and followed them with the rest of his body. He paused a moment to stretch again and then after locating his trousers and t-shirt from the maelstrom that was his bedroom floor; pulled them on and went downstairs to the living room.

When he got to the bottom of the stairs James was stood in the living room with one hand on his hip and the other hand scratching his head as he looked from one end of the room to the other. Keehan could see there was a look on his face that betrayed some deviation from his standard, quite placid and unruffled by life demeanour. He appeared to be agitated; or at least confused, it was hard to tell exactly.

James generally got up quite early in the morning. Most often he would be sat in the living room at the table by the window reading a book or the day's newspaper and having his breakfast. This morning he had been cleaning. The clean was not something he insisted on with rigorous consistency or regularity but all the same he liked to try and keep things relatively nice and tidy. If nothing else it kept the landlord off their backs. He was on his own in that respect as it seemed to be an area of life that wasn't even on Keehan's radar. James snapped out of his bemused surveying as Keehan walked in.

"Hey lad," he said. "Alright," Keehan replied. James' face maintained the same quizzical expression as he turned back to continue what he was doing. He was surveying the stereo, which rarely used was covered in a fine film of dust. Moving to lean in ominously over it, with what looked to Keehan like great difficulty, he recovered a mug that was lodged behind it.

"Here, ya may start cleanin' up after yourself a bit more," he appealed to Keehan over his shoulder as he delicately manoeuvred himself back into a stable standing position, the handle of his new discovery pinched delicately between his thumb and middle finger. "The place is in ribbons the whole time 'n I'm getting sick of lookin' at it."

He stood up straight and seeing the stereo with its new patch of sleek shiny blackness, looked down to assess himself. The dust which had been covering the stereo was now for the most part caked down the front of his t-shirt. He put the mug down and began to try to brush the dust off, almost immediately realizing the futility of what he was doing. "And could ya start bringin' the bags down to the recycling now and again," he continued, turning to Keehan and starting to sound more and more irritated as he began to remember more jobs that needed doing. "I don't think you've done it once since we moved in here."

Keehan, sensing James' growing irritation and knowing on some level that the responsibility would inevitably come his way, had been unconsciously summoning his defences. And now that the moment had arrived he dropped his bottom lip petulantly and rolled his eyes at James. "Sure I cleaned the place top to bottom last week," he protested, with the steady righteousness of someone knowing they've been wronged.

James, who was now on his hands and knees using the sweeping brush to fish under the bookcase for debris, stopped what he was doing for a moment and looked up. His face shifted from a look of focused determination to an incredulous smirk as he looked at Keehan and tried to figure out whether he was taking the piss or what. "Y'know that you can't just say that ya did something and then it *actually* happened," he queried Keehan after studying him for a moment. "Like the past suddenly changes on your decree and everyone realises that what they thought they'd experienced was actually wrong,". Keehan was resolute. "Well I did," he replied, and James, slightly amused and not sure if there was any point arguing with him, threw him the brush and told him to give the kitchen a sweep; which Keehan did uncharacteristically thoroughly and enthusiastically; as a small act of atonement or a gracious and generous favour to James.

Just after noon Lisa came over. She needed a new bike pump, and as it was shaping up to be a nice bright day outside, they all decided to take a stroll over to the bike shop.

The lunchtime rush was just beginning and the previously empty streets began to come to life as workers trickled out from shops and offices and made their way to the delis, chippers and coffee shops. Solicitors and checkout attendants, tattoo artists and pharmacists, out to beat the wave of teenagers from the local secondary school; queued up in tiny shops and sat outside at tables and smoked. The three headed down past the daily stream towards the bike shop. Simply called 'Bike', it was the newest occupant of a block of commercial units that had materialized some two years previous and for the most part still lay dormant and unused.

They walked in and gazed around aghast at the cornucopia of bikes and accessories that was nestled, hidden away in this ghost block in their little town. There were Mountain bikes, Racing bikes, BMXs. Ones with chopper style handlebars. There was even a two person tandem bike. "Fuckin' hell," Keehan muttered, sliding the tips of his fingers along the crossbar of a particularly sleek bright red mountain bike with thirty two gears, "who's buyin' all this shit?" James nodded in agreement as he continued to look around and take it all in. They'd known the shop was here, they'd seen the sign a hundred times. But none of them had ever imagined that inside that dull, unimposing glass shopfront there could be a world so elaborate. Aside from the bikes which took up most of the floor space of the respectably large unit, there was all the special aerodynamic clothing, the protective gear, helmets, gloves and knee-pads. There was a large portion of a wall covered with lots of various little mechanical knick-knacks, and finally in a corner at the back were the pumps. Keehan and James continued to admire the gadgets and gizmos while attempting to figure out the situation that would require a pair of battery powered socks, while Lisa headed over to look at the pumps.

Her eye was immediately caught by a beautiful shiny red pump that hung on the row just above her head. She reached up and pulled it down and turned it over in her hands enjoying how the light glistened in quick darts off its sleek surface. Hopefully but warily she upturned it to observe the sticker on the bottom, which as she had suspected revealed it to be well out of her price range. The supermarket where Lisa had worked evenings and weekends during her school years had had to cut down massively not long after she finished school, leaving all one hundred or so employees either without jobs or on drastically reduced hours. A lot of other places around were going the same way, with either massive cutbacks, if not closing down completely. It was an epidemic; like a plague that was wiping out the economic life of the country. The more places closed down, the more people were out looking for jobs; and with fewer and fewer jobs available and less money to spend; more and more businesses crumbled. Lisa's disposable income was therefore meagre, consisting of a paltry wage for whatever hours she could get, supplemented by whatever benefits she could get on top of that; a portion of which she contributed to her mother for housekeeping. She had pretty much given up hope of finding any sort of decent job and had mostly just resigned to living without and making do with what small amount she got.

She shrugged and replaced the red pump back on its hanger and picked up the cheapest black plastic one that was hanging just beneath it. She held it and waved it through the air like a baton. It felt like it could cave in with a tight enough squeeze. *Who cares*, she thought, *it's just a pump.* And it would do the same thing whether it was shiny and pretty or not.

She went up to pay and chatted for a moment with the guy behind the counter, who she vaguely recognized from school. After arranging to meet up for a drink sometime she slipped the pump in her jacket pocket, said her goodbyes, and headed out the door; where the other two were waiting leaning against the wall in the now diminishing sunshine.

As they were already out and about they decided to head

into the pet shop across the road to look at the rabbits and gerbils and some especially cool fish. The fish in the pet shop were always fun to look at, whether it was lots of little tiny ones of all different colours and weird patterns, or bigger ones with bulging eyes or with weird whisker-like barbels that trailed off their faces. They found the tanks and stood watching, waiting for something new to emerge from the greenery or for something else to disappear. Or for two fish to almost come in contact with each other but somehow at the last moment manoeuvre around each other with an ease and fluidity that seemed almost like a synchronised dance.

After a time spent watching the hypnotic drifting of the colourful creatures, James, now examining a chewy inflatable pizza slice, mused in the direction of the other two who had also ceased watching the fish. "Maybe we should get a dog? That'd be kinda fun." Lisa was knelt down with her finger sticking in through the bars of a cage containing a fluffy ball of rabbit, that seemed wholly ambivalent to the intruding digit and the girl at the end of it. "Dogs are cool," she said standing up. "I think I prefer cats though." "Meh," said James, and Keehan grimaced. "What?" Lisa asserted. "Cats are cool." "No way" Keehan retorted, vainly attempting to spin a pink and green tennis ball on the end of his finger and just catching it before it spun off and almost knocked over a nicely stacked display of birdseed. "Cats don't give a fuck about you," he continued, composing himself. "They just turn up when they want food and warmth." He conceded defeat with the tennis ball and replaced it on the shelf. "Dogs are loyal. They'll lie beside their owner if they die and guard the body. A cat will eat its owner if they die."

Lisa screwed up her face. "I don't know if that's true," she objected, "And I like dogs too. But I know cats can be every bit as loyal it just like sometimes takes 'em longer to warm to you." Keehan raised an eyebrow sceptically but didn't say any more. Having seen enough of the pet shop, and about ready to go back home, they headed towards the door.

"I had a cat once when I was younger called Lucy," Lisa began, stepping outside and squinting in the murky brightness that greeted her. "And she'd sleep in front of the heater and whenever I came home from school she would always get up and come over and rub against my legs and purr and then go and sit back down or get up on my lap and play with me. When my ma let her in in the mornin' she would come straight down to my room and get up and lie on my head." "Fair enough," James said, smiling. "Well we probably couldn't afford to keep a dog anyway. Or a cat... Would be cool though."

They walked up the street each in their own musing. The sun was gone completely behind the clouds now and it looked as though rain was imminent. The freedom of the continental morning had dissipated and it was turning into just another grey day.

They headed up towards the local primary school which was in its first week open after the summer. It was emanating an incongruous clamour that rose and dispersed into the quiet streets around it, and which as the three approached; began to clarify into the sounds of many individual children shouting and screaming for all their worth; as they kicked and bounced footballs, and ran and climbed things.

Looking over the wall the three almost simultaneously

spotted amongst the maelstrom of chasing and kicking and screaming a smartly dressed young boy with deep brown eyes. He was wearing a peculiarly fashionable pair of bright red trousers held up with braces over a crisp, black polo shirt and had his hair neatly parted on one side. A gang of young boys surrounded him and were pushing him back and forth between them. One of the bigger boys who seemed to be the ring-leader, slapped the books that the young boy had been holding under his arm. They scattered on the ground as the rest of the boys laughed and cheered.

The little maneen with the red trousers bent to pick his books up off the ground, and after gathering them up, stood and clenched them tightly up to the front of his chest. His eyes were wide with terror and confusion as he continued to be bounced back and forth between the group, attempting to maintain his footing as they laughed and cheered. "Have fun kid," drawled Keehan sourly, watching on with an equal measure of sympathy and self-pity. "These are the best days of your life…"

He jumped at the shock of a sudden loud noise by his ear. "Hey!!!" Lisa let out a loud yell at the gang of kids. They all spun around, shocked from their primitive and savage ritual by the surprising and imposing presence of an adult voice. "Leave him alone!!!" They all scattered across the playground as she made as if to climb over the wall after them.

The kid, left standing alone, his eyes now glassy with the tears that he had managed to hold back, proceeded to pick up his books which had again been knocked to the ground. He glanced soberly at Lisa for a moment, too numb to express gratitude, or to even feel it properly at that point. Regardless it was there, nestled away, ready to expand fully as soon as the inner tumult of anxiety had settled. He turned away, hesitating momentarily, and then began to walk slowly and preciously back into the classroom past a middle-aged woman wearing a navy pencil skirt and a grey cardigan who was leaning against the wall sucking absent-mindedly on a Benson & Hedges.

Lisa, Keehan and James continued their walk back towards the house. They stopped briefly on the way at the local supermarket hot counter to get some soggy potato wedges and slightly dried out sausage rolls, before heading back to settle down home for the afternoon around the TV; Lisa using her new bike pump to occasionally blow jets of air into Keehan's face; only continuing because of the fury that burst from his eyes each time.

At about ten past three there was a knock on the door. The three of them looked at each other expectantly to see would either of the other two possibly have been expecting a guest? Or if not; were they bothered getting up to open the door to some unknown and unwelcome intrusion? After a momentary stand-off James finally got up and opened the door.

Standing out on the footpath was a tall, skinny girl with long blonde hair and gangly flamingo-like legs. Standing beside her was a smaller, stockier guy with a broad face and hair styled into a Jimmy Neutron quiff. They both appeared to be in their late twenties and were both smiling brightly. "Hi, how are you today?" the boy chirped, smiling eagerly at James. "Not too bad," James replied hesitantly, eyeing them for clues as to what their purpose could be. "Basically," started the girl, after they had finished their greetings and established that everyone was in decent form, "we're here today to spread the word of the light of Jesus Christ." James felt a wave of relief as he realised it was a meeting that could be ended immediately and resolutely without any further imposition. "Ah no we're grand thanks," he mumbled making to close the door. The boy stepped forward, raising his hand in a gesture of respectful interjection. "If we could just have a moment," he persisted. "It won't take long," added the girl, smiling reassuringly.

Seeing that they were not intent on moving and not wanting to actually slam the door in their faces, James decided to relent and allow them in for a minute, if for nothing other than a little entertainment in an afternoon that would be like every other. "Do ya's want a cup of tea or anything...?" he asked, gesturing them towards a couple of chairs. "No thanks we're fine," the boy replied and the girl smiled.

Lisa and Keehan who had been sitting facing the television with their backs to the door now turned around to inspect the new arrivals. The boy and girl seeing them greeted them warmly. "Hey," Lisa said and smiled. Keehan eyed them with a sulky expression and said nothing.

The boy paused for a moment as he looked around the room taking in his surroundings. He'd not long been in this line of work and was finding that with the constant encountering of new people and new environments there was always the potential for distraction. "I'm Liam by the way," he blurted, suddenly snapping back to his purpose for being there. He gave a little greeting wave to the three who were sat around, still eyeing the new arrivals in varying measures of anticipation and curiosity. "And this is Kate," Liam continued, gesturing with an open palm towards the blonde girl. "Hi," Kate said, and smiled at them each in turn. They both took their seats and the room settled into a more casual ambiance.

"So do any of you guys go to church?," Liam began. "No," answered James. He glanced at the other two who were totally unresponsive and realised that the responsibility for their side of the conversation was going to be directly and solely on his shoulders. He shifted uncomfortably in his chair. "I useta when I was a kid," he added. "Oh right, so how come you don't go anymore?" Liam continued. "Dunno, don't see the point of it." "Do you pray?" "No, I don't believe in God," James answered resolutely. Liam continued unabashed, addressing the three of them at once and earnestly; "We believe that we are a generation that needs a leader, someone to provide guidance in our lives." He began to count on his fingers as he continued to address them. "Politics constantly lets us down. We choose leaders to run our lives and they continually fail to deliver on their promises. Banks lose our money. The poor and oppressed in society are continually overlooked. We are adrift and the world is in upheaval." Kate took over now and continued. "God doesn't want us to be leaderless, to be without hope. That's why we he sent his son, Jesus, to lead us."

Lisa interjected now finally, as though she'd been waiting for the chat to pick up some momentum before hopping on. "But sure there's been no sign of Jesus for two thousand years. How is that leading anyone?" Liam smiled reassuringly, and calmly met Lisa's sceptical gaze. "Jesus is always here and has always been here," he began. "If you want to know him you only have to accept him into your heart as your saviour."

Lisa raised an eyebrow. "And what if ya don't want to know him?" she objected. Liam smiled again, "All those who accept Jesus as their saviour can know what it is to belong and to be secured a place in heaven."

It was his facade of utter confidence and the script-like nature of his replies that was starting to irritate Lisa a little as she continued to question them more and more fervently. "Well," she began again, "What about all the Muslims and Jews and other religions? God just sends them all to hell?" Liam hesitated for a moment. Sensing her growing hostility he seemed to lose his resolve for just a fraction of a second. "Only those who follow the one true path can be promised eternal salvation," he continued.

There was a slight note of hesitation in his voice as though he knew they were the words he was supposed to say but he hadn't quite gotten behind them as much as he thought he had. Lisa continued, picking up steam. "Well if he created the world why would he deliberately deceive most of the population?" Liam smiled again. "All people have the opportunity to accept Jesus into their heart." "But they don't really do they," Lisa was starting to get on a roll and turned to kneel up on the couch leaning her elbows on the back and facing the others who were sat round the table. "It all depends on where you're born," she continued. "Most people don't get to choose what they want to believe do they? It's just something thrown onto them when they're born. You're generally just told what to believe by the community around you when you're a kid and you can't really differentiate, while your mind is still forming..."

James, sat listening, began to recollect a conversation he

had had with his sister Ciara some months before that remained vivid in his mind. He had gone to collect her one day after school when their father was in work and their mother had gone to visit their granny who had taken ill. James was waiting at the gate of the school with the other parents when the crowd of children began to stream out the door to the clanging of the bell. He remembered seeing his little sister trudging out among them with her backpack on, carrying her Sponge-bob lunch-box. Generally a chirpy and excitable young girl, this day she had looked pale and distant. He took her bag and her lunch-box and rubbed her on the head playfully and she smiled weakly as they began to walk.

After talking for a moment without much responsiveness James asked her if she was okay. After hesitating for a moment, she turned to him, her eyes wide with terror and asked, "James, is the devil real?" "What?" he replied, a little thrown. "Where did that come from?" She told him about how Miss. Redmond was teaching them all about Heaven and Hell. "What did she tell you about the devil?" He asked. "Nothin' really," she replied, her eyes becoming moist and glassy, "Just that he lives in hell and if you're not good you go there when you die and he traps you there forever."

Her voice had started to crack a little and James could remember feeling a burning anger in his stomach, a remnant of which had stayed ever since and began to be stoked in him again. He continued to recollect Ciara's panicked questioning as the discussion continued around him. "What if I go there? Is Granddad there? What if you just made a mistake, like you didn't mean to do something bad, if it was an accident?" He had put his hand on her head and stroked it and trying to sound as resolute as he had been able, told her that the devil was just an idea someone came up with to make people afraid. "To teach them or whatever. The truth is no-one really knows," he told her. "How could anyone know unless someone actually died and came back to life and told them what it was like." "But does that mean there's no heaven either?" She had asked him then and he smiled now fondly to himself at her sharpness. "Aaaahhh, yeah, well, I suppose," he had fumbled for an answer that was somewhere between comfort and the truth. "Well no-one knows. For all we know it could be something amazing that we could never have even thought of. That's the way I think about it anyway."

She hadn't appeared to be totally convinced by his explanation but had at least seemed a little less frightened. Lost in recovering the details of this moment and a little bit in his own pride at being able to help his sister, James continued to recollect how he had told her that "Anyone that tells her that they do know for definite is a complete liar and you should kick 'em in the balls!" He shouted "Hiiiiiii-ya" as he delivered a swinging kick to a dock leaf sticking out of the ditch, knocking the leaf off its stalk and getting his foot stuck in the briars. He had almost fallen over before managing to pull his foot out and regain his balance. Ciara had laughed at him and they had walked back home laughing and joking and blowing dandelion heads in each other's faces.

Many times since, James had thought about his own religious experiences growing up. The nightmares and the fear that had never really left him fully. It pained him to think of that crap rolling around in the heads of little children, especially Ciara; and the half-lives quashed by fear that lay before them on account of it. It seemed to James like his brain had been moulded with that stuff. It had its own niche that fit into his mind with its own parameters, its own links, its own particular space and everything he knew had been moulded around it. Once God went that space was always there. You could find something to believe in here and there, something to cover a few bases, but nothing ever fit it exactly or conclusively. Certain chemicals had appeared to fill it at first but it would quickly wear off leaving the hole even more gaping and obvious. Still, it seemed like the farther he had gotten away from the loss of God, the more he had learned about the world; the more he felt like he was beginning to discover a voice inside himself that was like his own. Chipping away at what he knew was unreal he felt he was progressing towards something important, if only in rare but increasing glimpses.

As James' attention returned fully from his pondering to the ongoing discussion Lisa was asking the two newcomers "How'd you get into this anyway? Were your parents religious?" "My parents are Christians, yes," Liam answered. They looked to Kate. "I actually wasn't religious at all until a couple of years ago," she began. "Then one day I was crossing the street and I was hit by a car." Lisa and James sat and listened. Keehan's interest was piqued slightly by the mention of a car accident. "I was in a coma for about two weeks,"she continued. "I had a crushed lung, three broken ribs and a broken arm. Once I woke up I was there for almost two months. That's when I found Jesus, while in the hospital." "Oh yeah?" queried Keehan, "what was he in for?" He sat grinning to himself.

Lisa and James both turned and glared at him half-heartedly. Had the girl been like some of the more overbearing and obnoxious proselytizers they had come across they probably would have burst out laughing. As it was they both concluded that this girl seemed fairly genuine if a little naive. It was quite understandable that someone undergoing such a frightening experience would look for some comfort, for something to ease her fear. The two of them both had at one time or another questioned the silence just hoping that something or someone was taking care of everyone -although that time was long gone now. Once they had discounted the purely coincidental and the minds natural reaction for coping with fear; showing you what you needed to see; there really didn't seem to be anyone in particular looking over things. Or if so, they seemed to be either hard of hearing or just plain ambivalent. Keehan pouted at Lisa and James and turned back to the television.

"Well how about we leave these leaflets with you," Liam said as they both got up. "You can read them or throw them out if you want." He gave a shy smile. "Oh yeah thanks," Lisa said with only the vaguest curiosity as to the content of the pamphlets but having grown to quite like the two of them all the same -or at least feel a slight sympathy for them. James got up and opened the door for them and smiled at them as they headed out.

He closed the door behind them and returned to sit down in his usual seat beside Lisa on the couch. Lisa was sighing. "Jaysus," she muttered. "Those two weren't the worst I've come across, but can these people not just keep their beliefs to themselves... They have to bleedin' shove it in everyone's face."

"I dunno," James mused, "Maybe they really think they are trying to help. Like when you try something different that's really good, eat a food or hear a song or something and it's like, *hey you have to check this out, it's amazing!*" "Yeah," Lisa replied as she considered this briefly but remained unconvinced, "But that's an actual tangible result. What's gonna happen if I start goin' to mass and prayin'? Not a damn thing. I don't know what they're tryin' to achieve."

"Yeah I guess," James replied losing interest as the tiredness from all the days activity and emotions began to catch up with him. He slumped back down on the sofa and stretched his feet up on to the coffee table. "I think I'd like to worship sometimes, I just don't know what," he added as a half-hearted conclusion. Keehan who had been sulking since his attempt at wit had not received the rapturous audience it had deserved, now suddenly re-emerged to chip in to the conversation as it had died off. "People just believe in God cos they're afraid of goin' to hell," he interjected, surprising the other two, who both cocked their heads in his direction. "Them lads are just lookin' for brownie points."

As Lisa and James looked to Keehan, then to each other and back to Keehan, he turned back to the telly and picked up the remote to flick through the channels, his bottom lip curling in the beginnings of a scowl. Now with his audience all ears, he continued to spout words that he'd probably heard somewhere or even thought once or twice himself, but all the same wasn't even sure he believed. No matter, he was on a roll. "The same reason people help each other too," he continued. No-one gives a shit about anyone else really. There's no God anymore and no rules. It doesn't matter what you do.

You might as well do whatever the fuck ya want. It makes no difference."

"Jaysus," Lisa eyed him amusedly, "Where did that come from? A bit nihilistic isn't it." Keehan looked confused. "What?" "A bit hopeless, like." "Well it's true," he continued testily. No-one gives a fuck anymore."

"Well I mean I wouldn't go writing everything off," Lisa countered, scrunching her eyebrows together and stroking her chin as she gathered her thoughts. "Like, people are generally pretty cool, I don't think God has anything to do with it. And anyway, some of the atheists can be as bad as the god-freaks. I mean they're still clinging to dogma and shovin' it down people's throats. I'd be on the side of no god or at least no definitive conception of god but..." She stopped suddenly, a puzzled look on her face. She turned to look at Keehan. "Did I not see you wearin' a chain with a cross on it here before?" Keehan had indeed found a crucifix on a chain in his parent's house one day and had put it on and had been wearing it on and off since then, for reasons even he was not quite sure of. "Uhh, yeah," he replied a little flustered. "I was just jokin'." Lisa looked at him. "You've a quare strange sense of humour."

Shrugging it off Keehan turned back to the TV. The world began to fade into background noise as he saw Kara Hughes on the screen posing for photographers, and his mind became consumed. Kara was one of the people that seemed to be famous for being famous. That hadn't seemed to have actually done anything more spectacular or important than turn up at places. She kept turning up and people kept taking her photo. She had her own show now where they filmed her all day turning up. The draw was that after she showed up all glamorous, people could then see when she went home and was just a messed-up train-wreck like everyone else. *She wasn't quite like everyone else though*, Keehan thought. *She was on television...* That's what made her misery enviable and special. At least it was important enough to be shown on TV. People took notice. Whereas Keehan Dang had to sit there in just his own normal, boring, everyday misery that no-one knew or cared about; and which would be forgotten and lost in the tide of the world like all the rest of the misery belonging to all the rest of the sad saps around him. He got up off the chair and went into the kitchen to pour himself a drink. "Bit early isn't it?" Lisa called into the kitchen on hearing the clinking of the bottle. "Ah what's the bleedin' difference?" Keehan replied with a rare peaceful ambivalence, and wandered back in to slump back comfortably into his chair.

This strange resignation that almost pointed to happiness would pop up briefly for a moment now and then but never really lasted long. Neither did he know where it came from. He never really questioned it too deeply but generally in what had become an almost instinctive routine, he would douse it in alcohol. In vague hope of keeping it trapped, safe from the interference of the world outside; and even vaguer knowing, that by now he'd become genuinely petrified by any extreme of feeling. Even sober happiness seemed to him something strange and uncomfortable. The world in his mind was the only one in which he could hold on to any sense of pride or usefulness, the only one he felt was likely to pay dividends; and so it was the only one he really invested in. His body and the physical world it pertained to was merely a screeching irritant: a continued nuisance, which he had ceased to understand and preferred to ignore.

He sat now gazing at the screen with detachment, his mind content to quietly and freely play without striving, as his body disappeared in the warmth of the chair and the alcohol. *Kara Hughes*, he thought, enjoying his current lack of aspiration. *Who gives a shit...*

CHAPTER 3

That weekend, the first weekend of September; a fairground in a muddy field on the outskirts of the town was having its last busy Saturday. It had been in full swing for the last two weeks of August, and would be taken down on Monday to disappear again for another year.

There was a small selection of rides -enough for an evenings entertainment; which included a Miami Trip and a Freak-out swinging and twirling, as well as an Orbiter and a Topspin and hovering above everything, a 40 metre high G-Force tower; which stood garish and erratic against the empty green hills stretching out forever behind it. On the ground were a few booths with different games such as ring toss and fishing for ducks.

Although hardly spectacular it was the kind of event that provided a welcome novelty and drew people of all ages out of their homes to have a look, and to hang out somewhere different for the last time before the summer ended properly. To some of those whose worlds had been confined by choice or destiny to never exceed the nearby streets and countryside it was almost exciting.

Michelle and Sharon, who were set to return to college

in two weeks after their summer spent at home, were stood leaning against the railings by the waltzers, which were spinning vigorously to the strong distaste of a young boy in one of the carriages. He was bawling his eyes out and wailing with a relentless vigour, producing a kind of anguished banshee Doppler effect as he passed every ten seconds or so.

Michelle, her eyes painted dark, her lips bright pink and the fringe of her long, shiny hair cut in a drastic line just above her eyes, was scowling, trying to pick out someone cool among the plebs. Sharon stood beside her. She was wearing an emerald green, knee-length summer dress which was almost casual enough to be in harmony with her surroundings. With her clear, natural and slightly pale complexion, she had the appearance of a living porcelain doll; particularly now in the colourful, shifting neon lighting that was giving everything in the field an eerie resonance. She was anxiously eyeing the mud around her small island of grass.

Michelle groaned. "Eughh, the state of this place. There's no-one here." She stood on her tip-toes to try and get a better view of who was around then turned back to Sharon. "I thought you said Adam was gonna be here." "He said he was coming," Sharon murmured as she attempted to use the gates as a hand rail to step tenderly to an area of ground that was a little drier and less unstable. "Maybe they left already..." Michelle looked around again. "There's nothin' but bleedin' crusties here."

Sharon squinted in the lights as she looked up at the giant metal contraptions towering above them. "Are ya goin' on anything?" she enquired, without a particularly positive expectation. "Are ya jokin' me," Michelle balked, still scanning the crowd. "Who puts these things together anyway? One screw out of place and yer gone." She turned back to Sharon. "I just got me hair done anyway, it'd be all over the place." "D'ya wanna just head back to mine, stick on a DVD or somethin'?" Sharon offered, seeing that it was not going to be much fun. "Yeah I suppose," Michelle sighed. "Jesus I can't wait to get out of this dump."

Just as they were about to make a move Sharon spotted a guy they knew from college. He was walking towards the exit chatting to Lisa. James and Keehan were just behind them. James was ragging Keehan, who had bragged about his experiences on some of the world's largest roller-coasters before arriving and informing them that "I'm not afraid, I'm just not bothered going on anything..."

"There's Kehoe," Sharon said, turning to Michelle. Right at that moment Kehoe happened to look up and spotted the two of them stood by the waltzers. He waved. Gesturing to Lisa and the lads to come with, he began to head over towards Michelle and Sharon, having to negotiate his way through the streams of people who were milling around, eating hot-dogs and candy-floss, interspersed with little kids darting gleefully in and out of the crowd. "Alright what's the craic?" he asked, finally managing to cross the stream of traffic to the two girls. "Nothin' much," Michelle sighed, still looking around her with a vaguely disdainful scowl. "We're probably gonna head. This place is fairly lame." Kehoe looked around at all the people meandering about, some stuffing their faces, some in groups chatting and laughing animatedly; most of them pottering along to each ride or booth in turn, with the colourful flashing lights illuminating their faces open and beaming.

He grinned to himself. "Ah it's a bit of a laugh sure," he concluded. "Somethin' different anyway." He turned back to them. "When are ya's back in college?" "We're both back the twenty ninth," Sharon replied. "How about yourself?" Kehoe clasped his hands together elatedly and grinned again. "Not 'til the thirteenth of October," he announced. His eyes sparkled at the thought of the coming adventures. "Gonna spend the next few weeks gettin' off... me... face." He emitted a joyfully stuttering laugh that sounded something like a chainsaw attempting to start on a freezing cold day.

Michelle stared blankly at him, an unintentional and very subtle smile momentarily cracking her rigid facade as the corner of her mouth turned up almost by its own volition. Sharon laughed politely, unsure as to whether it was a topic she wanted to pursue or even could, to remain within the bounds of respectability. "Ah yeah why not sure," she replied, not committing herself to anything in particular, "Has to be done." "What have yous been up ta anyway?" Kehoe asked trying to contain a smile again at Sharon's formality and the warm competency of her social grace. "Ah nothing really," she replied. "Just hanging out." "Not a lot else to do round here," Michelle interjected. Kehoe laughed. "Sure there's mass and the pub. What more do ya want?" Sharon smiled. Michelle was scowling again though a little less fervently. "Anyway," he continued, "I'm bringin' these lads down-town if yez want a lift anywhere." Michelle's slowly softening demeanour momentarily cracked into a beam before returning to its usual state of composed neutrality. "Nah it's okay cheers," she said as she nodded her head in the general direction of

Sharon's house. "We're headin' up the other way." Kehoe nodded. "Right see ya's later then."

They said their goodbyes and turned to head towards the exit. As Sharon began to walk away, distractedly trying to fit her phone into the pocket of her bag, she dropped it. The phone bounced off her knee and landed beside a huge puddle.

Keehan, though never having had so much as a word of conversation with Sharon, had been in love with her since his last year of school when he had walked past her one day and saw her placing her books in her locker with what seemed to be the care and diligence of someone who didn't need to be anywhere but where they were. Her eyes to him had seemed to sparkle and shine for nothing but the objects surrounding her, and they still did -though not quite as bright as he was sure he remembered. He had been standing beside her as this conversation with Kehoe had taken place, trying to maintain the right balance of watching her so intently that he soaked in every detail of her, without coming across as some kind of demented potential serial killer. He was finding it extremely difficult. If only he could say something to her, he thought *But what?* He'd probably just embarrass himself. Say something stupid and weird. He always did. Or start stuttering and look like an idiot. Or just say something pointless. He pictured the scene. He pictured her grimacing and retching at the verbal diarrhoea he'd just spewed in her face. *God what a moron.* She'd never want to look at him again. His need to say something right now; to finally be part of an actual, real conversation with her, began to press harder and harder on him as his fear of dissolution and the loss of dignity fought against it, and his stomach began to constrict with anxiety. He seemed to forget how to breathe and began almost to choke on the air around him. As Sharon began to walk off Keehan saw her phone drop.

With a laser-like acuity he grasped the chance he'd been waiting for to find some relief from his emotional turmoil and to be known, acknowledged by her in some way however small. He dived over and picked the phone up almost before it hit the ground, almost before she realised she had dropped it, and held it up to her. She looked up, a little surprised by his sudden appearance then took the phone from his hand. "Thanks," she said and smiled politely, and Keehan was sure he saw that same vivid sparkle as he'd seen before.

He nodded bashfully at her, feeling his cheeks begin to flush, as she turned and headed out to follow Michelle who was waiting on the road. Keehan jogged to catch up with the others who had headed out the gate already, his face cracking into a broad smile he could barely contain.

Kehoe's battered Toyota Corolla was parked just outside the gate. Lisa hopped into the passenger seat while the two lads got in the back. There was a session on in Duckie's which was where Kehoe was headed. Lisa was heading the same direction. "Ye sure ya's don't wanna come in for a while?," Kehoe asked, puffing on a cigarette as they cruised down the almost empty streets. "Apparently it's a fairly mad one down there." "Nah we're cool," Lisa replied, and turned to look at the two lads in the back to confirm. James confirmed with a shake of his head while Keehan didn't even seem to be listening. Lisa turned back around, "Not really into it any-more," she continued. "I'm just gonna get a bag of smoke off him 'n head home." "Cool," Kehoe replied, and tapped the indicator deftly before swinging the car abruptly across the deserted road.

They pulled up right outside the house where they all stumbled out of the car and up to the door, and Kehoe knocked sharply on the white PVC. After a couple of seconds in which the clatter of voices inside became slightly hushed, the door was opened a crack and a bleary head poked around it and looked searchingly out. Immediately recognising them the bleary head pulled the door open fully and greeted them with a dazed but warmly welcoming smile. "A-right lads," he drawled as he stepped back to let them pass. "What's the craic? Come on in."

Lisa looked around tentatively as she stepped inside before unconsciously taking a deep breath, as if wading through this atmosphere might deprive her of oxygen. Beckoned by Ducky, and followed by Kehoe, she headed through the party to a room just off to the left. Keehan and James hesitated sheepishly until some lad they vaguely recognized addressed them, "Here lads close the door will yez."

They stepped in and closed the door. They were now standing in the main room which was a kind of living room and dining room in one and was almost identical to their own. Scattered around the room were twelve or thirteen lads and girls of varying levels of inebriation, some sprawled across chairs and couches, others sat on the floor. One guy, his eyes bulging maniacally out of their sockets, was stood pumping his fist in the air to the quarter note pulse of the techno mix that was thumping from the stereo in the corner; seemingly oblivious to everything else that was in the room including the two new arrivals. Judging from the muffled thuds and chatter emanating from the ceiling there were obviously more people upstairs. From the doorway Keehan and James could see through to the kitchen where another three lads and a girl were sat around a table, one of the lads using a razor blade to chop up some white powder on an empty CD case.

The atmosphere was dense and the two of them willed Lisa to get a move on with her transaction. The more they stood there the more they began to feel as objects of suspicion, separate from the unity of the crowd, like narcs with no business being there. James looked over at Keehan who turned to look at James. They nodded at each other in an awkward attempt of reassurance and both went back to trying to appear casual, trying to blend in; as though they belonged there, as though they were in on the joke.

This appeared to be a session that had passed its initial stages of buzzed happy mayhem on full stomachs and well rested nervous systems, and was reeking a little of desperation. The breaking down of boundaries, the making of new friends and the epic conversations about nothing at all had long since fizzled out and it seemed to have gotten for the most part to that backwash stage that often followed: of sinking moods hanging on to the initial taste of euphoria that was days old now and was getting harder and harder to recreate; as their bodies weight of collapse was becoming more than their spirits could support much longer, even with chemical help. It was a scene that though relatively familiar to them from the inside, was never really comfortable to view now that they were outside the loop. James, fighting a pressing urge to integrate or get out and not wanting to leave Lisa here alone, decided he'd probably take a line if it was offered to him just to keep everything cool. One line. Then he didn't have to come back here again. He wouldn't be around it. He wouldn't be able to get any more even if he wanted to. And he knew he'd want to.

Just then he recognized a sweaty guy who was sitting on an armchair facing away from them absent-mindedly puffing on a rolled up cigarette. He edged over behind the guy. "Alright Puds," he interjected keeping his voice low despite the clattering, thumping noise that filled the room. The lad turned around and seeing James, raised his eyebrows in recognition as a tired smile crossed his face. "Alright lad, hows it goin'? Ya here for the sesh?" "Nah just passin' through," James replied. "How's things with you?" "Ah grand," muttered Puds. "Same old."

He turned looking for something to tap his ash into and finding an empty cider can he held it in his left hand as he flicked the cigarette with his right, dropping the ash on the carpet beside it. He put the empty can back on the table and turned back around. "Hows yourself? I haven't seen ya round in a while." "Nah," James replied. "Kinda takin' a break for a while." Puds turned and nodded sagely as he took a slow drag on the cigarette and looked for the can again. Managing to flick the ash in this time he turned back to James. "D'ya hear about Kev?" James shook his head. "Ee was out last night after leavin' here," Puds continued. "Micky Roche started a fight with some big burly lad. Kev got involved in it. Dunno if he wuz joinin' in or tryin' to break it up." He turned away from James for a moment again and coughed a dry rattly nicotine cough into his hand which he then rubbed on the knee of his trousers before turning back and continuing; "Anyway next thing a couple of mates a' this big lad turn up in a car. The lad in the passenger seat grabs Kev through the window and drags 'im back agains' the car and the other lad tears off. They dragged him down the bleedin' road hangin' outta the side of the car about as far as the roundabout before they dropped 'im." "Jesus," James said feeling his chest begin to tighten. "Was he badly hurt?" "Ah nah," Puds replied, taking another slow drag from his rollie which had deposited beads of grey ash all over the front of his white Lacoste tracksuit top. "He just had a few bruises and scrapes." "He was lucky," James mumbled softly, as he began to feel once again the urgent need to leave this house and this life, propelled by an almost overpowering sadness for Puds and many other genuine, cool, mixed up people he knew that probably never would. Maybe he would be one of them. Those that would still be here in years to come, with the same tales of woe and misery: still just trying to laugh and find a way out of the shit that surrounded them and seemed to pervade their whole existence.

"Yeah he was," Puds mumbled absent-mindedly, as he slowly blew a cloud of smoke up towards the ceiling, which hung in the air above them and drifted and curled into itself before fading into nothing as they both watched it disappear in silence. James stood up and looked over at Keehan who was still standing in the same spot shifting uncomfortably.

Keehan's eyes suddenly lit up and a wave of relief appeared to pass through him as James followed his gaze to see Lisa emerging from the back room. She appeared considerably more relaxed than when she had walked in initially, having met some people who had been in her class at school and having a chat with them. After saying her farewells to the rest of the gang in the living room, some of whom noticed, some of whom didn't; she followed the lads out into the street.

Keehan, followed by James, had almost dived out the door as soon as he had caught sight of Lisa. He stepped outside onto the pavement and took a big gulp of air. The glacial night had never tasted so good and he sucked in the cold, feeling it expand in his lungs. He noticed now how fast his heart was beating as it began to slow down. He knew the powder the lad in the kitchen had been cutting up. They had experienced its effects first hand. Keehan himself had tried it a few times. Almost every time he had felt so nervous and panicky he thought he was going to have a mental breakdown. At the same time he had experienced such unbelievable feelings of near omnipotence that he knew he could well spend the rest of his life filling his nose and never bother doing anything else. It was this thought that made him panic most. The glimpse of a life of artificial happiness that could soon become his only source and take over the one he dreamed of -take over *him* completely. For although Keehan's life now seemed to him to be becoming for the most part shit to the point of pointlessness, there was something inside of him, diseased now and clinging on for dear life; but that nevertheless told him that he would one day do something worthwhile; and that he would have to be ready for his opportunity when it arrived. He decided after those few times to leave it alone and just stay at home.

Lisa and James on the other hand though had had quite an extended experiment. For a period of a few months in the spring and summer the year before, they had been among the regulars at the numerous sessions that had been going on all over the town; as well as having their own personal stash at home for the occasional day or two of sitting around watching DVDs or listening to music. On at least two occasions they had spent almost a solid week snuffling up the powder, taking occasional brief breaks for whatever food or sleep they could snatch. After a while they had begun to become gaunt and thin and listless. James had begun coming home from work on his lunch-breaks to do a couple of lines to relieve the tedium.

After a couple of months of this though they had grown weary of it. Lisa had given it up completely having become bored of the whole repetitive cycle and also a little scared of how dependant they were becoming on it. James stopped attending the sessions, stopped going out; though had continued to use it for some weeks after on his own. He found the powder had in its initial stages the power to completely obliterate all the voices of criticism that rolled around his head from morning to night. The payment for these periods of absolute freedom of mind however was nights spent recovering, too tired to do anything but too wired to sleep. Unable to eat but with a stomach that hadn't seen food in days. Increasingly the highs were not quite as high and the following lows became crushing.

One evening late the previous summer, after a particularly lengthy binge, he had been suddenly hit by an attack of panic about how his life was going. Nauseous and numb with terror he had gone and lay on his bed at about six o'clock, the muted sunlight still creeping in the cracks in the curtains. He lay there for the whole night as the light gradually dimmed to pitch black: neither able to close his eyes and go to sleep nor to get up and do anything. He could remember that night vividly. How he had lay there for hours feeling so low he wished he would die; until eventually sometime around five the next morning as the tension in his body and mind began to dissolve, he had managed to nod off and get a few hours of deep sleep. After that night he had given it up completely.

As much fun as it had seemed initially and despite the good times they'd had and the people they had met, it had after a while ceased to look to them like the answer they had been searching for, and seemed on the contrary to be most likely the path away from any chance of real happiness. They preferred to keep that life for now at least as memories of a distant past; some aspects treasured in a way but mostly mementos of a scared and turbulent time, all tinged with darkness with the advance of perspective. The three walked back through the cold night wanting nothing more than to hide away from it all.

After an hour or so sitting on the couch watching mindless television, their spirits had begun to rise again. *Search for a Superstar* was on. Lisa and James had been casually following it for a few weeks. Keehan was sitting pretending to not be interested in it.

"Jesus," he growled, scowling at the television. "Look at some of these tools. All these fuckin' idiots gettin' the royal treatment while I'm sat here in this shithole. I could sing better than most of them." Lisa was sat bent over the coffee table rolling a joint, her attention halfway between the TV and Keehan's bemused and bitter ramblings which had barely stopped since the show had begun. "Why don't ya enter next year?" she suggested, more as a retort than a genuinely expected possibility. Keehan nodded to himself with a facile determination. "I will," he said. "I could probably win it too." He paused to reconsider, then continued, "Or at least get to the finals." "Yeah be realistic," James chimed in, looking over at Keehan and grinning at his affected air of resolution. "Ye wouldn't want to overreach yourself."

At the next ad break Keehan got up to pour himself a vodka and orange juice and James decided to join him. Lisa watched Keehan from the corner of her eye as he ambled in from the kitchen and plonked back down in the chair with his trusty bottle of red label in one hand and the carton of orange juice in the other. She had lately become a little wary of Keehan's drinking habits. James drank quite a bit but not so much and even then she knew that for all his problems he was somewhat more mature and self-possessed than Keehan was. She didn't feel like she needed to worry about him. Keehan now though it seemed to her was almost drunk or having a drink more often than he was sober.

Lisa having rolled the joint now lit it and took a couple of deep drags before offering it around. James took a drag and reached across the sofa to pass it to Keehan, who scrunched up his face and waved his hand dismissively at it. Lisa was now slumped down low in the couch feeling her mind drift into a meandering dance of colour and ideas. She looked over at Keehan and smiled. "You'd be better off smoking this now and again than drinking so much," she said holding up the joint to show him. Keehan shrugged his shoulders. Lisa continued, sitting up a little straighter. "You can still function with this if ya don't get the really strong stuff, and you won't be killin' yourself either." She began to root in her pockets. "I'll leave ya some here and some skins n stuff."

"I don't like smokin' that stuff," Keehan asserted, still gazing at the TV screen. Lisa shrugged in slight agreement. She'd seen him smoke once or twice before and it hadn't appeared from the outside to have been a pleasant experience for him. She continued, still searching her pockets for the bag of weed which had fallen off the coffee table some time ago and was now sitting on the floor by her feet. "If you've a tendency to get lost in your own head it will kinda make it worse alright."

Keehan turned to look at her, his eyes narrowing suspiciously, disgruntled that she should claim to have any knowledge of the workings of his mind that he didn't have himself. Lisa ignoring him continued; "Y'can kinda spiral off. You have to relax and be focused on the moment. Then it feels good."

Realizing the weed wasn't in her pockets she had a quick scan around the immediate vicinity and spotted the baggie sitting on the floor. "Ah there we go," she said picking it up and putting it back in her pocket before turning back to him and continuing, "It'd be healthier than drinkin' all the time."

Keehan hadn't really been listening to anything that followed the comment about him being lost in his own head. Not having a sound reply his mind had been working furiously on hypothetical scenarios in which he had, and was now just playing out the different variations, crafting the moment in which he would have the exact response to give himself the upper hand once more.

His spiralling thoughts were interrupted by the sudden re-emergence of James into the scenario. James had been slumped quietly between them, casually drifting back and forth between listening to their conversation and enjoying the fuzzy feeling he had from the mixture of the weed and the vodka. "I don't know," he chimed in now, "they're kind of a different buzz. I go back and forth with it. Sometimes it's great, like I can think really clearly and focus longer but other times, yeah, I get really paranoid." He looked as though a grin was attempting to climb out of his face if only the required muscles could find the motivation to move into proper formation. Finally they jumped into position, as he chuckled, "Half the time I get so paranoid I can barely move." Lisa laughed and took another deep drag. After a lengthy exhale she stubbed out the half-smoked joint in the ashtray before settling back down comfortably on the couch. She continued dreamily, "It just enhances whatever way your mind is at the time." She looked over at Keehan and paused, and for a moment considered the repercussions of Keehan's mind being exaggerated in any way. "Okay," she admitted, "It's probably not a great thing for *you* to be doin' often... Not yet anyway... You still should ease up on the drink though."

Keehan nodded agreeably as a concession for the sake of peace, and continued to drink his vodka and daydream as they all sat back and relaxed; content at last to find the point in the day where their various addictions and neuroses became tomorrow's problem: to be dealt with in the realm of the living, on the other side of sleep. They sat around watching TV until about half one in the morning when James and Lisa went up to bed and Keehan, after polishing off the bottle of vodka, stumbled up not far behind them.

CHAPTER 4

He could remember hearing his footsteps echo as he walked through some huge warehouse; what looked like an abandoned factory. He looked around, seeing nothing but blank walls and doors sealed with brutishly intimidating padlocks. He spotted one room that appeared to be open and went towards it.

As he cautiously peered around the door which had been left slightly ajar he saw that the room was completely empty save for a hole in the floor. Two metal bars protruded from the hole, which on further inspection revealed themselves to be the top of a ladder just jutting up over the edge. Not knowing why; not really seeing any other option; he climbed on to the ladder and began to step carefully down towards the ground below.

All of a sudden the floor that had been above him vanished into a black nothingness. He was still on the ladder but now the ladder was attached to the side of a huge metal silo, that was extending both upwards and downwards at increasing speed. Keehan clung as tightly as he could to this ladder in an immense cavern of rust and metal. He looked down. There was a concrete floor beneath him but it appeared to be at least a hundred metres away and descending still farther at a rapid pace.

His head began to swim violently and he gripped the ladder even more tightly. Beginning to panic he decided to try and climb back up. He looked up at the top of the ladder and it too was extending away from him.

His arms and legs now started to go numb and twitch and shake nervously. He was stuck. Looking downwards just made him sick. He wanted to climb up but felt as if he was losing control of his limbs. He felt like the relatively tight grip he still had on the ladder was the only shred of hope he had left and if he tried to move in any direction he would surely fall. Every time he looked down his stomach lurched up into his throat so he looked up. As he looked up he was overwhelmed by the looming monstrosity rising above him and felt the strength in his arms begin to ebb away even further.

His head continued to swim and his panic rose and rose and became more manic and unbearable as his mind ran faster and faster away from him; pure terror now building and suddenly he jerked up in his bed, sweat pumping, his heart racing, almost frozen with shock and gasping for air.

It was the first truly memorable nightmare Keehan had had for a long time; the most vivid and terrifying since he was a child, when a devil from a cartoon he'd seen had reappeared in his sleeping consciousness to keep him awake for days in fear for his soul.

He sat for some time in his bed, feeling his heart beat manically as he surveyed his room, trying to convince himself that he was safely back in reality again. He choked on mouthfuls of air as his lungs constricted and expanded erratically in fitful spasms. His forehead was damp and clammy and his cheeks burned red hot.

He continued to sit upright looking around the room, waiting for everything to make sense again. He looked around at the furniture. His wardrobe. The clothes scattered around the room. Objects of his everyday which all seemed strange and unreal and yet gradually poured back into him a sense of the comfortingly mundane. He sat looking at all the objects that he had barely noticed for some time now and allowed their solidity to take him over. He sat for quite a while just looking around and reacquainting himself with normality, and began to feel like he had regained himself somewhat. He caught his breath again and his heart slowed back to the point where he could again lie down and go back asleep, warm and safe in his bed.

He slept relatively peacefully for the rest of the night and barely stirred again until noon, at which point he woke up, not frightened; but with a vague feeling of unease: the night's events still fresh somewhere in his mind.

Lisa meanwhile, after staying the night at the lads' house had gotten up around eleven. She had gone downstairs and opened up the windows in the living room to air it out, and after making herself some toast proceeded to tidy up a bit.

Whereas James was quite tidy and generally kept the place relatively neat, Keehan, as she often pointed out to him, was like a child who had to be badgered and harangued to perform such simple duties as putting his dishes in the sink. He also seemed to insist on throwing down indiscriminately whatever he had on him, be it clothes, DVD's or anything else he happened to be momentarily interested in.

Lisa would not generally have been in the habit of picking up after Keehan but as yesterday was dole day she knew that if she delayed a little, her father would almost certainly already be in the pub by the time she got home. It was not that Stephen was unnecessarily mean to her or treated her badly, it was just that in her eyes he was a loser and sometimes she just couldn't be bothered to be around him.

Her mother's father Cyril lived just on the other side of town. Cyril had known Stephen Mulcahy since he was a boy. He had known about all the thieving and vandalism. He had been a witness to the state of the young Connell lad who after a relentless course of bullying at the hands of Stephen and another couple of lads, had eventually been beaten to a point where he had to be hospitalized and had almost died. When Stephen was in his early twenties, he along with the rest of his family had moved away from the town to a village a few miles outside for a period of a couple of years. From what Cyril had heard about him from his various sources, from friends and from general talk that went around, it seemed he had continued down much the same path in his new community. From the time Stephen and Josie first started going out together Cyril had made clear his objection to it and his wish that his daughter stay away from the lad and the trouble that constantly followed him.

The relationship had continued regardless, and Cyril, respecting Josie's wishes and wanting to keep things civil, had reluctantly put his misgivings aside. Cyril had watched as his daughter started working less and spending more time in the pub; and he tolerated Stephen with gritted teeth and probably would have avoided them entirely if it wasn't for the grand-daughter he adored more than anything in the world. The money he had given them over the years to help out he was certain had mostly disappeared into the pockets of the local bookies. But he let his suspicions slide; not having use for much money and operating under the hope that at least some would end up contributing to the household and to a somewhat better life for Lisa and her mother. But although generally managing to keep up a veneer of civility along with genuine concern and love for his daughter, his grief and what had become positive loathing for Stephen was not easily hidden.

One night some years before, under the influence of a few too many whiskeys, it had all risen to the surface, in an outpouring made vicious by repression. Grievances that had lain dormant for years were finally aired and things were said on both sides that could not be easily taken back. Consequently Cyril was no longer welcome in the Mulcahy household; and he had barely seen his daughter since that night. Lisa though was old enough and headstrong enough to make her own decisions and she still visited him regularly regardless of what her mother said.

Sure enough, when Lisa got back to the house her father was nowhere to be seen. Josie was getting her things together to go to work.

Lisa sat down at the kitchen table, looked forlornly around the dilapidated kitchen and sighed. The house depressed her to no end. The lino in a corner of the kitchen had been torn in a couple of spots allowing patches of grey concrete to peek up through the beige and brown geometric design. Above the patches was a bunch of coloured wires sticking out of the wall where a light switch had been broken off and had never been replaced. Putting her elbow on the table, she leaned her head onto her open palm and looked across at the cupboard by the fridge on which one of the hinges of the door had at some point become broken off and never fixed, leaving it hanging off limply and pointlessly. The whole place just had an air of futility.

"D'you stay over at the lads' last night," Josie asked as she pulled a freshly ironed t-shirt over her head; bright red and bearing the small logo on the left breast of the national chain of discount stores whose local branch she was currently working for. Lisa who had been beginning to drift off into an impromptu nap, snapped back to reality and sat up, stretching sleepily. "Yeah," she answered half-yawning. "We watched a bit of telly." Josie coughed raspily, a chesty rattle caused by years of heavy smoking. "So what are you up to today then?," she asked as she cleared her throat and began to pull a set of cotton sheets from the tumble dryer, the enamel coating of which had once upon a time been sparkling white and had now faded to a musty yellow; its performance having faded alongside it. "I'm headin' over to Grandad's for a bit," Lisa replied, attempting to affect a nonchalance that was almost convincing. Josie tutted as she squeezed the sheets checking to see if they had dried fully and seemed about to start protesting. Lisa ignored it. She'd had this argument a million times before and wasn't in the mood to have it again. "What time are ya workin' at?" she asked, deflecting the conversation. Josie, now persuaded that the sheets were adequately dry began to fold them and place them in a neat pile on the counter-top. "Late shift," she replied staring at nothing as her hands moved automatically to perform the task at hand. "Starting at two." "Cool," Lisa replied, dreamily watching her mother fold the sheets. "Ya comin' back here after?" she asked. Josie turned to look at her. "Of course," she replied, her voice pitching up slightly with the subtlest hint of indignation. "Where would I be going?" Lisa, ignoring the question simply nodded acknowledgement and stood up to leave, a brief twitch in the corner of her mouth betraying the vaguest hint of hopeful satisfaction before returning to the deadpan but bright-eyed neutrality which characterized her countenance for most in the world. "I'll see ya tonight so," she replied and smiled warmly at her.

She headed outside pulling the door behind her and wondered what it was that made her mother so blind? Why she couldn't see what everyone else saw so clearly? She pulled the hood of the jacket over her head and took a small joint out of her pocket, a one-skinner. She stopped a moment to light it, shielding it from the wind, before continuing up the path to her front gate.

As she approached the gate she met James bouncing up the footpath. He was walking in the jaunty manner that indicated that his anxiety, for whatever reason was today at a tolerable level and was almost akin to excitement. "Alright," he chirped and gave Lisa a playful jab in the stomach with his finger. Lisa, mid-exhalation, spluttered a dense cloud of smoke into James' face. "Hey," she greeted him between convulsions of coughing and laughter, "What's up?" James' face was contorted in mock disgust as he used his hand to fan the smoke away from his face. He smiled at her. "Nothin' really, whatch'ya up to?" Lisa handed the joint to him. "Just headin' over to me Granda's for a while," she nodded her head in the direction of uptown. "Ya comin'?" James took a couple of quick tokes on the joint and handed it back to Lisa. "Yeah, sure." They set off down the street chatting.

The side streets were quiet, punctuated by the occasional appearance of a vaguely recognizable face and some unknowns; some of whom smiled, and some who carried on about their business. Due to accommodation prices in the capital rising to exorbitant levels in recent years and their town's connection to it through a recently built dual carriageway, they had seen the population swell with an influx of commuters who lived on the outskirts of the town and made the daily trip to the city by car, bus or train. Consequently it was as though a whole new community with its own identity had begun to envelope and permeate the town. More and more people they had grown up with had moved away; to be replaced by strangers who had their main lives in the city and were looking for somewhere affordable to sleep at night or somewhere a bit more peaceful to raise their families.

"Man I wish we had something to do," Lisa said as she took a drag and sighed and looked around at the rows of houses stretching along the road. "I'm getting so sick of just pissin' around here." She handed the joint to James who took a deep drag and held the smoke in his lungs as they walked in silence. "What do ya wanna do?" he asked finally, sending the question out on a cloud of smoke. Lisa screwed up her face and shrugged. "I dunno," she replied and sighed again. "That's the problem. Like I wanna do stuff; write maybe, or travel... Make an animation show. Learn how to write music, etcetera, etcetera. But ya need money to live, and to get money I've to get a proper job." She took a long drag and exhaled slowly, then pushed a stray strand of golden hair off her face and back behind her ear. "Then you're stuck in some fuckin' job eatin' up all your time. And when you've got time off you're recoverin' from your weeks work, 'til eventually you just forget about doin' anything else and concentrate on just bein' able to work. It's like, how do ya get out of this fucking circle."

James considered this for a moment then shrugged. "I guess ya just have to pick the circle you wanna be on."

"Yeah that's exactly it," Lisa agreed, turning to him and holding her hand up in an emphatic gesture of understanding. "How the hell do ya do that?... Just pick something? Like there's a million different things I'd like to try but it's just not practical. And it seems like the older you get it's like, well either pick something soon or you're left behind."

She turned to face forward once again as she almost tripped over a giant granite flowerpot filled with brightly coloured geraniums. Unimpeded, and becoming more fluid as her views seemed to crystallize, she continued; "Then you just spend all your time workin' some job you never wanted. Too tired to think of tryin' something else. And all you can do to stop your dead dreams from eating at you is spend all your time off drinking or eating pizzas or makin' your own kids and fuckin' shoutin' at them all day to make em do what you couldn't." James chuckled and added wryly, "Or convincing yourself that it's all God's plan." "Yeah," Lisa laughed. "God created me so I could spend my life pissing around in total confusion doin' nothing of any value. Nice plan."

They continued to chat as they turned the corner onto Cyril's street and headed down towards his house, which was the second last on the row. It was one of the old streets, the original core that the town had been built around, with all the old town-houses with thick granite walls and big sturdy wooden doors with brass letterboxes and door knockers. The houses here stood in marked comparison to the newer houses; the estates on the edges of the town that had in the preceding years begun to shoot up like mushrooms in an empty field, but had lately begun to falter and decay; the finished ones with their plastic doors and windows that looked as though they could have been made from cardboard. Lisa lifted the big brass knocker on Cyril's door and tapped it three times.

They stood and waited. After a good minute or two they heard the latch click, the door creaked slowly open and Cyril appeared, squinting out in the daylight. Seeing Lisa and James standing there the wrinkles around his eyes, already quite deep, became even more pronounced as his face lit up in a broad smile. He greeted them heartily and ushered them both inside.

The two stepped in to the musty smelling hallway with the deep shag carpet patterned with floral designs of brown and charcoal and deep maroon and the walls that had most probably been white at some point that were now a kind of browny-yellow. Cyril closed the door and they headed through to the small but cosy living room where he spent most of his days sitting by the fire watching the sleek black Panasonic television Lisa's uncle had bought him some years before, to replace the small black and white set he had been using; with its wood panel veneer and the small clicky dials for manually changing the channels and adjusting the volume. James, as he stood in the doorway of the living room becoming increasingly dazed, was observing to himself that Cyril, like his own late grandfather and a lot of other old men, was wearing a suit as he seemed always to do, even when just sitting in the house. Cyril had on a white shirt, parts of which were beginning to resemble the same musty colour as the walls in the hallway. Around his neck he had on a nice silk tie with a brown and navy paisley pattern on it and over the shirt and tie he was wearing a light grey v-necked cardigan. His jacket was light-brown tweed and was laid over a nearby chair with a trilby-type hat on top of it. James looked down at his own tattered jeans and t-shirt and thought he might like to wear a nice suit sometimes and a trilby hat. Not an old man suit; definitely no paisley patterns or cardigans. But a cool one, like the pictures of F. Scott. Fitzgerald in Paris in the 1920's, or like Johnny Depp or something.

Cyril who had been discussing the upcoming local elections with Lisa, went into the kitchen to get some Ribena and biscuits for them. James, realising he was still standing erratically in the doorway, took a seat beside Lisa, who was already sat comfortably on the couch engrossed in an advert on the telly for car insurance featuring a talking telephone.

James bounced gently a couple of times as he sat on the springy couch which was a kind of dark olive green corduroy and had patches almost worn through. The chair opposite them was where Cyril always sat, beside the fire facing the TV. He lived here alone now, his wife Catherine -Lisa's grand-mother, having passed away almost seven ago years now. Save for Lisa, occasionally accompanied by James; he didn't have many visitors, and he mostly sat watching the television, occasionally nursing a glass or two of stout. Now and again of a fine day he would go and sit in the park and watch the people going about their lives: going to work, bringing their kids out to play or walking together just enjoying the fresh air. During the summer there would always be lots going on: now that the autumn was coming in and the holidays were ending, the park was becoming quieter and the amount of people generally out and about was slowly dwindling.

James and Lisa made themselves comfortable and looked around the room as they always did. The various shelves and dressers around the room were filled with knick-knacks and curios. The little bits and pieces that had been collected over a lifetime, each little thing holding its own memory and all playing their part in the story of the life of an old man. There was the little porcelain pig that had sat on the shelf above the television smiling down at them for as long as they could remember. There was a little cartoonish figurine of a Native American girl with big round dark eyes and a plait going down her back. Some weird coloured glass balls, probably old Christmas decorations. Some silver tankards with engravings on the side that had pens and pencils and various little bits and bobs in them. There was a big sea-shell that Lisa had brought home from the beach one time that was vibrant shades of pink and orange and had little jagged spikes along one side. There was an old barometer, an old typewriter, and scattered around them, various different McDonald's Happy Meal toys. These were all interspersed with various religious figurines and photos of Lisa and the rest of her family.

The effects of the weed were beginning to hit James hard now and he was starting to feel a little uncomfortable. His leg began to twitch anxiously. Lisa looked at him and smiled. "You okay?" she asked him. "Yeah I'm okay I think." Just then Cyril came in with a plate of Jaffa Cakes. "Biscuit?" He said holding the plate up to James. "Aaaaah, yeah, please thanks." James took the plate and set it down on the table. Lisa leaned over. "Just take a breath," she advised him as Cyril went back to the kitchen to get the drinks. "Try and empty your mind." "Easier said than done," murmured James and then at a loss to understanding what he himself had just said, suddenly burst out laughing. Lisa began to laugh as well, quickly clasping her hand over her mouth to prevent the Jaffa Cakes spluttering all over the floor in front of her.

They sat stifling giggles and just managed to calm down and regain some semblance of normality before Cyril came back again. "Cold out there today isn't it?" he said as he slowly lowered himself into his chair by the fire until adequately positioned then dropped with a heavy plonk. Taking a moment to settle he reached behind his back to pull the cushion that was lodged there into a more comfortable resting place. "Yeah it's startin' to get a bit chilly alright," Lisa replied still smiling. "Are ya alright for sticks an' coal and everything here?" "Yeah Johnny Casey br..., ya know Johnny Casey, lives over there by the monument?" Cyril jabbed his thumb in the air. Lisa and James nodded. "He brought me over a trailer full of sticks there the other day. He does be out up the woods choppin' up the trees that are knocked down." Cyril took a white handkerchief from his pocket and coughed raspingly into it before continuing, "I wouldn't mind only they're takin' lumps outta that forest. There's gonna be nothing left of it if they keep on."

He put the handkerchief back in his pocket and sat back in the chair. "Still, Johnny's decent enough to bring me a few sticks over. No use in it goin' to waste."

He picked up the remote control and examined it for a moment through squinted eyes before finding the required button and pressing it to switch over to the horse racing. "What are you two up to today?" he asked, slowly but resiliently pulling himself up out of the chair again. "Ah nothing much," Lisa replied as she stared at the horses running in circles on TV with a palpable disinterest. "Just hangin' around. How are you getting on?" She turned to him, "Apart from decimatin' our natural resources." Cyril laughed dryly to himself as he poked at the fire which was smouldering under a blanket of ash. James got up gingerly and went to get a couple of logs from the kitchen. "Ah sure I'm grand as always, no news thank God," Cyril replied. His joints creaked like a rusty door as he pulled himself up from where he was hunched in front of the fire and dropped himself back into his chair. "My legs are painin' me a bit with the cold weather comin' on," he continued. His face straightened and his voice became soft and touched by nerves. "How's your mam and dad?"

Lisa was now observing the myriad colours and patterns on the silk shirts of the jockeys as they sat on top of their ambling horses preparing for the next race to start. "They're fine," she replied, "Same old, ya know," She turned back to Cyril. "Me ma I think is goin' to be getting another couple a' days in the shop." "That's good," Cyril replied. "And what about you two? Have yous any luck with a job or anything?" He looked back and forth between Lisa and James who had returned from the kitchen with two logs, which he placed on the hearth before taking his seat back on the couch. James shrugged. "I've a couple of days a week. It's enough to pay the rent an' all... just about." "Sure ya mustn't have a lot of spendin' money do ya?" James shrugged again. He had regained himself and was feeling a lot more relaxed and comfortable. "Ah sure I've nothing to spend it on anyway," he continued. "A few drinks and a few books. A bit of food occasionally." "An' what about you?" Cyril turned to Lisa. "Ah, is it wooorth the aggravaysheeeeooon...," she half-sang in a whining faux-Mancunian drawl. James joined in, *"To find yourself a job when there's nothing worth workiiin fooooor."* They both laughed.

Cyril looked at them, a slightly bemused expression on his face. "An Oasis song," Lisa clarified. "Ahhh them fellas," Cyril replied nodding. "Ya still following them?" He smiled to himself. "I remember the t-shirt you got one Christmas when you were about ten or eleven. You were wearin' it for about three weeks solid. Ye must've had to scrape it off with a chisel." He smiled as Lisa and James burst out laughing.

Cyril took a sip of tea from the Bugs Bunny mug Catherine had gotten years ago by collecting tokens from a Weetabix box. "Have you any plans to go back to college then or are ya still going to be a rock star?" he continued, placing the mug back down on the coffee table in front of him. Lisa and James laughed again. "Ah I'm not really bothered," Lisa said. "Why not?" Cyril asked, turning to her and raising an eyebrow. "I dunno...," Lisa replied, sighing and looking down at the floor as she tried to wrestle an answer from herself. "I didn't really like it. It seemed a bit rigid n' like, professional or something. Like they're just givin' ya more ideas to learn and formulas to use. Could do without it." Cyril pondered this for a moment, slightly unsure as to whether he should support her or convince her otherwise, and between his heart and his head unable to find a compelling or definitive argument either way. "I suppose it just doesn't suit everyone," he answered in an attempt at diplomacy. "Everyone has their own ideas." "Yeah, and sure I couldn't afford it anyway," Lisa added. "So what are the two of ye plannin' to do with your lives?" Cyril asked, looking at the two of them.

Lisa and James looked at each other then looked back at Cyril. "Dunno," they said in unison.

CHAPTER 5

"It's important to be doing something with your life. When I was your age I never had the opportunities you have." Sharon's mother Julie called in to her as she stood in front of the bathroom mirror applying her lipstick. She was getting ready to go to a party, a work related affair thrown by her bosses at Collins' estate agency. "I'm not going to have you bummin' around wasting your time."

Sharon was sitting on the bed in her room across the hall from the bathroom. "But it's so boring...." She looked down at the carpet, at the monotonous shades of bluey-grey that enveloped her feet and stretched across the room to meet the bevelled white skirting board. "I don't know if I can do it the rest of my life." "Well what are you going to do then?" Julie queried her. Sharon hesitated, knowing what she wanted to say but not quite sure how to say it; or whether at this stage it would even be worth the bother. "I don't know," she mumbled, nervously poking the carpet with her toe. "I was thinking of maybe doin' photography or like photo-journalism or something like that. I thought maybe if I could have a year then I could build up a pretty decent portfolio and then..."

"Don't be ridiculous," Julie called in from the bathroom. "Where's this come from? You're not an artist…"

There was a silence as she popped the lid back on her lipstick and dropped it in her handbag. "And how do you expect to make a living from that?" she continued, now scanning through bottles of creams and ointments that were scattered haphazardly all over the bathroom counter-top. "Why not?" Sharon replied feeling the hope that had been none too resolute to begin with, wilt even further. "I could try couldn't I?" she attempted to argue, her voice beginning to crack as her chest constricted to further diminish her resolve.

Her plea was met with silence and a subtle metallic rumble from a radiator in the room next door. Putting her feet back flat on the ground she turned to look out the window at the swirling clouds in the deep blue sky, like a living moving picture framed against the yellowish-beige expanse of her bedroom wall. Lacking any definitive answer she returned to the same conclusions she always reached, the only things she was really sure of. "I don't know what I am," she said out loud but mostly to hersel;, unsure if Julie was even still listening to her. "How am I supposed to know that now?"

Her voice became calm again with certainty as she regained herself and lowered her gaze back once again to the mottled carpet. "I know I don't want to sit in some office all day every day." "Well that's the way life works," Julie called back unfazed from the bathroom. "Sometimes you have to sit in an office all day. Where do you think the money came from to buy this house?" She snapped her compact closed and put it in her handbag. She then picked up a small white bottle of pills that was sitting on the counter beside her and threw them into the bag behind it as she stepped out into the hallway. She turned to Sharon, feeling an unexpected thump in her chest as she saw her daughter's forehead knotted in confusion, her eyes downcast and almost mournful. Taking a deep breath she continued; "Finish your studies. With any luck Michael Stewart'll be able to give you a good job. And once you have a job then you can do what you like. Take photos or whatever you want." She raised her eyebrows conclusively. "Alright... Let that be the end of it."

After one last quick check of her make-up in the hall mirror she picked up her bag before poking her head back in Sharon's doorway. "There's dinner on a plate in the fridge. I shouldn't be back too late. Okay." Her eyes were dull and the muscles of her face heavy to move as she just managed to flash Sharon a tired smile before heading out the door.

Sharon leaned over to her dresser where she had some leaflets and prospectuses with some courses marked off. She cursed herself for not being more forceful as she browsed through the leaflets. She probably should have shown her mother her research. Maybe then she'd have been taken more seriously. Most probably not though, she thought as she lay back on her bed and stared up at the ceiling. She knew her mother was very stubborn and once she had a plan in mind there wasn't a lot that could derail her. There was always the chance she might set her off on a mood as well. It was generally just better overall not to push things too much. To try and maintain some kind of stability. There was certainly no use in stirring things up for the sake of something as vague and impractical as artistic aspirations. Not that Sharon wanted to be an artist particularly. She just wanted to see things, take some photos. She'd spent her whole life since she was five years old sitting somewhere, listening while people told her what's what. And it was beginning to seem now as if that would be a pattern that would continue through the rest of her life. Of course college was expensive as well, she thought. More than she could ever afford working holidays. She had to be grateful for the fact that her parents were giving her this helping hand. She had opportunity. More than a lot of people in the world. Maybe changing her mind now was just being ungrateful. Wasteful. Maybe she was just spoiled?

She pulled herself up off the bed and went downstairs to the living room where she took a seat on the edge of the massive, plump white leather couch and sat looking around. It was a lonely house. Her father was travelling quite a bit for work and her mother also worked long hours and so the house was empty for large portions of the day. It was nice and big, with more rooms than three people needed. They had a huge thirty inch plasma screen TV. Most of the house had been re-decorated the previous year and all the carpets and wallpaper were fresh and clean. It was a nice house, Sharon thought. A nice, pretty house. Still, she wondered, wouldn't it be cool to see some marks on a wall or stuff laying around or anything really that betrayed the fact that there were people actually living here? Some sign of life and not mere existence.

She'd had a pretty good life all in all, she thought. Nothing she could really complain about. She hadn't been abused. They'd always had enough money to live well and buy everything they wanted. She had good food, nice clothes, a nice house. And yet it all seemed so dull and lifeless. She couldn't get away from this feeling of being somehow disadvantaged in life and at the same time constantly felt ashamed of herself for feeling this way. When she tried to examine herself to find the cause of this restlessness and saw nothing but a pretty girl and an easy life it made her feel all the more like a horrible, ungrateful person.

She decided to go for a walk, to get out of the house and get some air. Pulling on her coat she stepped out into the brisk evening and began to make her way towards town.

As she was passing the entrance of her road onto the main street she passed two guys she recognised from school and said hello. Two dorky guys. She liked them though. They seemed like fun. They were constantly laughing at each other. Even though they probably weren't the type to have hundreds of friends or be invited to the good parties, it didn't seem to bother them at all. They did what they liked. Sharon often wondered if she wouldn't rather to just be having fun like them and laughing like they did at something pointless; than keeping up this facade and living everyday in view of her reputation and duties. Living like some pretty object, some sort of model of perfection; rather than a person with guts and flaws and weird thoughts she didn't understand sometimes. It seemed as though preserving herself took up most of her energy and although it had seemed important at one time she was beginning to have her doubts.

She continued down the cold, almost deserted street, beginning to feel weightless, as though she were evaporating. *The thing was,* she thought, *it wasn't even really herself she was preserving... Who was this person? The person that seemed to exist already fully formed, like a character already written; and she was now born to live up to it. Where did it come from?*

She had no interest in accountancy or anything even vaguely related to it. How was she now already in the process of working towards this career she didn't even want?

She turned to look back up the street where she could just make out the two lads off in the distance, still laughing heartily as evidenced by the shuddering and wobbling of their vague silhouettes. Harry and Piotr probably weren't expected to be cool and rich and part of the social elite and have respectable boring jobs and big clean houses and gardeners to keep their lawns tidy. They could just have fun. Be themselves.

She turned back around and continued to walk, bunching herself up in her jacket and thrusting her hands deep into the pockets as she began to shiver in the cold. She knew that probably wasn't true either. That things were never so simplistic. She knew there was something else to all this, something she was missing.

CHAPTER 6

"Fish-eye fighter-pilot, tree ballerina... Briight-sun lollipop. And so it begins; or not."

Piotr stared intensely down at Harry with a barely suppressed grin that trembled as though about to explode. "You're quare strange," Harry replied and eyed Piotr with mock caution. Piotr's grin finally did explode and a torrent of laughter burst from him and continued to flow as he stumbled along holding his stomach. "Bright sun lollipop!!!"

He continued to laugh for some time as they walked, passing rows of sleeping shops and offices, before the words eventually began to weaken and leave him, as other things fought for his attention; and his chuckles finally began to fade and succumb to the silence of the evening street. He let out a sigh. "I like it anyways," he added in conclusion. "Yeah it's alright actually," Harry replied, starting to smile, half at Piotr and half at his ridiculous poem. "So what are we watchin' tonight?" he asked, turning to his lanky friend who was trying hard to suffocate a second onslaught of crippling laughter that was beginning to build up momentum.

Harry and Piotr had been in the same secondary school as Keehan, James and Lisa, but a year below them, in the same year as Sharon Davies and Michelle Clarke. Consequently, their paths had never really crossed for the duration of that stint. They had met James for the first time at the beginning of that summer in the local Xtravision video shop.

James had gone in there for a browse and was perusing the back of a DVD case when a faux-Russian voice had suddenly boomed in his ear, making him jump. "VEEERRE'S DE FUCKIN' MONEY LEBOWSKI???" He turned around to see a six foot tall guy with blonde hair that was sticking up in random tufts, who was staring into his face and grinning like a lunatic. Another voice that was lower in register but with a slightly squeaky timbre joined him from somewhere. "We vont de fucking money Lebowskiiii." This time it was a smaller guy, who stepped out from behind a shelf of DVD cases and looked from Piotr to James, to the DVD case James was holding, and back to James again. The second guy was quite chubby, with a face that was almost blank but with what seemed like the smallest hint of a laugh about to happen somewhere within its deadpan features. James froze slightly, not really sure what was happening, and his mind barrelled in on top of him so as to smother his senses. "Some movie," said the tall guy Piotr, gesturing to the DVD case.

"Oh…," James replied open mouthed, and as it dawned on him that the previous threats had been mere references, began to feel an unthreatening reality flood back into him like a cool breeze in a stuffy overcrowded room. "I… I haven't seen it," he added and smiled as his breathing slowed to a calm, natural tide once more. "Oh man…" Piotr exclaimed and he and Harry looked at each other excitedly, sensing an opportunity to introduce someone to The Dude.

The three of them hung out at the video shop for some time that day discussing movies and then school and various other things before picking up some vodka, Tia Maria and milk and heading back to the lads' house to drink White Russians and watch The Big Lebowski. Harry and Piotr had become regular visitors to the house over the course of the summer, a fact that Keehan wasn't terribly pleased by.

Some weeks after the meeting at the video store, when the two had been relative unknowns to him, Keehan had come home expecting nothing other than his usual relatively comfortable and peaceful evening with some drinks in front of the TV. He had flounced in the door as usual lost deeply in thought and imaginings before stopping short as he suddenly realised the room was more crowded than it usually was. What he had come across was the four of them; Lisa, James and the two newcomers, who were there in the living room sat around the coffee table deep in discussion.

Piotr and Harry had been attempting different techniques for lucid dreaming. Lisa and James had both tried it numerous times for short periods and they were excitedly discussing their experiences. "Alright?," Keehan muttered, mostly to James and Lisa before he glanced across the two new arrivals with an attempt of cordiality that was peppered with an instinctive measure of suspicion as well as a little shock from the sudden forced transition from his reality to the other one; the one where people he was unfamiliar with turned up out of the blue to encroach on his space. "Hey," Harry and Lisa both said looking up at him and Piotr raised his hand in a gesture of greeting and smiled. "How's it goin' man," James nodded to him before turning back to the others to continue... "I never actually got as far as being able to control what was happening like, but I remember one really cool one where I was in a school gym, kinda like ours. I was standin' at one end and suddenly, out of no-where there was a T-Rex at the other end!!" His face began to shine with glee as the memory of the strange experience came alive to him again and he continued to recount his story. "It started coming towards me and I was standin' there shittin' myself, but then just as I was starting to run away I suddenly realised I was dreaming... Once I knew I couldn't get killed or anythin' I just kept running up and down the school corridors, ducking in and out of rooms with 'im following me." He started to laugh. "I was runnin' around the school playing chase with a T-Rex! It was some craic..."

Keehan pulled over a chair and sat down on the periphery of the group as they continued to talk about a subject that he was sure he'd had no experience with. As he sat quietly trying to be attentive, he began to feel more and more like a spare part. But he figured it would probably be rude to just walk off straight away. Not that he cared so much about being rude to anyone, he just didn't like to be excluded. He would exclude them as soon as he knew he was wanted. He decided to wait to see if someone would initiate him to the discussion.

As he continued to sit there the discussion continued as though he wasn't even there and he began to get anxious and fidgety. He began to feel excruciatingly pointless. That he needed vitally to contribute something soon or he would become forever the sad boring simpleton with nothing to say. His mind began to furiously rifle through arguments and possibilities and the conversation the others were having became an intermittent and unintelligible background hum.

Surely there was only so long he could sit there saying nothing without being weird? He couldn't leave now though could he, after sitting down for this long? He couldn't just get up and walk away, that would be really weird, maybe even offensive? He was happy being special, but he didn't want to be a weirdo. He began to get slightly irritated by the four of them rabbiting on and on and began to feel even more fidgety and uncomfortable as his mind frantically scrambled for a way to preserve his dignity.

Having gauged that the conversation was something to do with dreams he sat impatiently waiting for a gap in which to insert himself. As soon as James finished describing how he had once flown in through someone's window and how the sensation had felt like swimming, Keehan jumped in; and the others turned to listen to him as he blurted out the first thing on his mind that was even vaguely related. "I had a nightmare the other night, I was goin' down this ladder in this massive grain silo kinda thing." Having gained their attention now and caught up in the relief of having temporarily escaped his self-imposed solipsism he continued, relaxing into his position. "The ladder started gettin' longer and longer and it started shakin'." As he continued to recount the details of his dream he suddenly began to remember how terrified he had been that night. As he was not in the habit of divulging such vulnerable details he skilfully managed to divert to a more heroic ending, concluding; "But just as it was about to shake me off I managed to grab on to it and climb back up."

James, Harry and Lisa sat and nodded in deferred acceptance, each in their own way attempting to make sense of Keehan's tenuously related point.

Piotr looked at him, a thoughtful and earnest expression on his face before informing him solemnly, "I think that means you like to have sex with dogs." He continued to look at Keehan, who had been stunned into silence for some seconds, before his face broke out in a wide grin and the others burst out laughing.

Keehan looked around at them, his eyes for a split second widening in shock before narrowing contemptuously as he pursed his lips together tightly. The others continued to laugh, assuming Keehan would join them at some point, but his face retained the same hardened expression; his thin, crunched together eyebrows sunk deeply over narrowed eyes. His lips still pursed tightly as though his face had been frozen by furious indignation.

"Seriously," Harry turned to him after the laughter had eventually died down, and realising that Keehan was not partaking in the joke. "If you're going down a ladder or something in a dream it generally means that you're going into your subconscious. From what I know anyway... Like you're examining your underlying fears and motivations."

Keehan looked at him suspiciously, not sure if he should take him seriously or not. Harry continued, a twisted smile creeping across his face as he leaned forward and began to impersonate the raspy, tense whisper of the Crypt-keeper: in the process emphasizing the slight, intermittent squeak in his own voice, producing an unintentionally comic tone -as though it were battling for prominence with a demonic Powerpuff Girl. "All the daaaaAArk and unruuUUly impulses of your nAture lie hidden under the sUrface, reprEssed by the mind to keep them at bay... The hiDden vIolencccce and sssAVAgery that drives you. That drives aAAAll of us…" He burst out in a hearty laugh and his head seemed to inflate like a balloon as he laughed and laughed and the other three joined him, infected by his joyful exuberance. Keehan was silent as they continued to laugh.

Calming down eventually Harry turned to Keehan who was still sitting stony-faced, and summarised matter-of-factly, "And that's what you're connecting with when you go down a ladder or a stairs in a dream… supposedly."

Keehan had already decided now that he wasn't going to give any credence to all that hippy crap about the meaning of dreams. He just wanted to say something. And he could do without the bloody performance as well. He nodded and immediately decided to ignore Harry's interpretation, logical as it may have seemed on another day in another context.

From that day on whenever Harry and Piotr came over to the house Keehan generally rebuffed them with sarcastic retorts or ignored them and skulked around reluctantly find-ing alternate ways to amuse himself, or playing his PSP as they all talked and laughed among themselves. Spending his time with himself, having the conversations he could've had with the actual people around him. But it was easier that way. Things went the way he wanted. He could revise and refine what he wanted to say -what he would say if he could live how he felt when he was alone; with no pressure, no anxiety.

"What's Keehan's deal?" Harry quietly asked James and Lisa one day some weeks later as Keehan sat in the kitchen sip-ping vodka and orange juice and listening to his mp3 player through a small white cube speaker; whilst also surreptitiously catching snippets of conversation that drifted through from the living room. "Ah I don't know he's a bit weird some-times," James replied, not really thinking too much about it as he gazed out the window at a dog in the car park across the street who was running in vigorous circles for no apparent reason. He smiled and turned back to the others. Absorbing the question more fully he continued, "He acts cocky, but like, really I think he just gets anxious around new people." Harry's brow furrowed. "Like he's just shy or somethin'?" He paused for a moment to attempt to digest this possibility before continuing unconvinced, "He seems like a bit of a mouth." He quickly held up his hands in a gesture of apol-ogy. "Y'know... I don't mean that in a bad way." He smiled as James and Lisa laughed. "Just. I mean...I just wouldn't've ever thought he was shy." He scratched his chin. "D'ya know the Myers-Briggs test?" he asked Lisa and James. Lisa shook her head. "That's that personality test," James replied. Harry nodded. "Ah yeah I've heard of it," said James. "Don't know much about it." "Based on what I know of him," Harry con-tinued, "I'd have thought that he'd probably score pretty high on extroversion on the Myers-Briggs." He scratched his chin again and looked off thoughtfully. "I suppose maybe it's pos-sible for someone to be shy and extroverted at the same time?" "Yeah maybe," Lisa replied as her attention turned back to the TV. Piotr laughed. "That test iss a load of rubbish, it's not even recognized by the psychological community. He scoffed disdainfully. "Why do you have to be one or the other?" "Ooh the commuuuuuunity," Harry crooned at Piotr in mock respect while waving his hands in the air. "Mr psychology student." Piotr laughed again, "Yeah, well."

Keehan was no longer listening to them. He had been

listening more intently ever since the subject of himself had come up and he was not terribly impressed with the image that was being portrayed, or even the fact that they thought they had the right to try and define him at all. Of course he probably wouldn't have minded that so much if their definitions had at least been overwhelmingly positive. *Bleedin' dorks and their theories and equations*, he thought as his mind began to go into overdrive. *Bloody college boys... They probably don't know half what they're talkin about...* He took a hefty gulp of vodka and orange juice. *It's real geniuses like me that don't need to go on about it,* he thought, his heart beginning to beat faster. *Livin' in the real world. Not some phony bullshit system.*

There had been times when Keehan had considered fearfully the possibility that he might just be a bit of a dork. He'd seemed to have flown under the radar as regards the popular groups in school. Also he did seem to be more attracted to the esoteric in life, which as a young child had seemed unimportant, even quite endearing; but had seemed to become more of an issue the older he got. As everyone started to divide into groups it seemed that in some groups certain interests became valued while others became something to be embarrassed by, and that if you couldn't find the way to be what you wanted to be; then skill at being part of the general community became the only important thing and the gateway to success and survival. The skill of being the same as everyone else. Of doing what everyone around you did. Of always being confident even if you didn't know. Of lying if the truth was inconvenient. Of never being weird or showing interest in things that weren't deemed important or thinking in any way differently. The skills of easily and happily pissing your time away talking to other people about the weather or some bullshit. The skill of unquestioningly following all the other sheep into churches and colleges and offices. If you could be enthusiastic about it then even better, you'd do really well.

The truth was he had at one point liked to learn, to know things. But somewhere along the way real life had intervened and that kind of knowledge had seemed to become a game played for kicks by those who'd learned how; while the rest concentrated on trying to be good at life and to not look too stupid without looking too smart either.

He was sure he'd managed to adapt quite well and separate that geeky, bookish, weirdo kid from the charismatic stud he was now, although he still had the occasional surfacing of some secret passions or forgotten hobbies he just didn't act on anymore. A sort of shameful inner dork like a Mr Hyde that he kept hidden, from himself at least; and just generally avoided having any meaningful contact with: in a blinkered attempt to spare himself the pain of knowing his true passion and how it was slowly dying to nothing. He didn't really read anything anymore except on the rare occasion when the world felt inviting or he had nothing left to lose. He hadn't the attention span for it anyway. Not since he left school. His mind was too occupied by other things. He decided books were for losers who had nothing better to do and that would end his dilemmas and settle him again.

Sitting alone in the kitchen now and drinking his vodka and orange juice he continued in the theatre of his mind, and his anger began to rise higher and higher as he continued to mull over the others and their obvious disregard and disrespect for him: and their and everyone else's obliviousness to the great guy Keehan knew that he was. Desperate to be seen as the person he wanted to be; instead he was just some clump of animated matter with no real life worth mentioning, and a self created fictional biography that existed only in the reality of his own mind. He resumed crafting his plays, real-life situations in which he, in the course of his everyday life gained the upper hand due to his intellectual prowess. He found different settings and different audiences, but the basic premise of his session now; the thread that ran through all scenes was the same -the humiliation of Harry and Piotr by him. He gave them words, set them up so he could knock them down. His own words; his every gesture; he crafted and changed and revised and revised again in order to wring the greatest amount of glory from each situation. To make the people watching laugh harder, or to make them whisper to each other in awed amazement at his genius. He sat and spiralled again, the tension in his body feeding the poison in his mind, in turn feeding the tension in his body, and so on, reinforcing each other; balancing each other; like dancers that could not stop but only get more energetic and more frantic as they spun; taking on a life of their own; attempting to maintain their equilibrium as the music became more riotous and the tempo increased more and more. It was times like these Keehan sometimes wished he could just put a bullet through his head, to end the torment once and for all. He never seriously considered it, in fact it frightened him a little the fact that he could have these thoughts; but at the same time it went some way to comforting him even as a thought -to know that he could. Of course it was his own mind that was his torturer, the thing he needed to obliterate. All he *truly* wanted was to live in peace.

Even now as he focused on his own death, on the end of it all, the images began to slow and become less vivid. The real world around him began to come back into focus. Meanings faded and the tension in his body with them. Keehan began to pray to no-one and nothing in particular that they would stay away; but his will was faint and was being slowly forgotten. He continued in desperation even as the thoughts began once again to bubble up inside his head, the residue of anger left behind, spurring his mind to whirl once more and swallow him up in his own darkness.

CHAPTER 7

Monday, September 8th.

Keehan was awoken by the dampened glare of sunlight attempting to push its way through his curtains, and the sharp twinkling of birdsong in his ears. It was just a little after nine, and as much as he tried he couldn't get back to sleep. Despite the fact that he'd just woken up, he was already feeling restless and slightly anxious.

He had been finding of late that the sedentary, work-free lifestyle, rather than nourishing his legs which he had always assumed would be the case; seemed in fact to be the root cause of a growing tension and discomfort. He'd been feeling the effects increasingly of late as the muscles in his calves and thighs had begun to develop a tremor akin to a nervous twitch, that had started in intermittent phases and now was becoming an almost constant trembling numbness. He had begun to accept begrudgingly that an increase in physical exertion would be necessary to rid himself of the aggravation of his throbbing limbs, and he decided he would go for a walk sometime later that day. He continued for the time being to lay in bed, staring at the ceiling as his mind drifted in and out of lucidity: occasionally twisting and stretching when a certain position began to cause his legs to become tense and cramped again.

Eventually after almost an hour of this he could lie there no longer. He managed to pull himself up out of bed with difficulty and headed downstairs to get some breakfast. He ate a bowl of cereal and sat and watched a little television before he began to feel the trembling restlessness come on again. Finally at a point where he could no longer ignore it, he got up and grabbed his sunglasses which were lying on the coffee table and slid them on. He picked up his mp3 player and headed towards the door, plugging the headphones snugly into his ears as he stepped outside; his mood lifting considerably as he looked forward to getting lost in some music and the breaking up of his regular routine of pottering around the house. He decided to head to the supermarket on the other side of town. Not for any particular reason; he had scant money to buy anything. But it was somewhere to go. A destination. He closed the door behind him and locked it and turned to stroll off in the direction of the shop.

He passed a couple of streets at increasing pace and soon enough his legs began to relax to an extent: the tension in his joints began to loosen and he slipped comfortably and happily into his mind wanderings; the music blaring from his headphones blocking out all unwanted distractions from the world around him.

He skimmed his finger lightly across the music player which was nestled snugly in his pocket until he found the dial. He clicked it three times and waited for the split second until the crisp, warm opening harmonies of "Nowhere Man" came glistening into his consciousness. This was the song of the moment, the one he clicked back to repeat on endless loops again and again. As much as he'd listened to the album here and there over the years, the song had never really stood out to him. There were many like that on many albums that had been the same initially. There were the instant and obvious hits, the ones that had always been around and always would. And then there were the others. The supporting players. The ones he would have skipped over usually. It seemed that at different points in the course of his life, in certain moments; one of these songs that he'd heard but never really listened to, would suddenly for some reason become illuminated. Like it had contained a vial full of perfume that had suddenly been released and had wafted through him with something more profound than he had ever known was contained in what had previously been merely a pop song; a nice, jangly tune that had never really had anything in particular to say. Often he could remember a particular time a song had changed for him; had suddenly become important. In some cases he could remember the exact moment. That was the case with this song. He could recall the moment it changed, as though he were watching it happen on a screen in his mind: could almost live it again, but without all the monotonous reality that surrounded it. Cleaner, tighter; more epic.

It had happened one night only a few weeks before as he lay on his bed too drunk and lethargic to move. He had spent most of the day in the house alone drinking Jack Daniels while James was at work. That evening as it began to get dark he retired to his room to continue to drink and wind down with some music. After an hour, finally unable to drink any more, he put *Rubber Soul* on; skipped to the second track

"Norwegian Wood" and lay back on his bed, mentally exhausted and heavy with alcohol. He lay back on the soft duvet feeling a numbness crawl over him as his mind switched off completely.

The album played on as background noise, one track following another as he lay in a daze hearing nothing in particular; but lost in a jumble of sensory information. Gradually out of the fuzz of his experience the words of this song had seemed to appear. They had crept into his awareness to re-ignite something in him and had suddenly become clear and bright as polished crystal: as though traced with a wet finger through the dust which had previously obscured them. He could remember suddenly becoming more and more awake and once again becoming present in the room and the world around him, as the words seemed to speak directly to him at his deepest core. He lay there until the song ended, then reached over to the player to skip back to hear it again, and then another time and another; and he lay back and wondered about his life and his dreams, and whether they were for anyone or anything in particular, and whether someday he would begin living for real.

Listening to his music and unobscured by company on the quiet, almost empty street, he was making great time and was beginning to gain momentum in his stride. He passed another two streets as if they weren't there; when suddenly his headphones began to crackle and fizz. Slowing down, he gripped the headphone jack where it was plugged into the player and jostled it back and forth a few times. The sound recovered its clarity and he resumed his pace, happily settling into his stride once more. Just as his mind began to drift off again there was a loud crackle in his left ear like the pop of a tin-foil balloon and with that the sound cut out completely. He let out an irritated grunt and stopped walking. He took the player out of his pocket and checked to see if it was still playing, the small triangle in the top corner indicating that it was. He grabbed the headphone jack again and more aggressively this time began to twist it and press it and pull it in a desperate attempt to wring some sound from the jaded wires, but nothing came through. In a fury he yanked the headphones out of the player, almost snapping the jack in the socket. Indignantly he stuffed them into the nearest bin.

He was supremely irritated that his walk had been ruined. Muttering curses under his breath he began to walk on again in a huff, his mind racing to try and find some way to justify the senseless cruelty of the world. He continued to walk, his jaws clenched tightly and his eyes glazed, still muttering in his mind; charging blindly against the sunshine which had begun to form a wall in front of him. He just wanted to listen to a bit of music. *Was that such a fucking tall order? Could things not just go right for once? No. Nothing could be relied on. Nothing could be depended on. Why bother? Why fucking bother...* He continued to walk, no longer even thinking of his headphones, just spinning off into scenarios and possibilities that were becoming ever more distant and pointless.

As he continued on his journey the loss of his music gradually became less and less important as the world around him began to crowd in. His anger, with nothing to attach itself to, gradually began to run out of steam; and as it drifted he began to feel the warmth of the sun on his face. He began to feel the warm rays permeate his body as if he were a sponge.

The autumn air was crisp in his nostrils and despite himself he was beginning to feel content and even buoyant. He felt lifted up by the world, and his tense, resilient stride relaxed into a casual, bouncing stroll.

He passed two women who were talking outside a newsagents. One of the Ladies was grasping the handle of a buggy which was turned away from her facing out into the street, as she chatted animatedly to the other woman about the previous night's episode of Coronation Street. Inside the buggy was a small girl with wispy blonde hair who was sat upright with her elbows perched on her chubby thighs, a plush grey donkey held tightly in her hands. She had a sun hat on and was peering out squinting from underneath the peak at the world going by her. She looked up as Keehan was passing, and seeing her sat there he smiled. The little girl looked at him blankly for a moment with big blue staring eyes before the corners of her mouth turned up ever so slightly as she smiled also, then watched after him as he continued past her down the street. As he strolled on, Keehan began to feel a trembling in his chest. It wasn't the bad trembling, the slightly terrifying trembling that came after too many nights drinking heavily or a couple of days on M-CAT; but the kind of trembling that felt natural and even beautiful.

Just then he spotted Mrs. McCarthy crossing the street. His feeling of satisfaction began to slowly dissipate with the sight of this woman. She was crossing to his side of the street: to the footpath that was too narrow to ever avoid a meeting. A strangling sense of trepidation grew in him at the possibility that he would end up having to have a conversation with her. It wasn't that she wasn't a nice woman. She was quite lovely actually. And she would almost certainly strike up a conversation with him. A conversation in which she would inevitably ask him what he was doing with his life. This was Mrs. McCarthy, whose son Brian had been a couple of years ahead of Keehan in school, and was now writing as a permanent staff member for a newspaper in San Diego, California -as Keehan's own mother seemed to find abundant opportunity to mention. And Keehan remembered that it wasn't enough for him to be a warm sponge soaking in the sun-rays. He sat down on a wooden bench by a bus-stop and breathed a sigh of relief as he watched Mrs. McCarthy turn down a side street and out of view.

He leaned back on the hard bench and lifted his sunglasses for a moment as he pondered on what he would have said to her if she had asked him what he was doing. How he would have explained away the empty days and nights of his life so far? What achievements he would inform her of now that he'd left behind his school days and their lack of obligation beyond day to day attendance; and taken on a future of striving and competition that everyone else seemed to find natural but that he just couldn't seem to find any real lasting passion for? Could he tell her that no; he didn't have a job or a girlfriend or any real prospects, but that he had however developed a great capacity for drinking vodka: and that he had some pretty cool memories involving The Beatles and loneliness...

Across the street almost obscured by the glass panels of a phone-box he suddenly spotted Sharon talking to some girl; the intruding glass panels of the phone-box painting her over with a warped and shimmering brilliance. He'd never know if it was the brightness of the sunshine, the weight of the moment, or the feeling of sheer worthlessness; but he instantly felt a clawing tightness in his chest as he realised that he couldn't possibly live the rest of his life without this girl. Just seeing her there he felt inspired. He felt the physical presence of life. The urge to be someone, to do things, to be great. And he felt charged with the electrifying possibility that he actually could be someone. He could be great. He could be charming or funny or daring or adventurous. If it was for *her*.

He peeked across at her through the phone box trying to not look too obvious, and he began to imagine a hundred pairs of eyes turning to look as he entered a room with her hand clasped tightly in his own. Maybe it was at an Oscar's ceremony, with him being the newest sensation having written the breakout movie of the decade. A movie in which he also starred, garnering rave reviews. He would walk in, dashing in his tux: Sharon alongside him dazzling and resplendent. Both at home together in the glitz and glamour of the show-business world. There was George Clooney sitting at the first table. *"Cloooonaaaay, how's it goin lad,"* he would wink and shoot Clooney a wave. There's Mila Kunis at the table behind... *Quare jealous. I'm sorry Mila,* he'd think to himself giving her a consolatory smile. *Sharon's the only girl for me, you're pretty cool though...* Without him noticing, Sharon had crossed over to his side of the street and was now walking down towards him.

As she approached him sitting on the bench she glanced at him as she would a tree or a post-box, not with any malice whatever but without much occupation either. Waking up just in time, Keehan in a state of shock managed to muster enough self-control to give her a casual smile; like one that might twinkle if he were the debonair and handsome leading man in a fifties movie. It manifested as little more than a barely perceptible twitch at the side of his mouth. Sharon vaguely recognized him and smiled as she did to most people she didn't really know yet; a smile that was polite and reserved but genuine enough as to never be cold. She carried on, her mind on other things; and Keehan debated to himself whether he really saw a special warmth grow in her eyes as she looked at him.

He pulled himself up off the bench, and no longer feeling the need to go as far as the supermarket he began to saunter casually home. He imagined waking up beside her in the morning, rolling over to see her face sleeping beside him. How amazing that would be. He thought of the days in school, the days that happened occasionally when he woke up in the morning, dreading the thoughts of it; trying to pull himself up; forcing himself to move; when he's suddenly realised, *it's a day off!! Oh God what a feeling!* And the whole day after that is a gift... The most important and valuable day there ever was. If only he had her in his life. Every single day would be a gift. He began to drag his feet now along the cracked paving slabs. *But was life even like that anymore?* he wondered to himself. *Could life ever be a gift now? Or were those days truly a thing of the past?* Reality began to creep in again as it always did.

Summoning hope he recalled the picture of her in his mind, the picture that changed resolution from time to time but always remained in some trace. The picture he kept that when clear and vivid, spurred him on relentlessly. By the time he got home he had managed to create a new, better reality; one that for once didn't piss on his dreams. And he decided conclusively that Sharon was in love with him.

When he got in James was there, sitting in front of the TV. He had on the table in front of him a fresh new refill pad open to a blank page with a new pen on top; and it lay there defeatedly as he sat scratching the label off an empty beer bottle that had been sitting on the floor for two or three days.

James, while having had a relatively easy life, being loved and cared for and being essentially happy with himself; had inherited a nervous disposition that had strengthened during the years of his adolescence: and while rarely proving completely incapacitating essentially preserved the boundaries of his life to a selection of people he'd known for years as well as a fractional discourse with the world outside. The tension in him only became more pronounced as he developed a love affair with Charles Bukowski and Hunter S. Thompson, and he dreamed of being a renegade writer; out in the world kicking up dust and chronicling his adventures. This led his mind to become in almost every waking moment the setting of an epic battle between his passion and his fear. A fear that was all pervasive and intangible and almost always won. After many years of this battling his passion was almost ready to concede defeat just for the sake of some peace, if only he could figure out how. The tension still resided in him no matter how he tried to ignore it and it manifested itself in his worst moments as scratching the labels off bottles, biting his nails, and various other fidgety behaviours.

"Well?," he paused his scratching to turn and greet Keehan as he walked in and closed the door firmly behind him.

"Alright?," Keehan replied, a little less morbidly than usual. James replaced the now label-less bottle back in the spot it had previously occupied on the floor. "Any craic?" he asked. "No not really," replied Keehan, taking a seat on the couch beside him. James was now absent-mindedly folding the paper label from the beer bottle into consecutively smaller triangles. He chuckled. "I was just out at me ma and da's. Me da was tellin' me he was drivin' home yesterday and, ya know that lad that's always sittin' on the bench on the corner down by Paddy Power, about early forties, always wears that green baseball cap?" Keehan nodded. "Well he came runnin' out of a house up in one of the estates and some wan -his girlfriend I think; came runnin' after 'im with a hatchet. Started chasin' him round the green. Me da had to let him jump in the car and drove off with yer wan chasin' 'em wit the hatchet." "Jaysus," muttered Keehan. "Someone rang the guards anyway," James continued, "and when they went back up they were throwin' her in the back of the squad car. Me da was still recoverin' today, I think he almost gave himself a heart attack,"

He laughed to himself as he fondly recalled his father's flustered re-telling of the story, which had been exaggerated for comic effect but hadn't quite managed to completely conceal the certain level of genuine trauma for a man of a gentle and quiet disposition. "Why'd he stop for yer man anyway?" Keehan asked. "Ah he knew him," James replied still unfolding and re-folding the piece of paper. "Used to work with him somewhere I think. Apparently he's a fairly docile sorta lad." He stopped folding for a moment and looked over at Keehan. "Why, would you not have stopped to let yer man in, an' the other one chasin' him with a hatchet?" Keehan scoffed.

"I wouldn't anyway. None of my business. I'm not riskin' getting an axe in the face for some douchebag." James smiled, rolled up the beer bottle label into a little ball and tossed it in the fireplace to nestle amongst the cold ash. Keehan glanced over at James who had now turned back to the TV. *He almost certainly would have stopped*, Keehan thought as he watched James who was still smiling to himself.

Despite how they'd grown apart in some ways over the years, there was something about James that Keehan had always secretly admired on some level. Something that had always attracted him. A kind of honesty. As much as he seemed to fade into the background of life and get tossed around, there seemed to be something unshakeable about him. A way of doing the right thing when it really came down to it. It had seemed boring at times in a perverse kind of way: in that you were always pretty sure he wasn't going to be an asshole, regardless of the situation. He'd never make a spectacle of himself, for better or worse, never be the guy who ruined the party. But despite that, Keehan enjoyed being around James and felt relatively comfortable in his company. It was some quality that James had that Keehan was beginning more and more to think he might like to have himself. To be able to trust himself to not be a dick at least, regardless of how the rest of the world was running.

"So what are ya doin'?" Keehan asked, nodding towards the blank refill pad, "A bit of writin'?" James pulled his eyes from the TV and looked over at the blank pad and the beginnings of a groan appeared to cross his face before morphing into a resigned smile. "Ah I've been trying to figure out some goals," he said, picking up the pen and tapping it rhythmically against the pages which sounded a hollow muted ricochet. "I dunno, I guess I was out at me parents, and seein' them and me little sister n' all, getting on with their lives and just doin' shit..." He scratched his cheek with the pen while narrowing his eyes and then squinted again at the blank pages. "I've kinda been feelin' for a while like I really want to start getting on with stuff. Like figuring out properly what I want to do with my life." He turned around on the chair to lean his arm on the backrest and looked over at Keehan who was staring blankly at him. "I'm tryin' to figure out what I want to do but, I dunno; it just seems like I can't figure out anything *in particular* to do. But I know I wont be happy just doin' anything."

He paused and lowered his eyes to the cushion beside him and scratched his chin thoughtfully. "Like isn't that why people end up hatin' their lives?" he looked back up at Keehan. "Cos they never chose what they wanted to do and just ended up somewhere? Living a life they never wanted?"

Keehan's heart, without him realising, began to beat the slightest little bit faster and he shrugged his shoulders in lieu of a committed answer. James continued; "I keep just thinking of stuff, like the cliché stuff -see the pyramids or whatever. And then I think like; do I really give a shit about the pyramids? Do I actually really care, or is it just a thing you do? To look travelled and adventurous? Like a sign of a good life. I mean..." He gazed vacantly up at the ceiling, and his eye was caught by the brown water stain that had been left behind when the pipe for the shower had burst some months ago. "They're cool and all," he continued. "It'd be deadly to see them. Actually yeah, I'd probably really like to see them."

Filled with a renewed conviction he leaned back down

towards the blank notepad and reached for the pen. He paused just as he was about to touch the pen to the paper and looked off again and scratched his chin with the butt of the pen. "But is it a goal?" he mused out loud, and Keehan began to wonder if he was even still necessary for the conversation. "Is it something to aspire to?" James continued. "Or is it just a great experience along the way? Maybe that's all your life is: a collection of random experiences. But how do you ensure you have these great experiences if you just fuck around and muddle along? Or does it even make a difference?"

He sighed and turned back around to slump back in the chair. Keehan shrugged as James picked up the remote and began ritualistically skimming through the channels, his eyes becoming glazed as he automatically slowed down around the usual favourites in the hope of something good grabbing his attention; which was still attempting to untangle the mystery of how to live. Returning to lucidity he let out another deep sigh and gave up. He turned to Keehan again, and tossed him the remote. "All I know is this shit isn't working anymore, like I can't keep living this life. Something has to change." He turned back and readjusted himself on the chair, pulling one leg up across the armrest and leaving it dangling idly off the side.

Nothings gonna change, Keehan thought as his stomach sank and he joined James in gazing glassy-eyed at the flickering light in the corner of the room. *It never does...* He'd heard this all before. From the other two and from himself. He had himself tried making plans before. He had at various points over the course of his years sampled some of the different techniques and systems; tried out some different ideas. He had felt good for a day or so, like he was going somewhere, like he'd found the answer. Then everything would just fall back to normal. Ultimately he knew there was no escaping the fact, as much as he tried; that they and many like them, were among the broken. The ones who'd already passed the point where life could ever not be a burden. The ones who'd never be free of the shit they'd accumulated, and would spend the rest of their days aiming only to minimize their pain; while engaged in futile attempts at forgetting how they once wanted to do something great.

The sky outside had by now faded to the murky grey of evening, and unnoticed by the two of them had begun to seep into the room, filling it with shade; and providing emphasis for the electric flicker of coloured light which emanated from the screen in the corner and had become now like a beacon, a focal point of prominence, in a room that was slowly disappearing into night.

CHAPTER 8

Needing some fresh air and a change of scenery, Keehan, James and Lisa along with Harry and Piotr decided to go camping in the woods for a night or two.

The area of woodland they had chosen was located about three miles away, beside the beach. A place they had known well as children but had not seen in some time. It was a secluded area, and would be even more secluded now that the holidaymakers who came to inhabit the beach and its surroundings for the summer months would by this time have packed up and gone back to their other homes in the city, leaving only miles of desolate and solitary nature. Keehan was adamant that they should get a taxi, bemoaning the fact that they would have to carry all their equipment such a distance. The others however were looking forward to the walk and the sense of adventure; and so they packed up their tents, sleeping bags, food, beer and firelighters and headed off: with Lisa insisting that Keehan leave his PSP behind.

About a mile outside the town the air began to get fresher and easier to breathe. The houses became less plentiful and began to stretch out from one another leaving vast expanses of green to fill the growing gaps between them. The road was quiet now and was becoming more rugged and worn as they left the town behind. Time appeared to slow down as the world of people and their strivings began to lose its significance in the growing presence of unbounded and untamed nature.

They were walking almost adjacent to each other now as they stretched across the deserted road laughing and talking. Keehan, becoming increasingly more comfortable around the new members of the group and maybe more freed by the peaceful surroundings, joined in the fun; although not without maintaining at least a quality of his usual bravado. "Yer one Sharon is well into me," he confidently informed the others when the topic of relationships came up, feeling that if even partially true it would be sufficiently impressive. "Sharon Davies?" Harry asked and raised an eyebrow sceptically. "Yeah," Keehan nodded smiling. "No chance," Harry replied, the corner of his mouth curling up in a smirk and his eyebrow arching sceptically as he along with the others searched Keehan's face for a sign of conviction. Piotr was the only one who didn't seem to mind. "She's really pretty," he interjected looking down at the road as he kicked a pine cone, which subsequently bounced a couple of times on the uneven surface before hopping gracefully into the ditch. Harry continued, "She was in a couple of my classes in school. I wouldn't have thought you'd have a chance with her." Keehan bristled for a moment but decided to forgive their ignorance and let it slide. "How do you know she likes you?," Lisa asked. "Have you ever even met her?" she added, her face screwed up in puzzlement.

Keehan, always certain as the nose on his face; having seen

the evidence play out on an almost continuous loop in his mind; as he often did found trouble retracing the source of his knowledge. "Yeah, well, we kinda, ah, yeah," he spluttered, before regaining himself slightly. "We met a few times like, in town. And I kinda knew her from school and that. I think I made out with her once..." He trailed off. He had been convincing himself up to that point but even he knew that was a step too far. "Ah that might have been someone else," he quickly added in a feeble attempt at recovering the situation.

The others again looked at him sceptically. Lisa tutted to herself. Piotr grinned. "Well we've only met a few times," he tried a different tack, "but like, it's the way she was lookin' at me, I could see it in her eyes. She was gaggin' for me."

"So what's the plan Romeo?" said Lisa and they all laughed; except for Keehan, who finding the truth unbearably stressful had already left them all behind again. "You gonna sweep her off her feet or what?" "Aaah." He was now zooming through the streets of Rome on a Vespa, helmet-less with a cigarette hanging languidly from his bottom lip; with Sharon sitting behind him, her hands clasped tightly around his midriff as her hair billowed in the wind. The Colosseum looming ahead of them as they wound their way in and out of the anarchic Roman traffic. "Yeah someday when I'm free I'll give her a call, head out for a meal or something... I'm gonna take it casual."

Not feeling the need to argue the point they all simultaneously decided to drop the topic on that ambiguous note, each individually making up their own mind as to the extent of the truth and none of them at that time really caring especially much either way.

They were entering the woods now, the sunlight breaking into miniscule darts and flashes as the trees began to envelope them. The rugged tarmac road gave way to a mud track with trails of sand carried up from the beach, which became increasingly obscured by foliage as they ventured further in.

There was a clearing further into the woods that opened right out onto the beach and on reaching it finally, they dropped their loads down with relief and began to set up camp there looking out across the sea.

James and Piotr began by digging a pit in the sand for a fire while Lisa and Harry went for a scout around the trees to collect some sticks. Keehan busied himself with pulling out their sleeping bags and with difficulty getting one of the tents to finally stand unaided.

By the time they got set up and got the fire lighting the sun was beginning to go down, and the sea on the horizon was sparkling orange like the flickering campfire glow on the grey sand. The atmosphere was so serene and peaceful that even Keehan, who had been fidgeting, pacing, poking and breaking branches; eventually succumbed to the moment and went to take a seat beside the others who were gathered around the fire.

"It's nice to see the stars," Lisa was saying as Keehan sat down beside them on the dry sand. "You can kinda see them usually but not as clear... or maybe you can always see them but there's so much goin' on around ya, you're too distracted to look up." Keehan produced a small flask from his pocket that was filled with Jagermeister and Coke. He took a swig before passing it around to the others who each in turn took a mouthful before passing it back. Keehan fixed the top back on and dropped the now half-empty flask on the ground between them. "We used to look up at the stars all the time," he began, his voice quiet and cracking a little: his eyes fixed down at his feet as he nudged a seashell that was almost hidden in the sand beneath him. "Yeah," agreed James nodding his head and smiling as he continued to gaze up into the luminous blackness. "And wonder about U.F.O.'s... and ghosts." The others laughed. "Yah this place seems to be full of ghosts," laughed Piotr, who generally didn't drink much and was beginning to look slightly dazed already. "Almost every house with a priest who killed himself or a black demon dog guarding the gates at midnight." "And fairy rings aswell," Harry added and they all nodded. James' brow furrowed as he looked down at the sand. "I still don't think I'd go into a fairy ring," he admitted as he looked back up to the others. Lisa laughed. "Really?" She opened another can, which fizzed up sending trails of white foam running down the side and over her fingers. She moved the can to her other hand and held it pinched between her fingers as she leaned over and wiped her wet hand in a nearby patch of crab grass. James smiled. "I dunno," he said, his brow furrowing slightly again. "Admitting it is like admitting you believe in magic. I don't believe in magic... Maybe it's just ingrained in me or something." "Probably," Lisa agreed. "Anyway it'd be Ciara's life I'd be riskin'," James concluded and they drifted into a momentary silence. "Everythin' was so much fun back then," Lisa mused, taking a sip from what remained of her beer. A gleam of joy suddenly flashed in her eyes and she turned to Keehan and James. "Remember that one day after school when we put the bottle in the stream and followed it all the way home?" She looked at them both in turn and was warmed by the almost instant recognition in their faces. "I actually just thought of it the other day for some reason," she continued, "Like it just popped into my head." James smiled. "Yeah, I remember." Keehan nodded and smiled, immeasurably happy that one of his favourite memories had been kept and treasured also by the ones he had made it with; in what seemed now to be almost another lifetime.

Lisa turned to Harry and Piotr to explain, "This one time after school when we were like, nine or ten or something, it was a really sunny day and we were walkin' home. And there's that little stream that starts beside the school and goes on the whole way down the hill runnin' beside the road; and in some places it runs under the road through a little drain and comes out the other side and keeps running. This one day we dropped a bottle in it just outside school and followed it the whole way back to town. Like, climbing in and pokin' it with a stick when it got caught in the briar's n' all. Watchin' it float into the drains and runnin' over to the other side to wait for it to come out. 'Til finally it joined the river and just floated off." She looked down and began to poke a hole in the sand with her finger, feeling it get colder as her finger pushed deeper through the layers. "It was like, that was your whole world," she continued as her finger pressed against the dense, cold, impenetrable sand which lay inches beneath. "Just a bottle in a stream. There was not another thing to think about... And it's so pointless but you never forget it, y'know. I'll probably remember that day for the rest of my life. And it's nothin'. Nothin' even remotely spectacular. We didn't achieve anything. Make any sort of mark on the world, or anythin' like."

She paused for a moment, then looking back up at the others continued, "Maybe it's just something to do with the distance of time, like how much has gone by; but it seems like none of my more recent memories come close to havin' the same kind of effect as those early ones... Like those special moments that make you kinda sad and happy at the same time but you just wish you could be there again. Or feel that way again."

"I dunno," Harry interrupted. "To me it kinda seems like my more recent memories get more and more like that the more time passes. Like you remember it cos it was a good moment and time kind of pares away the extraneous details and reduces it to the most important part." "Mmmmm yeah," Lisa partially agreed, the tone in her voice betraying a hopeful interest but a lack of any real conviction. "Like maybe twenty years from now we'll remember this moment and we'll re-member each other and the moon and the sea. And all the crap that was running through our minds; all the worries and stuff will have disappeared. Just got discarded along the way."

They all sat and pondered this for a moment. All except for Keehan who'd almost given up bothering to try and figure it all out. What he did know though, was that he felt closer to these people right now than to anyone or anything he'd felt in a long time. Maybe even loved them. Regardless, he was in no mood to think about the intricacies of memory storage. He'd just been reminded what it felt like to be connected to something; to be a part of the world -however small. And he felt so overpowered by the weight of the moment and his own feeling that his chest began to swell up, and his eyes became moist and blurried as he sat watching the waves break fractured slivers of the moon's glow for miles in the distance; and he listened to the others continue to chat and talk crap of no consequence as though it was the only sound he would ever hear. Feeling a tear roll gently down the side of his nose he managed to regain himself, wiped his eyes discreetly and returned to the conversation; taking a quick look around to make sure no-one had noticed; and smiling to himself as he realised he didn't really mind too much if they had.

The five of them whiled away the rest of the night laughing and joking, their worlds now confined to a patch of sand a few metres square and yet stretching beyond everything they could ever hope to know. As the night was drawing to a close, Piotr, under the influence of several cans of Bavaria and a substantial amount of vodka, decided to go down to the edge of the shore and dodge the tide.

As he show-boated to the others, dancing and skipping around, his foot slid on a wet rock. He fell flat on his face in the silty sand, at the precise moment that the tide rolled back in, saturating him from head to toe. The others fell around laughing as he flapped campily on the wet sand; scrambling to his feet just in time to avoid another soaking as the next wave came in. Soon after that, with Piotr in his underpants and a towel having dried off, and the evening having been brought to a suitably grand finale, they extinguished the fire and went to sleep, exhausted and happy, under the stars.

CHAPTER 9

"When are you going to start doing something with yourself?" Keehan's mother questioned him; her voice which tended usually to be a slightly unsettling balance of gentleness and sharpness, now leaning quite heavily towards the sharp side. Keehan shrugged. "Like what?" "I don't know," Helen continued, "Something decent." Keehan raised an eyebrow and his lip curled to affect a look of arrogance. "Sure am I not decent enough?" he retorted in a valiant attempt to bring humour to the situation. "Don't be smart." The half-smile that was attempting to creep across his face immediately sank back down. He thought he could remember a time when his mother would occasionally laugh or crack a joke but he wasn't sure now if he hadn't just gotten his memories mixed up with a TV show or a dream. "Sure what's the point of doin' anything anyway," he began, finally feeling the need to express his true thoughts on the matter, as the obligation to live and be so-called 'normal' was becoming more and more pressing. He leaned on the kitchen counter. "We're all just gonna die in the end anyway. Can I not just enjoy meself for a while?" Helen continued as if she hadn't heard him, exasperated in her own life and unwilling at this time to entertain his childish regression into airy-fairy nihilistic notions. "Alan will be back about two, he'll be bringing back dinner. Why don't you go and fill up that coal bucket and get a few sticks before he gets back."

Keehan picked up the coal bucket and shuffled out, furiously generating witty ripostes in his head and running through arguments philosophical and personal. By the time he reached the bunker he'd completely forgotten what he was doing. He looked around for a moment for inspiration before realising he was holding the coal bucket in his hand. "Fuckin' arseholes," he muttered to himself as he thrust the little shovel angrily into the bunker and loaded up the bucket with chunks of dusty, black coal. "Can they not just fuckin' leave me alone for five minutes..." He lugged the bucket back inside, forgetting about the sticks. Alan had just arrived home and was stood in the entrance hallway hanging his jacket on the rack as Keehan came grumbling past. "Here's Vanilla Ice," he remarked as Keehan sat the bucket down beside the fireplace. Keehan turned to him. *Vanilla Ice??* He repeated the name in his mind as he vainly searched within himself for a possible elaboration. Alan turned around to him, the corner of his mouth turned up in an insolent smirk. "Always walkin' around with your shades on. Mr cool." Keehan, incredulous, simply stared at him and wondered how the hell anyone could be so lame. *Vanilla Ice???* He shook his head in exasperation and went into the kitchen to give his hands a quick rinse in the sink. He picked up a ragged towel bearing a cartoonish image of the Cliffs of Moher and patted his hands dry with it before taking a seat at the table where his mother was placing plates of Chinese takeaway down.

"Awww chow mein," Keehan groaned, "I hate chow mein." "Pity about you." Alan had taken his seat at the table beside him. "Since when do you not like chow mein?" Helen enquired, as she stooped to pull condiments out of the press. Her irritation seemed to have passed and her voice had regained a calmness that was almost soft, even a little defeated. "Since ever like," Keehan replied, quite certain that he'd made this exact point at least a hundred times over the course of his life and quietly disheartened that it had never registered with the two people at least in the world that were supposed to know him; supposed to *want* to know him. "Oh," Helen replied vaguely.

Keehan eyed the veggie-noodle mix suspiciously and after poking and stirring it a few times reluctantly began to eat. He had to admit it was not nearly as bad as he remembered although he probably wouldn't eat it voluntarily. "You eat like a pig," Alan chimed in just as Keehan was almost beginning to not hate it so much. "What?" he exclaimed, looking up from his plate. "Stop slurping and take your elbow off the table," Alan continued. "You hold your fork in your left hand and the knife in your right. Didn't anyone teach you how to eat properly?" "But I don't use the knife," Keehan protested feebly as he wondered who exactly it was that was supposed to have taught him how to eat properly if not Alan himself. "It's feckin' chow mein..." he mumbled. "It doesn't matter," Alan concluded having already turned back to his paper and seeming to have not heard Keehan's last retort.

Keehan picked up his knife and resumed eating, his right hand poised ludicrously over his plate while he ate with his left. They finished their meal in silence and when they were all done Helen picked up the plates and glasses and left them in the sink. Keehan got up to carry his own plate over. "Five monkeys escaped from Dublin Zoo last night," Alan leaned back in his chair and began to read the newspaper out loud. "Jesus what kind of damage are they goin' to cause runnin' around loose. Can these eejits not manage to keep a few monkeys in a cage?"

Keehan sighed quietly to himself. "Well I'm gonna head back," he muttered, full sure he could have just left and they would have barely even noticed. For a couple of hours at least. He'd had about as much as he could handle for one day anyway and was looking forward to getting back to the relative freedom of his drunken hermit life; where at least the volumes of criticism he had to face were filtered down to leave only the ones in his own head. Alan was still reading the paper and didn't look up.

Helen walked Keehan to the door and they exchanged the usual platitudes as he pulled his jacket on. "Take care of yourself," she entreated him as he walked out the door. Her voice appeared to Keehan to be carrying a note of earnestness that was not quite familiar and he wasn't sure if she said it simply out of habit or if she actually was a little sad to see him leave. He erred towards the latter interpretation and gave her a tentative but warm smile as he said goodbye and turned to start the journey back to town. He pulled a knotted up pair of old earphones out of his pocket that he'd found after a quick rummage in his old room and began to attempt to untangle them as he walked.

Something about the way Helen had said goodbye stuck with Keehan as he turned out onto the road and headed towards the bus-stop. He wondered if maybe she was genuinely worried about him. He began to feel a little bad. Being a screw-up had a certain kind of romanticism about it when no-one really gave a shit: but if she genuinely wanted him to succeed, if she actually cared -for his sake; then it gave the whole thing a new veneer. He saw in himself and in his life now for the most part an overarching theme of petty selfishness, although luckily with just enough genuine care left as to have prevented him from ever doing anything really dreadful. He began to feel a little ashamed. But not in the way that trapped him and held him down. It wasn't shame for shame's sake: the self replicating nightmare of fundamental inferiority. It was more like the motivation he needed to finally pull himself up out of this shithole life he was leading and actually do something meaningful with himself. The motivation to not be fragile and helpless anymore. He got on the bus and began the journey back into town, his dreams inspired with a new sense of responsibility.

"Do you have to be so hard on him?" Helen enquired tentatively after Keehan had left, her eyes flickering briefly at Alan before she resumed tidying away the bits and pieces from dinner. "Weeeeelll...," Alan replied, scrunching up his nose. "What age is he now? It's about time he started to cop on a bit."

Helen had to admit she had at times felt exasperated with Keehan's drifting. However, whether deserved or not, she had acquired for herself a large measure of blame and she felt Keehan's troubles at times as a mirror for her own feelings of inadequacy; consequently seeing him -in a way she had never been consciously aware of; as a way of righting the shame she felt herself and giving herself the love and encouragement she had not received from her own parents. They had been cold and distant, rarely betraying any real emotion or feeling. Helen's mother's speciality had been bouts of rage alternating with silent treatment; often making a point of going hours or even days not even acknowledging her children's existence if they had in some way transgressed, with the consequence of raising a daughter that was concerned about pleasing her to the point of terror.

On the occasions where she had excelled in some way, Helen was doted on by her mother; further exacerbating her need to conform to certain pacifying behaviours.

Her father had been a hard working man: she sometimes had thought perhaps the reason he worked so hard was to keep away from the house and the dark cloud of anger that hung over it. Some part of her held a deep resentment towards her father for abandoning her and her siblings or at the very least; not doing more to protect them from the toxic environment she had had to endure. Of course she was not fully aware of all these dynamics; as like so many others, her way of getting through life now and the way it had been for a long time; was to shut off that part of her life and thereby shut off a part of herself. Without realising, she had become her way of coping.

She had tried to encourage Keehan, to push him gently but it hadn't worked. He had just drifted off, had seemed to lose his will. It had been different with Kevin -Keehan's older brother. She had been stricter with him. She had pushed him harder, and when he had begun to play up she had made it clear who was in charge. And of course now he was gone. She had barely seen him in the eight years since he left to live in the city. She felt as though she was just unable to do it right.

"Ah but he's not a bad lad really is he?" she continued to Alan and she looked at him in hope of verification, as he continued to read his newspaper seemingly uninterested. "He's a bit lost but he'll find his way eventually," she persisted getting no real response. "He just needs a bit of time to sort himself out." Alan sighed and folded the paper, the words of which had now ceased to register with any clarity. He twisted around in his chair to meet Helen's imploring gaze. "Look," he finally sighed. "We've all been through it. I wasn't given time to sit around findin' myself. I was told what to do. I was made get up and work. And that's why I'm here today." He turned back to the paper, the expression on his face harsh and bitter and matched increasingly by the tone of his voice. "Life is tough, that's just a fact... He needs to know that and get used to it. It'll help him in the long run. When he learns to look after himself."

He fixed his eyes resolutely at the paper, looking at the words but continuing to no longer register them as Helen, lost in her own thoughts, made tea.

Helen and Alan had been married almost eight years. They had been seeing each other for three years before that, having met at the wedding of a mutual friend. Both survivors of marriages that had broken down, they had found solace and comfort in each other in a time of great upheaval for them both. Alan, like Helen, also had emotional scars from a difficult childhood; his father being the domineering presence in his case. His and Helen's relationship was one built on much pain and dysfunction, but they had found support in each other and built a relationship that was loving in its own unique way. Keehan, having been quite young when Alan had been introduced to his life, and having been barely seven years old the last time he saw his birth father; had made a relatively straight-forward adjustment to the new dynamic and the presence of Alan in his life, and had almost never known any different. Kevin however had taken an instant dislike to Alan and had rejected his presence outright. The pair had never seen eye to eye and that fed into Kevin's relationship with Helen as he began to rebel more generally and she in turn had been the one trying to bring the new family in line and create balance between them. Alan, feeding on his own insecurities had not helped foster any reconciliation; with the outcome of Kevin feeling more ostracised and ultimately, following the announcement of Helen and Alan's impending marriage; packing his bags and leaving for good.

The house was empty when Keehan got back and he went straight into the kitchen to pour a drink. He was certain there was a half-litre of vodka left around somewhere. He opened the fridge. There were some cans of cider, a bottle of Malibu, a half bottle of Pernod. *Where the fuck do we get this stuff?* he muttered out loud to himself, holding up a blue WKD as if expecting to see the name of the owner written on it. He found the bottle of vodka nestled in behind the two month old eggs and looked for something to mix it with. The best he could find was an open carton of grape juice. Reluctant to go back out to the shop to find something more conventional he decided to give it a try. *Could be interesting?* he thought. *Maybe like light wine?*

He coughed and retched as the first tentative mouthful hit

the back of his throat. It wasn't like light wine. It was more like cheap vodka with grape juice in it. But once the first couple of mouthfuls had given his gullet adequate lubrication, it began to go down nicely enough; the grape doing just enough to balance the burn of the vodka and take some of the edge off it. After polishing off the glass he poured another and headed upstairs to his room, peering into James' as he passed.

James was sat cross-legged on the floor in the middle of a pile of books. *What a dork*, Keehan thought to himself with a mixture of condescension and slight affection. The vodka was making his head feel airy and light. He went into his room and set the glass down on his bedside locker then lay down on his bed and closed his eyes. Before he knew it he had drifted off into a deep sleep.

He awoke abruptly just over an hour later; lay for a moment as he regained his bearings then stretched and reached over to pull the blind open a crack to peer outside. What sun there had been was gone but it was still relatively bright. Still slightly groggy from his short but effective nap he pulled himself up and went downstairs. James and Lisa were sat on the couch watching telly. "Alright man," James greeted him and Lisa nodded hello. "Alright," Keehan replied sitting down. "What're ya watchin'?" "Ah nothing really."

Around seven o'clock the doorbell rang. James got up to answer it. Stood on the other side of the door was a slightly dishevelled looking guy wearing a black t-shirt and black jeans with grey Adidas trainers that had seen better days. He was stood with his back to the door poised and squinting intently away down the street. "Alright Dave," James addressed the back of the guy's head. Dave turned back slowly, still looking confused. "Thought I saw something," he muttered. He smiled wryly and nodded at James. "Alright bud."

Dave Horan was a workmate of James' and occasional drinking buddy of theirs. He managed the storeroom in the supermarket, taking in the deliveries, checking them off and packing them away in an orderly fashion. The two things he was most passionate about in life were Liverpool F.C. and The X-Files. He followed James into the living room and nodded hello to Keehan and Lisa. "Alright Dave," Lisa said. "Yeah," he replied. "How's yourselves?" "Ah grand." They sat and continued to watch TV in silence.

"How was work today?" James turned to Dave when the ad break came on. "Aaah...," Dave looked blank for a few seconds as he attempted to drag his awareness back from the blinking colours. "Ahhhh. I lifted up some boxes." He turned to James. "And put them down somewhere else... That's about it." James laughed. "Is Larry back yet?" "Nah," replied Dave, "I think he won't be back 'til Thursday or so. You could probably get another day or two in there if ya wanted. 'Til Larry's back." He turned back to the TV as his attention was piqued again by a new yet familiar sound. "Naaah," James sighed as he gave it fleeting consideration. "I'm not really bothered. I've enough to pay the rent and everything. I don't really want to be there anymore than I have to." "Yeah you're probably right," Dave agreed.

He cast his eye over the pile of papers on the coffee table. On top was a leaflet that had been left by a canvasser a couple of weeks previous. One of the guys they recognized from the posters scattered around town. A career politician; like his father before him, and *his* father before that. When James had opened the door he was stood there with his greying hair neatly combed to one side and the same poster grin –the grin which he probably hung in the wardrobe along with his freshly pressed grey suit and purple tie, and brought out with the same intention of bedazzlement. With a brief glance at the beer bottle in James' hand and consequent quick scan of the living room, still scattered with the innards of a cushion that had burst during some drunken hi-jinks; along with several boxes full to the brim with beer bottles and cans; his smile had dropped to a barely concealed repugnance. He handed James the leaflet, gave a perfunctory nod and muttered "Vote for Fitzgerald in the upcoming election," before continuing briskly on his campaign without another word. "Are ya's voting in the election next month?" Dave asked, picking up the leaflet and casually perusing it. "Ah probably," Lisa said. "Yeah I suppose," said James. "Naaaah," said Keehan. "You know everyone says you should vote," began Lisa; "You have to make your voice heard and everything. But sure you just end up with the same twats over and over again. You're given a bunch of lads in suits that are all the exact fuckin' same, and it's like, pick one and go home." "Yeah I know," agreed James, running his eyes once again over the leaflet full of promises that would inevitably never come to fruition."It's hard to see what difference it'd make if you didn't bother." Dave nodded. "I know what ya mean..." He leaned forward to place the leaflet back on the pile of magazines and papers. "They all talk the same shite."

Keehan felt his eyelids getting heavy and he began to drift off again into a nice, deep sleep.

He awoke half an hour later and the other three, who had been beginning to drift off themselves, had decided to get up and head up to the pub for a couple of drinks. Supposedly there were a couple of bands playing, and although Keehan wasn't really bothered listening to a bunch of crusties he felt like he was decomposing in the house and figured at least there'd be a bit of life outside. They all wrenched themselves up and grabbed whatever bits and pieces they would need in order to venture outside.

As Dave pulled himself up off the couch his knee made a cracking noise. He'd been starting to notice more such cracks and creaks lately as his body was beginning to betray its almost thirty years on the Earth, despite the fact that he still didn't feel like he was ready to be alive yet. "That's it," he sighed wearily. He shook his leg out. "I've already begun the process of dyin'... I'd be as well now just tryin' to find a decent burial plot while I have the chance, start figurin' out me will." The others laughed and the four of them headed out and began to make their way up the street.

It took them no more than five minutes to reach the pub and they walked in and looked around. Their eyes adjusting to the sudden darkness, they could make out that there were about ten people scattered around from the top of the bar to the bottom end. "We must be early," Dave suggested, although the tone in his voice did not betray confidence. "Yeah," Lisa agreed, her eyebrows furrowing. "I thought it started at nine last time I was here." They moved over to the area containing the pool table which was the only part of the pub that didn't resemble a piece of the set of Nosferatu. A number of quite pretty lamps with multi-coloured, stained glass shades hung above them and there was a fruit machine in the corner, its neon lights flashing excitedly in intermittent bursts.

James got the balls out and proceeded to set them up while the others went up to the bar to get drinks. The barman was moving around casually picking up glasses and wiping tables. "Alright Barry," Lisa greeted him. "Is there no live music on tonight?" Barry turned around from the table he had been wiping and flung a damp cloth over his shoulder as he pinched the remaining two stout-stained glasses in his fingers. "Well lads," he greeted them warmly. "No the music's finished now for the summer." He gave a consolatory smile as he shuffled back in behind the bar and stood expectantly opposite them. "Grand," Keehan drawled, rolling his eyes. "Sure we've just to find somethin' to keep us occupied 'til next May then." Barry eyed him with suspicion and Lisa stifled a smile. Barry continued, "No point havin' anything on now at this stage sure the crowds wouldn't be here. All the college students are headin' back now in the next month." He shrugged. "The summer's over."

They ordered their drinks and brought them down to a small table near the pool table where James had the balls set up and was holding two cues, one of which he handed to Lisa. "Oh my god like," Keehan took a seat beside his glass of Jack Daniels and Coke. "There's never anythin' happenin' in this place." He leaned back on his stool and stretched his legs out in front of him. "Ya know," Lisa interjected hopefully, "we could try organizing something ourselves? Like I'm sure there's loadsa people around who'd play a few tunes. I know a few people that are in bands. We could ask around." She was met with a stony silence and half-hearted shrugs and she sighed with resignation. She knew in her heart she probably wouldn't have followed through with it anyway. "Fuck sake," Keehan groaned and pouted. "Can we not go somewhere where people are cool and sophisticated and rich and they party all the time." Lisa rolled her eyes. "Sure thing Gatsby," she chirped sarcastically; "We'll just head over to West Egg for a few jars and a bit of a dance." She swivelled the cube of chalk vigorously on the tip of her cue sending a misty cloud of blue dust floating into the air. Keehan squinted at her suspiciously and the other two laughed. Lisa smiled and blew sharply on the tip of the cue to send any excess dust flying, then leaned over the table and with a deft jab sent the white ball flying fiercely into the triangle of interwoven red and yellow, sending them ricocheting in all directions as they clicked off each other and thudded against the green baize along the sides of the table. A couple of hollow thuds followed by rolls indicated that at least two balls had arrived at their final destination. Lisa went to the side of the table and peered in through the glass. There was one of each colour. "Breaker's choice!" she exclaimed taking a quick scan of the table. "I'll take yellow." They played a few games of pool and had a few drinks and after a few rounds the absence of a band wasn't felt terribly badly. Their own world weary company was sufficient to pass a night and provide entertainment, with the aid of alcohol and a different set of walls to look at.

CHAPTER 10

The next morning Keehan was awakened by the rain, which was thudding against his window with a relentless ferocity. He got up, made himself some breakfast and sat down on the couch to eat it. The house was quiet. James was in work. Lisa, he assumed was at her own house. The day held an uncanny presence: the town was still and quiet, hiding from the rain. Keehan felt listless and ready to move but at the same time could feel the familiar tightness of anxiety in his chest constricting him. It was a more exaggerated version of the state he spent most days in. A kind of inability or unwillingness to relax, for fear of life slipping away; and yet without the slightest inclination or even belief in the usefulness or importance of any specific task or activity. He couldn't quite sit still but he hadn't the energy or motivation to actually do anything either.

Finishing his breakfast, he got up and put his bowl in the sink and stretched for a moment, clenching his face in a tight grimace as he felt the blood rush to his head and the aches in his arms and back pulled momentarily into a euphoric state of calm readiness. He opened his eyes and felt a slight nausea as his head swam and his vision blurred before slowly focusing back to its normal clarity as his muscles relaxed back into their usual shape. Shuffling back to the living room, still a little light-headed, he picked up a book of James' that was lying on the table.

James always bought the used books off Ebay as he liked to see if the names of the previous owners were written in it or if they had left any notes or highlights. He said it gave them character. Keehan had to agree it was vaguely interesting although he would never admit it out loud. He had on occasion been prompted to pick up a dog-eared and yellowing paperback that had been lying around and leaf through it to see what clues were left to its previous life or lives. He turned the book over in his hand. On the back sleeve was a photograph of some guy he presumed to be the author. On reading the notes below the photo he discovered that the man was a French-Algerian writer who'd won a Nobel Prize in the fifties. *He looks pretty cool*, Keehan thought as he nodded his head in approval. He looked *important*. In the photo on the sleeve he was wearing a black overcoat with the collar turned up and was looking over his shoulder, gazing at the viewer nonchalantly but with a subtle intensity.

Keehan knew James had a jacket that was just like that one only maybe a bit shorter. He went and got the jacket off the rack where it was hanging by the door. He pulled the jacket on and gave it a quick few swipes with his hand to rid it of the various loose fibres and dust particles which peppered its surface; and turned up the collar. He picked up a cigarette from a box that was on the table, which he presumed to be Lisa's, and put it in his mouth; letting it hang languidly from his bottom lip. He stood in front of the mirror drooping his eyelids sexily and attempting to affect a look of knowing nonchalance. He began to mumble incoherently at the mirror, gesticulating as if he were making a very important point. His audience of four walls was replaced by a crowded lecture room, filled with all the smartest people in the world. All sat enraptured as he turned their world's upside down. Showed them all what true genius was. Of course his audience was all ears. They realised now that he had the answers, that he could see what everyone was missing.

The faces began to fade: the images becoming translucent and dissipating to be replaced again by the greasy mirror on the magnolia wall; ominous in the darkness, as the rain like gravel pittling around him, again clattered in to crowd his senses. He slumped down in the armchair, letting the cigarette drop from his mouth onto James' jacket from where it rolled down and dropped neatly down into the side of the chair cushion. He was beginning to feel nauseous and slightly dizzy.

He reached over to pick up the book again from where he'd left it perched on the arm of the sofa. As he grabbed it, a piece of notepaper slipped from between the pages and floated feather-like down to the floor. He reached over and picked it up. There was writing on one side that on first glance appeared quite messy and erratic but on closer inspection was just about legible enough for him to read through. As he did, his heart began to beat faster. The combination of words on the paper gripped him with a primitive power. Like clasping and clinging fingernails in a handful of raw muscle fibres and nerve endings. He saw that though unfinished and a little incoherent, it was quite clearly a suicide note.

He read through it a few times more, his hands beginning

to tremble slightly, then reached again for the book and flicked as carefully as he could through the pages to see if he could find any clues as to the identity of the previous owner or any further notes.

Though quite musty, the book had no names written on it or indeed any marks of any kind, save for some slightly dog-eared page corners that were the only indication of previous use that he could find. Retracing his steps back to the table where he had initially picked up the book, he spied a torn envelope, which had taped to the side of it an Ebay sellers docket. James had obviously just received the package that morning before work and taken a moment to have a quick look at his purchase before heading out the door. He probably hadn't even seen the note, Keehan surmised.

He took the docket and the note and after reading through them a couple more times, took them up to his room. After taking a moment to decide what to do with them he eventually folded the two pieces of paper together and put them in the bottom of his bedside locker drawer, stuffed deep beneath some notebooks and old empty pizza boxes. Keehan decided then and there not to show anyone else this note. It had stirred up something inside of him. For some reason the mere presence of this note seemed to lay bare all his fears, all his insecurities and all his conceived weaknesses. It pulled them out onto the surface so there was no-where to hide. He wasn't sure why, but an overpowering sickly feeling in his stomach told him that it needed to stay hidden away where only he knew. Something else however, told him it was too important to discard completely; a conflicting sense of unnatural peace that seemed to elucidate his mind and banish a weight that had been stockpiled over years of misery. It was a peace that scared him, that felt like real control at last. And it seemed to be so inviting, pulling him towards it while his stomach churned and resisted. He lay back on his bed for a moment breathing deeply and trying hard not to vomit.

After a few minutes of staring at the dusty lampshade hanging from his roof he had managed to settle himself and relax a little bit. Though he still felt slightly dizzy, it was no longer accompanied by the nausea, and had become a somewhat pleasant -if unnatural, feeling of lightness.

He leaned down over the side of the bed to lock the drawer containing the note, and having done that and deposited the key in the upper drawer; rolled the rest of his body off the bed to land squatting on the floor. He stood up straight and gave his legs a little shake to release the tension from his knees, then headed back downstairs to the living room. He picked up the book again which was laying open on the couch and lobbed it into James' open backpack on the floor as he looked for something to distract himself. He turned on the X-box and sat back on the couch to tap away contentedly on the controller for the remainder of the day, with every passing moment the clawing sickness fading back to a manageable numbness.

With the note out of sight Keehan managed to block it from his thoughts and returned to his general state of delusion, with only everyday routine terrors which were easier to coat over. Life slipped back on its groove; empty and unfulfilling but leaving him ample opportunity to dream, and the deceptive comfort of routine. He turned his attentions back to his burgeoning celebrity career and to Sharon, and again lost himself in visions of the future life they would lead.

The mornings when he would wake up with her held tight to him with the smell of her hair in his nostrils; the sun bowing gracefully along the contour of her neck and filling his eyes with radiance. The things they would see together and the adventures they would have together. The simple pleasure of holding her hand and feeling her hold it back. The mahogany dark pools of her eyes reflecting him back to himself with the love he wished he could feel for his own existence. He carried on.

CHAPTER 11

Saturday evening, Dave turned up to the house about seven o'clock. Clasped tightly in his hand was a plastic shopping bag containing a small selection of cans and a bottle of spiced rum. He looked slightly flabbergasted. This wasn't taken to be anything unusual by James, who opened the door, it just seemed to be an effect of the specific combination of Dave's facial features. "Alright Dave," said James. "Alright lad," replied Dave. "Come on in." Dave came in and said hey to Lisa and Keehan. "I'm just gonna throw these in your fridge alright," he said holding up the bag. "Yeah work away," nodded James, taking his seat back on the couch. "Have ya's got any Club Orange?" Dave shouted in from the kitchen as he headed towards the fridge. He pulled open the door and the first thing he saw was a full two litre bottle lying on the bottom shelf just as the shouted reply came from the other room, "Yeah, should do…" After depositing his drink in the fridge Dave joined them in the living room and slumped down on the couch beside James and Lisa. "You's headin out tonight?" he asked. "Yeah reckon so," said James. "We'll probably go for a few quiet ones in Millie's and see then after that."

Keehan got up to pour himself a drink and the others soon

followed suit, starting off with a couple of cans to warm up before cracking out the rum and orange. At about nine, all feeling pretty buzzed they decided to make a move, gathered themselves together and headed out.

There was a decent crowd in Milligans already as they entered, running the spectrum from barely eighteen-year-olds all the way to the three old fellas pushing eighty who were sat on a small table by the empty fireplace. Lisa took a seat at a table beside them which from what they could see was the only one available, and the others took a seat beside her -James having to borrow a stool from the old men's table which was happily obliged.

They had a couple of rounds in the pub before Keehan began to pester them to head to the nightclub. James and Lisa hadn't ventured that far in a while, usually preferring the more chilled atmosphere of the pub and being happy to stay there: but as they were on a good level and feeling energized they conferred and made the unanimous decision to head over for a change.

They polished off their last round of drinks and headed out and crossed the street which was getting quite busy now, to join the line outside the door of Mac's nightclub. After about ten minutes of shuffling incrementally towards the entrance they got to the door, paid their five euro admission and went inside where there was quite a crowd already dancing and shouting to each other over the din of the latest chart R'n'B. They got some drinks and went to hang out in a less crowded corner.

On the opposite side of the club, Michelle and Sharon were already in with a couple of friends.

Michelle had been drinking since three o'clock and had already been quite drunk when they had met up at seven for pre-drinks at their friend Lucy's house. She was now blurry-eyed and wobbling. Her make-up was smudged and her eyes glazed and red, but she was enjoying herself and they were having fun. Leaving the girls for a moment on the dance-floor she went to get another drink, accidentally kicking her toe against the step leading up to the bar and stumbling slightly. Out of the corner of her eye she noticed some girl looking at her with what she felt was a look of repugnance. The girl turned back to her friends standing beside her and they all began to laugh. Michelle suddenly felt that everyone in the club was talking about her. A cyclonic mixture of anger and embarrassment swelled up inside her. She was being singled out again. *As she always was.* Taking a deep breath, she managed to brush it aside and calmed down a little. Looking around she could see now clearly that all around her people were falling around like crazed lunatics, shouting and yelling and cheering and knocking over glasses and bottles. Someone having a little stumble on a step was hardly noteworthy. But despite her rationalizations, the buzz she had been on had become more empty now. The feeling of comfort that under-scores all the best nights had disappeared leaving a hollow-ness. She continued up to the bar to get a drink, hopeful that another one would put her back on the right level.

Thereabouts, Keehan was still moving around, on the lookout for Sharon while the others had found a table and had met a few old school friends and were laughing and chatting and having a good time. Keehan had had a few drinks and was feeling pretty brave. Having rehearsed the possible scenarios so many times in his head now, his version of the future was becoming more solid reality than possibility. Knowing that Sharon would probably be out and knowing that he himself was currently at his most charming level of drunkenness, he was absolutely certain that this was the night his plans would come together. If he could only find her. 'Accidentally' bump into her maybe. Then offer to buy her a drink. *Maybe there'll be some big tough asshole trying it on with her*, he thought. *She'll obviously be desperately trying to escape his attention. That's when I'll step in. "Hey what's the problem here guy?" The guy will back off when he sees the calm but steely look on my face. And then I'll turn to her. "You okay?" She'll smile at me, gaze at me with those sparkling eyes and then wrap her arms around me... Or maybe we'll meet on the dance-floor..."* He watched himself throwing shapes, body-popping, the whole lot... Bathed in the flashing coloured lights, heads turning to watch in admiration. The fact that he had never actually learned to dance in any kind of elaborate fashion was merely a trifling and irrelevant detail. *She'll see me as I'm bustin' some pretty slick moves*, he thought. *As she's looking over all coy, our eyes will meet. And we'll both move closer and closer to each other... Yeah...*

Michelle's night had taken a nosedive. Where previously each drink she had taken had made her head light and her energy rise, now she had crossed that threshold where every drink she had just made her more sloppy and miserable. She made her way over to Sharon and the girls who were drunk but still quite merry. On her way she stumbled again, more heavily this time; and almost collided with a guy by the bar who was half sitting, half leaning on a stool; chatting with a group of three other guys. He was well dressed in a pressed white shirt beneath a well fitted grey jacket and matching grey pleated trousers and very handsome; with jet-black hair that was slicked back neatly, just a hint of stubble and deep green eyes. Michelle was sure she'd never seen him around before and wondered who he could be. She tried to regain her composure, and attempting a seductive smile, blabbered something that sounded vaguely suggestive but was largely incomprehensible to anyone listening. "The state of ya love," one of the lads from the group shouted over to her and they all burst out laughing. "Fuck yous!!!" Michelle slurred as she stumbled off and sat back down beside the girls, feeling like she wanted to fall down a hole and disappear.

Her head was swimming slightly as she sat and quietly drank her vodka and coke, silently fighting her prodding embarrassment with a resolute anger. Sharon noticed that Michelle had been slightly detached for some time. "Are you okay?" she asked, "you seem a bit quiet…" "I'm grand," snapped Michelle in a clipped tone that indicated an un-willingness to discuss the matter any further. Sharon smiled reassuringly at her. Having dealt regularly with Michelle's at times seemingly erratic mood-swings; and knowing the best way to deal with this situation was not to poke any further, she turned back to Lucy to resume their chat; adjusting her chair to create an openness for Michelle to not feel excluded and to know she was still part of the group. Michelle, despite not being in any mood for talking, did eventually however turn back to join the other two at least spectatorially and gradually regained her usual sense of hard-headed composure, even as the earlier upset continued to simmer underneath.

At the end of the night as the house lights came up and the concluding bass note of 'Creep' by Radiohead faded out into dull chatter and erratic shouts and yells and bursts of singing, they all filed out down the stairs and onto the street.

Keehan had rejoined the others and as he still hadn't found Sharon was reluctant to go home yet. The others were having fun and were also in no rush to go; and bumming some smokes off of Lisa they hung around with the rest of the loiterers, smoking and chatting and winding down their night. Sharon and Michelle were outside too. A former neighbour of Sharon's had met them at the door as they were exiting before the end of the last song. Having caught up on what they had been doing for the last while, what their plans were, how their respective families were doing; the guy had somehow veered onto the topic of the moon landings and was currently explaining to Sharon in relentless detail how they had been obviously staged and filmed in a studio in Hollywood; painstakingly detailing the many inconsistencies in the footage they were all familiar with.

Michelle, ready to go and having distanced herself fully from the conversation, was becoming increasingly cold and irritable and had moved to lean against a nearby wall, glaring furiously at the guy as she moved on. Her temper continued to grow as she periodically looked back to see him continuing to drone on with what appeared like no intention of stopping. The fact that her absence from the conversation had barely been noted didn't help matters much. Keehan was with Lisa, James and Dave again. Paying little attention to the conversation that was going on between the others, he was scanning the crowd still, as he had been all night, when he caught sight of Michelle leaning against the club doorway.

His heart began to rise. Feeling the opportunity he had been waiting for to finally make an approach, to begin in some small way to make some kind of reality of the dreams that had occupied his mind, he steadied himself and marched boldly up to Michelle -in his slightly panicked state not registering the impatience bordering on disgust that was characterizing her current expression. "Hey," he blurted, attempting to appear calm and in control of himself even as he felt his nerve wilting in this sudden exposure. "Is Sharon around? I've been waitin' to see her all night." Michelle turned to face him, the look of disgust on her face deepening even further into fury as she looked him up and down. "Who the fuck are you?!!!" she exploded.

The others standing nearby heard and turned to look as Michelle continued to unload, the nights trauma now finding fruition in a dynamic assault. "Sharon's busy, and if ya think she'd go near you anyway you're deluded! Go back to your fuckin' ugly crusty mates..."

Keehan, almost frozen to the spot with shock and confusion, searched for somewhere comfortable to fix his gaze, finding nothing but Michelle's aggressive glare, now softened slightly with a tinge of regret but nonetheless resolute -and rubberneckers turning back to each other and giggling or rolling their eyes or simply resuming their conversations after the momentary burst of aggression had cut through the vibe, threatening to become an incident. Looking over Michelle's shoulder, Keehan suddenly caught sight of Sharon just behind talking to her friend; who had turned and moved towards them when they heard the shouting. Seeing her with this other guy his heart fell to his stomach. His dreams in an instant shattered and dropped in pieces all around him. The life he'd envisaged usurped by some asshole as it always was and always would. They'd probably get married and move away and have kids and live happily ever after far away just leaving him there to rot; forgotten, abandoned, never to be seen again. "Fuck you bitch!" Keehan shouted at Sharon, his heart in his throat now and his senses having disappeared as he was overcome by waves of emotion, a turbulent mix of bitter anger, sadness, loneliness and confusion; until he didn't know what he was saying or doing. "Fuck the two of ya's!!!"

Sharon stood dumbfounded, her eyes wide open in shock and confusion as Keehan turned and strode furiously down the street, incensed with the whole world.

CHAPTER 12

In the days following the nightclub incident Keehan's ego was in overdrive, attempting to repair itself but limping painfully; and he was almost ready to stop caring. To discard it once and for all. Unfortunately without the weight of opinion to push around and tell him where he needed to be he was beginning to feel like he was disappearing. Left to his own choices he was sure to become nothing again. He needed *his* reality, however fractured, to ensure he didn't lose himself and lose the vision of how life could be.

This particular incident however was proving difficult to fight. The depressing truth was creeping up on him. It seemed to be everywhere he looked now. He knew she had not deserved that outburst. With the benefit of calm he could see now that nothing had happened. And even if it were happening as he'd imagined... What right did he have to get mad? No, it was him again, he knew. It was his own fault, as it always was, and always would be. For all his grandiose fantasies and visions, on some level he was sure all he really wanted was to be normal. To just do normal stuff and get on with life. It seemed so easy for everyone else. Why did *he* always have to screw everything up? *Fuck it!*, he decided after a while. *The whole thing is screwed up... Life... The World... She's an idiot. They're ALL fuckin' idiots...* He managed to regain himself, to cling to his fantasies, but he couldn't help but feel something simmering underneath, eating him from the inside. Life was returning to some approximation of normality: Boring, safe, distracting normality. But something had changed.

As Keehan was passing beneath the railway bridge one day on his way to the shop to buy a bottle of Coke, he suddenly noticed two figures just ahead of him lurking in the darkness.

They appeared to him to be in their late twenties, or in their early thirties at the very most. One of them looked a bit sullen but relatively easy going and was holding a cotton ball to the inside of his elbow and pressing it tenderly. The other one wore a grimace and a baseball cap, the peak of which pointed up over his curly, greasy hair and cast a shadow over his blank, staring eyes.

Keehan, strolling along in a world of his own, felt his legs go to jelly with the shock; not having noticed them until he almost walked into them. He willed his legs to move and continued awkwardly but the one with the cap had noticed him approach and stood out in front of him to block his path. "Hey," he said calmly but with an undertone of malice. Keehan forced a weak smile at him and attempted to keep walking. "Wait a minute," the lad said.

The other one had thrown the cotton ball on the ground and was rummaging in a plastic bag. Keehan was sure he recognized him now having seen him up close -possibly from school he thought, but he wasn't sure. He couldn't really think. He tried to say something to excuse himself but all that came out was a quivering incoherent mumble. As he tried to walk around, the lad with the cap stepped from side to side continuing to block his path in every direction.

"Give us a look at your mp3," he said to Keehan. Keehan moved his mouth but all that came out was a dry rasp. He tried again, his voice trembling as to be barely coherent. "N-n-n-n-no, I need it." The junkie in the baseball cap eyed him coldly. "Give us a tenner," he continued. "N-n-n-no I need it," Keehan just managed to stammer again, the only thing his paralysed mind could muster. "Listen!!!...," the lad's voice lost its veneer of calmness and was pure malice now, as he leaned in close to Keehan's face: so close that Keehan could see the spittle bubbles pop between his clenched teeth, "I'll break every fuckin' bone in your body and leave you over there by that train track!"

The lad's eyes now burned with conviction; the conviction of someone to whom consequences mattered little anymore, as he gestured perfunctorily toward the grassy embankment that led up above them to the rusty metal tracks where only trains went; and Keehan stood trembling and stupefied -unable to fight or run away. Unable to think or move.

At this point the other lad who had finished rummaging in the bag and was now leaning against the wall casually observing the encounter, stepped over. "Ah here leave 'im he's only a little twerp," he said gesturing dismissively at Keehan.

The guy with the cap after staring some moments at Keehan gave a little smirk and stepped out of his way, then eyeing him with a renewed anger almost spit in his face, "Go on ya little pprick!! If I ever see you around here again I'll fuckin' kill ya."

Keehan made to walk hurriedly down the lane exercising

every scrap of his willpower to try and regain the feeling in his legs and get them to move. His heart was in his chest and his head was swimming as he started to walk faster and faster until he was almost jogging: not slowing down until he got back out onto the main street where the usual hustle and bustle of everyday life was going on. Feeling a certain safety in the mundanity of ordinary decent people going about their business he relaxed somewhat, and his breathing returned to a more regular pace as he continued to walk briskly on.

By the time he got back to the house he had mostly calmed down. But he couldn't banish the sense of horror that was growing increasingly vivid within him. The horror of the world. The constant battling for survival and futile attempts to escape the misery that never ended. That came in wave after wave, day after day after day with seemingly no respite. The constant fear and anxiety and awkwardness and the regret and embarrassment that seemed to just accumulate and it seemed would never come to an end.

As he went to head inside he met Lisa coming out the door. "Alright?" she nodded. "What you up to?" "Nothing," Keehan muttered coldly, struggling to contain himself. "Right..." Lisa replied and eyed him with curiosity. "Well I'm just headin home now... Are you sure you're alright?" "Yeah I'm fine," he snapped, the words coming out with more force than he had intended. "I'm fine." He was already on his way to his room before Lisa could say goodbye. She faltered slightly, taken aback by Keehans brusqueness. He had never been overtly concerned with niceties and politeness but he'd never dismissed her quite like that before. She turned and headed home. As she walked home her confusion turned to hurt, which turned to indignation as she wondered what she had done that people could keep dismissing her so callously.

Still a little shaken, Keehan went up to his room, pulled the curtains closed and sat on his bed. His eyes began to moisten. He was embarrassed that he'd acted so pathetically and crumbled so easily. *A real man would have stood up straight*, he thought. *Looked the guy in the eye and told him clearly and calmly to take a hike*. It was so easy to know what to do, what to say from the safety of his aloneness. Why did his his body and mind have to betray him constantly? Why in every situation of the merest venture from comfort or the slightest confrontation did a flurry of nerves paralyse him and cause him to flap and stumble and break down into a pathetic wretch? Turn him into someone he never wanted to be? On top of it all had he now been a dick to Lisa aswell? He could barely even tell anymore. Could barely tell the difference in what he intended to do and what he actually did.

He lay back on his bed and with his whole body still trembling slightly he stared at the ceiling. At the glow in the dark stars left up on the roof by the previous tenants. He lay staring for hours until the green glowing stars eventually faded into complete blackness and his body had regained its calm and still he stared into the dark. He decided that he had to get away. That he had to leave this place, if only for a while.

He remembered the note in his drawer. In fact it was all he could do not to think of it over the course of the last few days. He leaned over to rummage in the top drawer for the key, found it and unlocked and opened the bottom drawer; where the note lay untouched since he'd hidden it away. He took it out and read it through again. He took out the order tracking notice that had come with the book and unfolded it. He wanted to get away, and he needed somewhere to go. He decided then and there, for reasons he wasn't quite sure of, but with conviction nonetheless; that he would track down the writer of the note.

CHAPTER 13

The next day Keehan woke up well rested after an unbroken night's sleep, which was a rare occurrence but always appreciated. He immediately remembered the decision he had made the night before, and though foggy and lacking the same panicked urgency with the night's sleep and dreams, it filled his mind to every corner. He told himself that if nothing else it would be an adventure. A cool story to tell. And he was sick of this place anyway. He needed a break.

He spent the rest of that day with some effort tracking down the address that the book had been sent from. It had come from the city, from an area he was generally familiar with but a street name he didn't recognize. He printed off a map and jotted down some information on the buses, trains and taxis he might need to get around once he arrived. He did some washing to have clothes to wear on his adventure and even did some tidying up.

Feeling a sense of prepared readiness he poured himself a drink and sat down in front of the telly to relax for the evening, feeling genuine comfort for once, with a day of achievement and purpose behind him and days of adventure and curiosity in front of him. He began to nod off peacefully in the chair and had already been snoring for twenty minutes when he suddenly woke with a start and decided to head up to bed to get a proper nights sleep, so as to be well rested for the journey that lay ahead. He went up and got into his bed, snuggled up beneath the covers and fell into a deep and peaceful sleep.

He awoke in the morning relaxed and energized, got up and packed a bag; threw in the note and the order with the address written on it, some clothes, and a bottle of vodka. He scribbled down a quick note for James explaining that he would be gone for a few days and headed out to get on the bus to make his way to the capital; a journey that would take roughly two hours.

As he got onto the bus and sat down he began to feel a nervous excitement. He always got excited going somewhere new and his mind dazzled, although underneath it was an awful sense of foreboding that was beginning to emerge through the excitement, and made his stomach lurch slightly. But he knew he couldn't turn back now that he'd gone this far. He knew that if he succumbed once again to the naggings of his nervous system, to the terror that invaded him daily, there might come a day when his own ability to choose his course in life would disappear forever into a current of rippling impulses and tides of vicious emotions -on which he would bob impotently before being submerged completely; until he was no more a person than is a flinch from the touch of a boiling radiator. He allowed the rising tension to subside without giving it any credence and busied himself looking out over the town as the bus pulled out of the stop.

As the bus crawled away, moving in increments to escape

the congestion of the small town, Keehan watched the old man with the constant look of fear on his face that walked his little dog every day and crossed the road back and forth as he attempted to avoid meeting another person on the path. He saw the man with the green baseball cap, who was sat where he was most days, on the bench outside the bookies alone smoking a cigarette and staring vacantly into nowhere. For some reason the sight of sad people made Keehan happy -maybe not quite happy, but a little *safer*. At first when he realised this he had denied it to himself, felt a little guilty about it; but he had gradually come to accept it. Knowing that everyone else was sad too made him feel a little more comforted, a little more solid, less alone. It's not like he was a weirdo. *Why did people love sad songs so much? Why did they go to movies to cry?* It seemed to him sometimes in what felt like rare moments of clarity that misery was some kind of secret that everyone knew but kept from each other because no-one wanted to be the one to shatter the dream. He lay back on his seat and turned away from the window.

They had left the town now and there was nothing much to see but green fields and trees, with the occasional house dotting the landscape. He stuck his headphones in and let his mind drift off, more content than he had been in a while. He liked journeys, especially on the bus. The trip to and from school had been his favourite part of his day. *The part when you're neither here nor there,* he thought. *Just somewhere nowhere in particular. Somewhere in-between. The same reason I like stairs. You're either going down stairs to do something or you're going up stairs to do something,* he continued to muse as he gazed out at the landscape flashing by. *No-one's ever just on *the stairs for its own purpose... It doesn't have a purpose... It's a place between purposes. A space without any obligations. Like bus journeys. Nothing to do but sit.* He sat staring blankly out the window the whole way up, lost in nothing and glad for the opportunity to not have to feel guilty about it.

He got off the bus outside the Museum, stretched his legs and looked around at all the people milling about to and fro like ants; bustling about, always busy, always going somewhere, always with things to do. The general pace of life seemed to be turned up a few notches from where he started and it excited him.

His older brother Kevin had moved up here about six years ago, soon after Alan and their mother had announced their plans to get married. Keehan very rarely saw him, although they did keep in sporadic contact and Kevin would occasionally send him packages and cards and pictures of his son Jake, Keehan's nephew. Kevin had an apartment in town near the quays where he lived with his girlfriend Melissa, and it was Keehan's intention to stay with them a couple of days -although he hadn't yet thought to inform anyone else of his plans. The apartment was further into town but there was plenty to see and he was in no rush so he decided to walk. He wondered briefly whether he should give Kevin a call and let him know he was coming but he decided in the end to surprise him.

Kevin Dang was not long home from work and was about to start preparing dinner when the doorbell rang. Melissa was off collecting Jake from the day care centre and hadn't arrived home yet. Kevin went to the door and opened it. To his great shock and surprise, standing on the other side of the door was his brother Keehan, who was nonchalantly peering down the corridor trying to see into one of the other apartments that had left their door slightly ajar. "Keehan!," Kevin exclaimed. "Alright bro." "Hey. What are ya doin here?" "I was just in the neighbourhood, thought I'd pop in." Kevin grabbed Keehan's hand and shook it warmly. "Aaaaaah..., he gaped, still quite taken aback. "C'mon in!" He ushered Keehan in to the apartment. "Sit down there," he gestured to the plush grey satin couch. "Uuuuuuuh," Kevin gawped around the room as he attempted to keep track of what he had been doing when this thoroughly unexpected guest had arrived. "I was just about to put dinner on," he said finally. "Chicken curry and rice, d'ya want some?" "Yeah cool if ya have some extra," Keehan replied. He was in fact ravenous, having come straight from the bus station and not having brought any food with him for the journey besides a pack of Tayto.

He looked around. It was a nice apartment. Modern. Blocks instead of patterns. Lots of glass and natural light. "Where's the other two?" he asked Kevin. "Ah Melissa's gone to pick the little fella up from day care. Should be back soon. So what are ya up to? Ya here on your own?" Kevin enquired as he went into the adjoining kitchen where a pot of water on the stove was beginning to gurgle and spit, while Keehan made himself comfortable on the couch. There was a small kitchen pass between the two rooms and Keehan turned to watch Kevin getting the dinner ready. "Yeah I'm up here on my own," he shouted in through the window, then paused for a moment. He had gradually become aware of the oddness of his spontaneously turning up at their flat for the first time ever and of the fact that they had their own lives going on and a baby to take care of.

"Listen," he began tentatively, "is there any chance I could stay here a night or two?" "Aaah," Kevin paused for a moment to take stock of the situation and simultaneously stir the curry that had begun to rapidly rise to meet the edges of the pan. "Yeah, sure," he replied, turning the heat down slightly and stirring the pot another couple of times as the sauce settled back in to its comfortable simmer. He turned to peer in at Keehan through the pass. "Is everything okay?" "Yeah, Keehan nodded. "I just needed a bit of a break away." "Ah right." Kevin didn't press any further. "Yeah well there's a spare bedroom here, well it's more of a box room. There's a load of cra..., *stuff* in there." Kevin smiled. He turned from the fillets of chicken breast he was now chopping to peer in again at Keehan. "I'm tryin' to clean up my language a bit with Jake startin' to talk an all." He chuckled and turned back to his slicing. "But yeah," he continued, "there's some stuff in there, boxes and clothes and that, but there's a single bed, made up and all. Ya can shove the bits off it." "Cool," Keehan smiled to himself and relaxed back into the plush velvet sofa.

"So what are ya doin' with yourself nowadays?" Kevin called in as he scraped the cubed chicken breasts off the chopping board into the pot. "Ah nothing really," Keehan replied. "Just hangin' around mostly. Mam's at me to get a job but sure what's the point?"

Kevin smiled to himself in remembrance of the heady rebellious nihilism of his own younger years. The strikingness of Keehan's physical resemblance to himself, having not seen him in person for many years; combined with the attitude, was creating a rather eerie effect for Kevin as though he were looking at a kind of mirror of himself from the past. Of course fond though he was of his memories of that time and age he had learned many lessons and been through many struggles in the journey to where he was now. Still there was a warmth and attraction in nostalgia that was only ever increased by sadness at the fact that it needed to be left behind. Being able to see it in someone else was a nice way of re-visiting his past, with the benefit of his current experience and the mindset of the person he had now become. Suddenly feeling a jolt of fear at the potential of this nostalgia to overpower his contentment in his current situation and the responsibilities he now had, Kevin's mind snapped back to the situation as it now stood and returned from a haze of emotion, filled with nights drinking cider stolen from his parents cupboard with his friends on an abandoned trailer outside town; meetings with girls after school; queueing up in the rain for hours to buy concert tickets: and the prescriptive and dull future that he was never going to let become his own.

"Have ya no ambition's or anything ya want to do? he asked Keehan. "It can't be much fun sittin' on your arse all day." "It's grand," Keehan replied and there was a hint of hurt pride in his voice. "Sure what else would I be doin'," he continued. "Sittin' in some place all day wastin' me time."

Kevin had the curry simmering now and the rice on the boil and he came into the living room and sat on the armchair opposite Keehan. "Well what are ya gonna do? Sit around for the rest of your life?" "I don't know like." Keehan was a little annoyed at being put on the spot and questioned so intensely.

But at the same time he was beginning to accept the fact that these were the kind of questions he was feeling an increasing need to answer himself now; although he wasn't quite sure where to start. "I'll figure something out," he sighed and then smiled reassuringly at Kevin. Kevin, seemingly satisfied that Keehan was at least taking his life somewhat seriously smiled back and didn't press any further. They both sat in peaceful silence, both surprised and gladdened by how good it felt to be together again after so long.

The peaceful silence they had been enjoying was suddenly broken by a rattling in the lock. Kevin slid off the arm of the chair to his feet and Keehan turned to look as the door slowly opened and Melissa shoved her way in with a duffle bag over her shoulder and Jake in her arms; who himself was holding tightly to a tattered looking plush rabbit. Melissa kissed Kevin who had come to meet them at the door and was about to mention how good the curry smelled, when over his shoulder she suddenly spotted Keehan sat awkwardly on the couch. "Hello," she said and looked at him questionably. "My brother Keehan," Kevin gestured at him to Melissa as Keehan stood up and stepped apprehensively towards them. "Keehan, Melissa," Kevin continued. Her face warmed slightly with recognition and almost instantly became tinged with confusion. "Keehan," she moved over and shook his hand. "Kevin's told me all about you. I didn't recognize you. How are you doing?"

She had moved over to the corner of the living room and was lowering Jake into a playpen Keehan hadn't noticed, the baby straining to keep his wide bright eyes fixed on the new arrival as Keehan watched him get set down gently before rolling onto his backside and grabbing the bars to haul himself up to his feet and peer over. *Behind bars from day one,* Keehan thought. "Ah I'm grand," he turned to Melissa, "just up here for a day or two to get away. How's things with yourself?" "Oh it's all go," Melissa turned to him smiling as she shimmied out of her jacket and turned to hang it on a hook on the back of the door. "Non-stop as always." Keehan knew Melissa worked in some capacity for a fashion magazine in the city. Kevin had told him before but all he could remember was that to him it had sounded convoluted and unnecessarily complicated, like most things in this world. "Do you want to hold your nephew?" Melissa smiled at Keehan seeing him eye up Jake who was continuing to stare at him. "Ah no you're grand," Keehan replied. Then sensing he probably was supposed to want to pick him up and make faces at him and stupid noises he hurriedly added, "Ah I'd be afraid I'd drop him or something."

He got off the couch and went over to the crib and stood beside Melissa. He looked in over the crib at the baby with its big dumb eyes staring back at him and noticed the vague family resemblance that hadn't seemed as evident in the photos he had seen; and he suddenly felt an overwhelming wave of sympathy. As much for himself as for Jake. He considered the fact that at one point he himself had been just like that. Just a little stupid lump not knowing a damn thing about anything, and staring around helplessly waiting for the world to reveal itself and put the foundations of his mind in place. Jake was somewhat lucky it seemed. He had a nice house. Two nice, loving, well adjusted parents. He might end up being relatively okay.

Keehan stretched his arm into the crib and extended his index finger towards Jake, wobbling it playfully. Jake hesitated for a moment before grabbing onto it and gripping it tightly. Keehan began to think of all the babies being born in war-zones and in places where there were famines, or whose parents were dicks; or just the whole general mass of confusion that surrounded everything. Just sitting there looking up with their big stupid eyes for the world to give them a mind, that for most would remain with them their whole lives; shaping those lives and moulding them. He sometimes felt lucky that at least he had had shelter and food and opportunity in comparison to what he could have had. There were no dramatic incidents, no beatings, no starvation, nothing he could put his finger on. But that just led to more guilt and frustration. That apart from a feeling of sheer hopelessness there was no tangible reason -no justifiable reason; why he couldn't get his life together and do something useful. Maybe do something to help the less fortunate. Or just be a little braver at least and stop whining. *I'm startin' to sound like a bleedin' sap,* he thought mockingly to himself and shut it all from his mind.

Dinner was now ready and he gently extracted his finger from Jake's tight grip and went to join Kevin and Melissa at the table where a steaming plate of delicious looking chicken curry had been placed waiting for him. "What d'you wanna drink?" Kevin asked getting up as Keehan came in. "We've got beers, or wine, and Coke aswell; or some apple juice if you'd prefer?..." Kevin had a nice frosty bottle of beer on the table and Keehan decided to join him. "Ah I'll have a beer thanks if you're having one." "Sure," Kevin replied, and got up to grab another bottle from the fridge drawer. He popped the lid off and placed it by Keehan.

It had been a long day for Keehan. He was tired and ravenous and was a long way from home. But being received so well and being welcomed in so readily by Kevin and Melissa; and now sitting down to eat some delicious food, had put him in a state of almost giddy relief. The beer was just the cherry on top of the cake, and any nervousness he had had before had been thoroughly erased as he enjoyed the novelty of his new surroundings, and the warmth of the connection with his long lost brother; and the family that had come along with him, that was now truly part of his own.

They chatted over dinner about this and that and after they finished, moved into the living room to sit in front of a movie and drink more beers and talk more. At about half eleven Kevin and Melissa retired to bed, both having work in the morning, as Keehan stayed up to finish his last beer and look forward to tomorrow.

CHAPTER 14

The next day while Kevin and Melissa were in work, Keehan went for a walk in the city. He had been here many times before and had always loved the sense of freedom he got, the feeling of mixing with the world. This time however something was not quite right, although he couldn't put his finger on it. There was a hollowness in everything around him and he began to feel more and more cut off from it all as he wandered the busy, bustling streets. It was as though someone had placed a layer of clear plastic over everything, and though it all looked the same as it always did and sounded the same as always; there was an eerie silence pervading it all. A distance that he couldn't explain. He saw people moving around him, just one singular mass like a giant amoeba; dividing, passing around him and converging again as he continued to walk.

He took a turn down a side street he was sure he'd never been down before. In the many times he'd been in the city since he was a child he had been led up and down streets that had had no names for him, just particular characteristics and items of interest; some of which stayed on permanently as fixtures or solitary beacons, the rest of which continuously shifted and changed around them as the years went by. As he'd grown older the actual names of some streets had fixed themselves into a kind of ever clarifying and interconnecting map he held in his mind, but a lot of it still was just a vast hodgepodge of individual curiosities, landmarks and prominent buildings; some of which were nothing more than vague memories to him now. He headed down the street a little way looking from side to side to see if any of the shops would trigger some memories for him, but nothing about it seemed familiar.

At the end of the street, rising up before him was a huge old building which appeared to contain within its hefty stone walls a newly installed nightclub that was preparing for its opening that night; as revealed by a massive banner which hung across the doorway. The facade of the building was Georgian, ornate with carved stone; impressive in its solidity and its subtle embellishment and symmetry, and even Keehan -never one to consider himself a connoisseur of the architectural, was impressed with its classic and elegant beauty. He walked up and leaned across the steps in front and pulled the massive banner aside to peer in through one of the windows into the downstairs area.

The first thing that caught his eye was a huge shimmering disco ball which was hanging from the ceiling. The floors were a mixture of polished wood and lush, red carpet. There were huge white leather couches in the corners. Everywhere was crystal and mirrors and neon lights, not illuminated now in the daytime but surely something spectacular at night. Keehan peered in with a wavering mixture of longing and bitterness. He watched himself bathed in the colours of the neon lights, surrounded by models and pop stars dancing and laughing. His hopeful premonition almost as soon as it had arisen began to wither away as he felt the cold solidity of the granite stone he was leaning on begin to burn his hand. He stepped back from the window and rubbed his hands together vigorously to get the blood flowing again. There were signs up outside the venue advertising the opening. Kara Hughes apparently was appearing. By all means it would be quite an event. Keehan, finding nothing in the day but a vague sense of disappointment, turned and headed back towards Kevin's flat.

He got in using the spare key his brother had given him to use and headed straight for his room and the bottle of vodka and Coke he had in his bag. He twisted off the cap of the bottle and began to drink as he leaned against the balcony and looked out over the city.

His mind was spinning. On his own all day pottering around, he had for the first time since he'd left home been hit with the randomness of the whole endeavour, as well as the whirlwind of emotions that came with meeting Kevin for the first time in so long, as well as Jake and Melissa. The previous day had felt like some weird dream at the time and now that he had a moment to stop and gather himself, the reality of it all was once again becoming clear and concrete. He was still quite exhilarated by the freshness of the whole experience and the bustle and noise and felt almost like he belonged again, as he surveyed the chic, modern flat and looked back out from the balcony, down at the city below. Still he couldn't quite dismiss a creeping sense of bitterness and jealousy that came with knowing that realistically, a life like this was something that was a million miles away from his own life. In his heart he felt the chasm that existed between the life he envisioned, the kind of life he was now a tourist in -and where he actually was now. Where he would be when the dream was over. The fact was he couldn't even begin to imagine how he could make a life like the one he was now briefly visiting. As much as he tried to find it, the bridge that should have connected the life of his dreams and those of his reality had been lost somewhere along the way and he was becoming more desperate for fate to swoop in and save him as he tried to obliterate the self he no longer believed in or trusted.

When Kevin got back from work that evening he walked in to find Keehan lying spread-eagled on the middle of the living room floor. His heart leapt in panic before he noticed the almost empty litre bottle of vodka sitting on the side-table beside the couch and he breathed a sigh of relief. His relief almost immediately turned to annoyance as he confirmed with a gentle push of his hand that Keehan had in fact just gotten paralytically drunk and passed out.

After being poked several times with Kevin's toe Keehan, still drunk and bleary-eyed, finally jerked awake. He slowly pulled himself up and looked around as he attempted to get his bearings. "What're ya at?" he heard Kevin's voice echoing from somewhere. "What're *you* at?" Keehan replied, groggy and irritated at being woken up with a toe in the ribs. "Get up off the floor will ya," Kevin admonished him sharply as Keehan began to pull himself onto his feet. "What'sh yer problem?" Keehan scowled, still quite drunk, as he looked around for his bottle. "What's my problem? Kevin asked, his eyes widening as his mouth dropped open. "I have a child livin' here. He'll be back in a couple of hours. He can't be comin' back to some drunken lunatic lyin' in the middle of the floor." "Jeshush you usheda be cool," Keehan slurred taking a gulp of vodka. "Remember when you used ta be out partyin' all the time an' takin' pills an' all. Now ya just work an' sit here wi' yer kid... Ya bleedin' sold out." "I grew up Keehan," Kevin replied calmly. "It's about time you did too. Start takin' a bit of responsibility for yourself." "Ah yeah, here we go," Keehan slurred taking another gulp. "Here," Kevin said making a grab for the bottle as he started to get irritated again. "You're not drinkin anymore of that."

As he made to take the bottle Keehan stumbled backwards to avoid him, knocking over a vase on the side-table, which smashed into pieces on the floor. "Jesus what are ya at," Kevin exclaimed as he went into the kitchen to get a dustpan and brush. "Put down that bottle and go lie down in bed for a couple of hours..."

Keehan, to Kevin's surprise and relief, immediately and without another word went off to his room. But instead of getting into bed he began to scoop up whatever meagre belongings he had brought with him and stuff them violently back into his bag.

He emerged from his room with the bag slung over his shoulder just as Kevin was throwing the remains of the vase into the bin. "What're ya doin'?" Kevin asked as he turned to see Keehan come striding out of the room with the back-pack slung over his shoulder. "I'm goin'," he replied. "Where? Kevin asked, with an eyebrow raised, as he sighed and turned to chuck the empty dustpan and brush back into the corner beside the fridge where it lived. "Just lie down there and sleep for a while." "No I'm going," Keehan retorted and jerked the strap of the bag up higher on his shoulder in a gesture of affirmation. He was starting to slightly regret how the situation had turned out but at this point was too far gone to turn back. "I know people around," he barked defiantly. "I'll be alright. See ya later." He strode out the door slamming it behind him before Kevin could do a thing about it.

Almost as soon as he got back out in the open Keehan started to feel his regret growing and began to assess the reality of the situation now that he had a moment to examine it from outside the swirl of chaos he'd found himself in. Kevin had always been cool to him and hadn't even gotten that angry. He knew if he had just calmed down and went for a sleep he'd still have a place to stay tonight. The shock had made his mind go blank that was the problem. *Yes, if Kevin had just let him sleep he'd have been alright.* He'd felt trapped, cornered. Even he knew that was a pathetic excuse. The truth was he didn't know why he lost control of himself. His mind just fell to pieces and got swept along by the reactive panic of his body and lost control of what he was doing. Started to react by some unseen force and then everything went to shit. *Why the hell can I not just be normal?* he asked himself for the umpteenth time. *Just be around other people and interact and be cool and have friends?"*

He reached into his backpack and took out the bottle of vodka which he'd managed to snatch on his way out, and took a swig. *Fuck it*, he thought. *I'm a rebel. A renegade.* He was a square peg in a round hole and he liked it. He liked that he didn't slot into things so easily. That he wasn't made to fit with this bullshit they called normal. Blinkered and sleepwalking like all the other happy people, that flitted around and chatted shite and did mundane pointless crap like get jobs and save up to go skiing or whatever so they'd have photos to shove in everyone's face to try and make them think they're interesting. *A renegade,* he thought turning the word over in his mind, fondling it and testing it like a ripe peach in a supermarket. *Renegade... Like the type people always dream of being, while they shuffle on afraid to really live... The romantic character not made for this world... That's what I am. And I'm gonna party with the A-list tonight.*

It was still several hours before the nightclub was opening so he headed towards the general area and ducked into the first pub he saw. He ordered a Jack Daniels and Coke and sat down at a table by the window. He sat there drinking and watching the people walk past, eyeing them with growing jealousy and disgust that was the product of his own tangled mind. After finishing the first JD and Coke he ordered another. The groggy feeling that had been threatening to escalate into a full blown hangover since he'd left Kevin's appeared to have been assuaged by the first drink, and his bitterness began to diminish.

Beginning to feel a little bored and restless he decided to pop next door and buy a pack of cigarettes to keep him occupied and headed back to the pub's smoking area. It was a small patio area, quite homely, complete with a weather-beaten picnic bench and surrounded by shrubbery. Over the sides of his enclosure he could hear the ambient noise of the city going on around him. He peeled off the plastic wrapping of the cigarettes and tore back the foil cover; took one of the cigarettes out and lit it up. He took his first drag, and the smoke hit the back of his throat with a force and a bitterness he wasn't quite prepared for. He coughed and spluttered and his diaphragm trembled as he did everything he could not to vomit: pushing his stool back and standing up, grabbing his stomach; hunching over; then standing up straight again and leaning on the table trying to breathe as deeply and steadily as he could until the tempest in his lower organs gradually settled back into their usual peaceful rhythm.

He took a minute to compose himself and looked around to make sure no-one had seen. The place was empty. The windows to the bar inside had been blacked out rendering him invisible to everything but the cold, uninhabited beer garden.

After a few deep breaths to settle his stomach he continued, being careful to measure his inhalations so as not to set off another fit of coughing. With the fourth and fifth drag though, he started to get the hang of it and relaxed into a consistent, mindless motion. His head began to swim and he started to feel a little sick. He tried to finish the last couple of drags but couldn't, and stubbing the cigarette out, he stumbled back inside and sat down again. He repeated this process numerous times as the bar slowly began to fill up with people.

Keehan shuffled back through the growing throng after smoking his fifth cigarette, now becoming much easier as the tar in his throat began to cushion the irritating effects of the smoke. His seat was still unoccupied and he sat down. The room was spinning now. He sat bolt upright with his hands planted firmly on the chair beside him for support and breathed slowly and deeply. When the room had once again stabilized and he had regained control of himself he pulled his phone out of his pocket to check what time it was. It was ten o'clock. Time for him to get going. He stood up and stumbled off out into the street, on his way to find the club; his sense of direction strangely efficient considering the circumstances. After recovering from his nausea earlier he was getting a second wind and was feeling refreshed though still quite drunk.

As he approached the street where he'd seen the club earlier that day he began to hear the thumping beat of the bass and the crackling hum of crowds grow louder and louder. The first thing he saw as he turned the last corner were the neon lights that earlier in the day had lain dormant and now were washing the pavement outside the club with colour. He began to feel a buzz of excitement and an increasing buoyancy as he approached the front door.

There was a huge man standing at the door with a skin-head and a goatee, wearing a black jacket and holding a clipboard. This giant man watched bemusedly as Keehan approached the club with inspiringly misjudged confidence and an apparent clear goal in mind; and he continued to watch as Keehan strolled nonchalantly up the steps towards the front door. Keehan was about to take his last step forward, to dip his feet into the pools of coloured light which emanated from inside and were bathing the floor in front of his eyes; when the guy in black took a single wide step to his right, stopping in front of him; blocking his entrance like a great immovable black obelisk.

Keehan's nose was almost touching the soft fabric of the man's jacket. He looked up. "Yeah?," the guy asked Keehan pointedly, staring down at him, his face blank and unyielding. "Alright," Keehan replied almost cheerfully; his swimming head failing to fully grasp the reality of what he was trying to do or to read the tone of the situation. "I'm just headin' in to the club," he continued as he moved unsuccessfully to try and get past, the great black wall leaning ever so slightly with his change of direction to block him again. Keehan looked up again now, beginning to finally grasp that his plan may have caught on a snag. The bouncer looked down at him and burst out laughing. He threw his head back and laughed. Then he took another look at Keehan then laughed some more. He looked around for someone to share this joke with. Some girl with a sparkly mini-dress and far too much make-up joined in the laughter as she tottered stiffly up the steps. "Just headin' inta the club," the guy nodded towards Keehan and the girl looked at Keehan. She rolled her eyes and continued to smile as she strolled past them unimpeded, as lightly as a breeze, as though she were walking in the front door of her own house. "Fuck off will ya," the bouncer finally said to Keehan as his laughter began to die down to a chuckle.

Keehan stood frozen to the spot for a moment, feeling the anger rise inside him. With no other option left to him he turned and stormed off, his jaw rigid and his teeth clenched.

He marched furiously off down the street not taking any particular notice of which direction he was going, and on turning the next corner in front of him he almost knocked over a couple of Spanish students who were standing awkwardly looking around trying to find their bearings. Regaining their balance and composure they turned to look at him go as he stormed ahead barely noticing them.

He made his way towards the park which was just around the corner, it being his only place of sanctuary and peace: his furious pace slowing down now to a more lumbering stroll as the tiredness began to creep up on him. On reaching the park he went in and found a bench and sat down for a minute to get his bearings and to figure out what to do with himself. His only goal had been to get in that nightclub, and the truth was he hadn't really thought any farther than that. With the day's exertions and the quite hefty intake of alcohol, his eyelids were beginning to get heavy. A wave of resignation washed over him and he put his feet up on the bench and lay down to sleep, surrounded by the comforting waves of rustling tree branches in the wind; supplemented by the occasional siren whoop off in the distance. What followed was a few hours of broken sleep where his exhaustion fought with the uncertainty of his surroundings. The bench was hard and it was quite cold, though luckily for him not as cold as some nights had been lately. He curled up as tightly as he could and tossed and turned for a few hours trying to protect his body's warmth as best he could from the harsh night. At around six in the morning as the air around him began to be warmed by the sun he had a good forty minutes of deep, uninterrupted sleep before waking for good with the sunrise stinging his eyes.

Sitting up, he rubbed his eyes and looked around. It was relatively peaceful still, save for the odd sporadic jogger who darted through the park, none of which paid much notice to him. All of a sudden he was hit with a blinding pain that pierced his head and sent a scream through every fibre of his being. He squeezed his head as if to attempt strangle the pain into submission. Almost as quickly as it had appeared, it faded back from its initial sharpness to more of a continuous dull throbbing. His eyes hurt with the sun and he couldn't find his sunglasses so he sat squinting. At least it hadn't rained, he thought.

He began to feel pangs of guilt as the memory of his encounter with Kevin pushed itself back into his consciousness. He couldn't go back there now. He checked his phone and sure enough there were missed calls from Kevin. *He actually cared, that's what made it worse*, Keehan thought to himself. *If Kevin had only been a dick then it wouldn't be so bad*. He was the one that had been a dick. He thought about going back and apologizing but started to feel a panic rise in him as he saw himself standing sheepishly at Kevin's door and wondered what he would say. Could he laugh it off as hijinks? What if he did and the two of them hated him? Then it would only be worse. Should he just apologize? Would they accept it? Would it lead to a big, drawn out lecture? *I'll give him a text later or something,* he thought and blocked it from his mind.

He sat considering his options for a moment, feeling like he wanted nothing more than to disappear down a deep, dark hole. As he sat for a while pondering his next move, he suddenly remembered a guy Gary Lynch who had been in a couple of his classes at school. He knew Gary had moved up here for a couple of years after they'd finished school. In all probability he still lived here. He thought maybe he'd give him a call and see if he could stay with him for a couple of nights. He knew there was no point calling anyone at this hour of the morning and so decided to go for a walk around town to while away a few hours and try and lose his hangover.

By around two o'clock, after a morning wandering around,

during which he'd gotten a bite to eat and some much needed hydration, he had started to feel relatively okay and he sent Gary a message asking did he want to meet up.

Gary was in work and had received the message with bafflement. He wasn't sure if he'd met or talked to Keehan Dang once since he'd left school, and even then hadn't even really hung around with him. He decided it might be nice to see him regardless and find out what he had been doing and as he had nothing on that evening anyway, he messaged Keehan with an agreement to meet up. He sent Keehan the directions for the restaurant where he was working and they agreed to meet outside at five.

Keehan had almost banished the previous day's events from his mind and was starting to feel slightly optimistic again about the future of his adventure. He sat in a cafe near Gary's restaurant with a coffee and wondered what the others were at now, and thought happily about being able to bring back some stories to brighten their grey lives.

CHAPTER 15

"Where's the other lad tonight?" Dave asked settling down on the sofa. "Aw he fucked off to the city durin' the week. I messaged him he just said he was gone up for a few days." James replied absent-mindedly as he struggled to gouge a couple of particularly obstinate batteries from the remote control using a butter knife. "What'd he go up there for, just the craic or what?" "Dunno he just went, never said." "Ah I dunno, Lisa added, curiously watching James's struggle with the batteries. "I'm glad to have a bit of peace for a while. He can be an awful tool at times."

James laughed and turned to Dave. "What're you up to? Any craic?" "I was just in askin' for more hours," Dave sighed. "Turns out Sarah's after getting herself pregnant." "Your sister?" James exclaimed as the batteries popped out of the remote and onto the floor and rolled across the room. "What age is she?" Lisa asked. "Fifteen." "Fifteen," James repeated. "Jesus when I was fifteen I was still playin' with Power Rangers." They all laughed half-heartedly. "Back in my day..." Lisa rasped croakily. "James joined her, shaking his fist in a curmudgeonly display, "You damn kids an' your baggy pants!!"

Their laughter didn't last long as the reality of the situation sat behind their jokes like a glaring presence. Lisa and James felt bad for Dave. His father had been laid off some years ago due to an accident, his mother being already unable to work; leaving Dave as the sole breadwinner, along with their various meagre pensions and supplements. Though they were a happy and tight little family Lisa and James both knew that things would be difficult for them to manage with a new addition to the fold. "So," James asked, "Do ya know who the father is?" "Yeah," replied Dave. "We do, but sure he's washed his hands, doesn't want to know. We went to his ma and da sure they were havin' none of it. So I'm gonna need the extra few hours if I can get it." He sighed resignedly and the other two smiled consolingly. "Anyway, are ya's headin' for a pint?" They decided to go for one.

They sat down at a table near the window and looked out on the street where the night was beginning. Lisa looking over towards the bar, noticed Sharon and Michelle standing there. It was the first time she had seen them since the incident outside the nightclub and her mind instantly went back to that moment. She had felt a little hurt at the time at Michelle's callous dismissal of them and it had played on her mind occasionally over the following days, although it had soon faded from her primary concerns. She had come to the conclusion that it was mostly a result of a bad mood at a bad moment. But still, she couldn't help but feel a slight resentment towards her. She watched Michelle and began to think of all the people like her she'd come across in her life. People who seemed to never have to worry or care about anyone else and could still be admired as an almost superior being. It seemed strange to her how some people could glide through their lives so flippantly, seemingly worthier than the rest. Picking and choosing what they want and leaving the rest to worry about everything.

She had sometimes wondered what if she just stopped thinking about stuff, stopped caring so much, could she have that easy life? Could it actually be that easy, and what would she have to discard in the process of gaining a life full of fawning admiration and pitiful respect? She was sure though that the losses would outweigh the gains. Something told her that she could never be comfortable living that way: or rather that to be comfortable living that way she would have to lose something that was more important than the status or respect she would gain. And though she didn't know quite what it was, she knew it was the only real important thing. It was really just a kind of interesting thought experiment and she had never considered it as ever being potentially anything more.

She turned her attention back to the lads. They were talking about work again, which it seemed to Lisa was all they ever talked about these days: James having recently accepted an increase in hours with the hope that the increased wages would expand the quality of their free time. As Lisa's attention returned to the lads their conversation gradually diverted to incorporate her and they began to laugh more as they left work behind and returned to other things.

After an hour or so, as the rest of the night's crowd in dribs and drabs began to file in, the room became full and the ambient noise around them grew louder. Conversation was becoming more difficult, and getting hoarse from shouting they decided to head back to the house and put a film on.

Lisa walked up to the bar to get one final round. As she stood waiting for the bartender and looking around, a group of girls she didn't know walked up past her. One of them turned to Michelle who was still stood in the same spot beside the bar. Michelle happened to look up as the girl approached, and her shoulders tightened almost imperceptibly as if she was sensing the approach of some malevolence. "Got enough eye-shadow on have ya?" Lisa heard the girl sneer at Michelle as the rest of her gang began to snicker and they walked on.

Lisa quickly turned back towards the bar but continued to watch Michelle out of the corner of her eye, making sure not to be obvious and attract her attention. For the most miniscule of moments; barely a split second that a blink would have obscured, she saw the soul in Michelle's eyes flicker softly and a wallowing depth open up in the black of her pupils before it quickly changed back to her usual sheen of haughty ambivalence. It was a different quality of ambivalence though –one that Lisa now realised she had seen before but had not really had the inclination to differentiate. It was an ambivalence that was slightly fractured, not quite real. "I'm just going to the bathroom," Lisa heard Michelle say to Sharon and the others who were chatting away, seemingly oblivious to the girls remark.

In the bathroom Michelle stood in front of the mirror and tried to figure out what was wrong. She took a tube of lipstick from her purse and began to apply the scarlet colouring to her lips which appeared to her to have become a little smudged. It seemed to her that the powder she always applied to her skin to give it its glow had been applied a little unevenly so she added some more and carefully blended it in. Still she felt as though something just wasn't right as she scrutinized her face from every angle, looking for the imperfection she could fix and finding just something that wasn't quite right somehow.

Sharon and the girls were just about to head in when Michelle emerged from the bathroom. "I'm gonna go home," she said as coolly as she could. "You okay?" Sharon asked, sensing something wasn't quite right. "Yeah I'm fine," Michelle replied. "I just don't feel well. Bit of a sick stomach or something." She managed to muster a reassuring smile. "I'll head back with ya," Sharon offered. "We can watch a film or something." "No I'm grand cheers," Michelle replied hastily, feeling more and more vulnerable to scrutiny the longer she stood there. "I think I just wanna go to bed. I'll give ya a call tomorrow."

With that she headed out and hurried back home, back to her sanctuary away from the eyes of the world and its power to praise as well as judge. To lift her high or drop her down. With her jacket pulled tightly around her in the cool dry September night, she wanted nothing more than to be left alone.

CHAPTER 16

The pigeons were gathering at Cyril's feet as he absent-mindedly scattered the crumbs on the path in front of him. He was sat in the park on a cold wooden bench just letting his thoughts wander. Behind him two young boys were throwing a tennis ball back and forth to each other. One lad, stick thin with bony elbows and a bowl haircut was standing just behind Cyril and was growing increasingly irritated as he maintained his chubbier friend with the Stone-Cold Steve Austin t-shirt was throwing the ball too hard. "Stop firin' it at me will ya," he shouted over at his chubby friend who was preparing to launch the ball back once more. Just then his attention wandered for a moment as he was distracted by a noise somewhere nearby. He returned to the game just in time to feel the tennis ball smack him bang in the middle of the forehead.

He stumbled backwards a step, in his confusion getting his legs entangled before falling back onto the grass; and he lay there dazed, looking up and blinking into the cloudy sunshine. His friend came running over to see if he was okay, his round, balloon-like face scrunched up with the exertion of trying to run while also trying to stifle a screaming laugh. The skinny kid looked up at him with a scowl, preparing to chastise him; before suddenly changing his mind and bursting out in a hysterical laugh instead. His friend burst out laughing as well and stumbled over onto the warm grass and the two of them rolled around on the ground trying to catch their breath from their hysterical laughter. Cyril sat only feet away, completely oblivious to their hi-jinks. His back turned to them as he stared into nowhere in particular, he dropped the last of his crumbs; then hauled himself off the cold bench and slowly hobbled off carrying himself like a sack of lead up the cracked and faded tarmac path.

He headed out through the park gate then crossed the road and took a left down the street towards Leary's pub. Finding the afternoons painfully long lately he had taken to dropping in to Leary's for a drink most days now to while away the time with a quiet pint in company with the rest of the broken and damned and those who just had nothing else better to do.

Meanwhile, Lisa was heading over to the lads' to see if James wanted to head over to Cyril's later on. As she walked up the Main Street and turned the corner she glanced across the road and saw Michelle coming down on the opposite side. She was walking down the street barefoot, fairly obviously hungover; with her heels hanging limply from her hand, smudged eyeliner, and with a short dress on that was erratically risqué for a Saturday morning in town. *She's obviously recovered from the incident the other night*, Lisa thought. *Like water off a ducks back...* Looking up suddenly from the pavement Michelle saw Lisa across the road and stared at her blankly before continuing on, stepping preciously on the cold concrete. Lisa paused before shrugging and continuing on to the lads house, where

James was sitting watching the telly with his blank notepad and pen sat on the coffee table in front of him.

Later on that day Lisa and James were sitting in Cyril's living room watching TV and drinking tea. Cyril was in a downbeat mood: a mood that seemed to the two of them to have been becoming more common lately. Sitting there alone day by day all he had to do was think, and his thoughts almost exclusively now would return to his daughter.

A part of him knew that he should just put his misgivings aside go and see her –a part that was becoming more desperate without becoming any easier to heed. The rest of him had decided that maybe he'd be better off just letting things be; to not stir anything up or cause trouble. Of course there was an element of pride too. He knew he'd been right all along and felt aggrieved at the reaction he'd received. He'd been spending more and more time in a resigned stupor. Conversation between the three was unusually stilted and James and Lisa both had picked up on the fact that something was eating at Cyril. "You alright Granda?" Lisa eventually spoke up. "Is something up?" Cyril let out a sigh and sat silently. A tentative smile began to creep across his face that seemed to be taking all his effort to manifest. His eyes glazed over and betraying his sorrow he answered almost to the room in general, "Ah, life's too short for petty squabbles." He realised immediately that he'd now entered a line of thought and conversation that he had tended to keep to himself and that there was no way now of returning to chatting generally about news and goings-on.

Without even looking he knew that James and Lisa had become quiet and still, waiting for him to continue. In a way he felt a kind of relief, like a door had suddenly cracked open that he had been struggling for a long time to keep shut, and he relaxed into the flow of his thoughts in a way he had only done alone before. He turned to James and Lisa so they should get the benefit of his hard-wrought smile before returning to examine his thoughts, with a bittersweet feeling that maybe there was now something positive to be gleaned from the misery he'd been enduring. James and Lisa looked at each other. "What do ya mean?" Lisa asked. Cyril looked over at them. "People are tough sometimes," he began. "They'll get on your nerves. You have te make sure and not let little stupid disagreements and irritations turn into anything bigger than they need to be. Sometimes it'll go too far, too far te come back from." He paused and sighed again and looked down at the floor for a moment before continuing, "And when you realise how pointless it was you'll be sorry you were so stubborn... and didn't take the time to understand what was really behind it. It might be so ingrained in ye that ye can't see around it anymore."

After another short pause he smiled at them again, this time a little more easily and naturally. Lisa and James didn't press any farther. They both knew what he was talking about. They also both knew their own helplessness in dealing with two people who were equally as stubborn as each other.

At half three James left to go to work for a couple of hours. Lisa stayed on for a couple of hours watching TV with Cyril. Though he said no more about Josie, his unhappiness seemed to permeate his entire being and Lisa could see that it would not be possible for him to be really happy again while carry-ing the burden of his estrangement. The issue had bubbled around in her mind ever since, even as they had settled back into a more casual mode, had had some lunch, some ham and bread and a tomato which she never ate but he gave to her every time nonetheless -and some more tea.

"Why don't ya just give me ma a shout," she blurted out, finally unable to skirt around the issue any longer and feeling the time had come to address the situation before it faded from view once again. Cyril sighed and looked at the ground, the wrinkles around his eyes ever more taut and sorrowful as he seemed to struggle for an answer. "And say what?" he finally relented. "I dunno, just call up and apologize or something..." "Apologize!" Cyril's bottom lip curled and with eyes deep and imploring he looked over at Lisa. "Why should I have to apologize?" he asked. "It's her that should be apologizing to me." The last sentence leapt from his tongue with resoluteness and determination.

Lisa rolled her eyes and looked him over. Saw his stubborn jaw beginning to jut out tensely. He had the hint of a demeanour that she had not seen very often before, a rare intensity behind his stubbornness. "Whatever," she replied. "I don't really want to get into it. But does it really matter? Why don't ya just say it anyway?" A part of Cyril knew she was right, that he'd probably be much happier if he just took the blame and made the first move. Unfortunately that part was buried under years of lonely solipsism and bitter pride. His inability to overcome this pride and his yearning to make it all better met in a deep sadness that was beginning to fill him almost to bursting. "Maybe," he sighed as he got up to poke the fire, his face now softened once more, his jaw having lost its tautness and his eyelids beginning to droop wearily. "Maybe."

Lisa shook her head in exasperation as she watched Cyril poke the fire mindlessly, his hands thrusting the poker in an automatic motion; just swirling it through the ashes and swelling flames, before finally after several minutes replacing it in its stand by the hearth and slowly and carefully lowering himself back into his balding old chair.

After an hour or so of sitting in peaceful silence with the only noise the buzzing of the television in the corner of the room, Cyril began to nod off in the chair. Lisa sat for a while, listening to him snore gently before getting up to put the fire-guard over the fire. She turned the volume of the telly down to a low murmur, gave Cyril a gentle kiss on the forehead and slipped out the door. She turned back for a moment, her eyes getting teary as she stood and looked at him sleeping in the chair and she felt almost mournful at the loss of the brilliant, witty man she loved more than anything in the world; and wondered whether he would ever be himself again. She shut the door gently behind her.

Her head full of thought she decided to take the long way home just to stretch her legs and get some air. It was all so sad, she thought, looking down at the pavement as she walked and recalling arguments she'd had in her life. People she'd hated at one point and the hatred that had often then been forgotten soon after. And the occasional few that never were. *So sad,* she thought, *the people that have always seemed so permanent through your life will someday just disappear. And how strange it is that you'll have spent the majority of your precious few years together pissed off over something pointless. And every-one thinking they'll live forever and that everyone else will live forever, will just push and grate off each other because of stupid little ideas they can't let go...*

Surprising herself she immediately began to worry about Keehan. He'd been gone for a few days now and she had no real idea where. She had casually wondered about him since he'd left, assuming that he was probably gone to see his brother or just gone away for a couple of days, but hadn't been sufficiently concerned to see what he was actually up to. Why he would have suddenly gone away alone for the first time ever. *But sure he's an arrogant twerp most of the time,* she thought, beginning an argument with herself. *He'd drive you mad with his carelessness and delusions. Why should I be worried about him? But that's the point isn't it? I suppose he's just a person too. He probably wouldn't be so annoying if he wasn't so hurt and damaged and scared. Like so many people. What if something happened and I never saw him again? Or anyone I know really?*

She thought how nice it would be right now to hear Keehan make one of his pissy sarcastic remarks and she resolved to give him a shout when she got back and see how he was and what he was up to. Continuing up the street, she remembered that Harry and Piotr were coming over to James' that evening, and she was suddenly overwhelmed with a sense of gratitude and excitement that she would see them soon, all illuminated and made more vivid by a deep sadness as she realised there would come a day when she would never see them again.

As she crossed the bridge she suddenly spotted Sharon sitting by the riverbank with her headphones on. She was sat picking up the daisies on the grass beside her; pulling the petals off and dropping them in the water, and watching them float off to have a confused and meandering race with each other in the slow current. Lisa walked over to her.

Sharon, seeing Lisa approach pulled off her headphones and looked up. "Hey," Lisa said. "Hi," Sharon replied, the invisible chasm that generally divided her from everyone else having temporarily drifted away with the daisy petals. "You okay? Lisa asked sitting down beside her on the grass. "Yeah," Sharon murmured without conviction. "I don't know. Just thinking." "Yeah?" Lisa replied, running her fingers through the crisp grass beside her. "About anything in particular?"

Sharon gently lobbed a daisy stalk into the clear water and sighed. "Just wondering what my life is going to be like," she replied watching the daisy stalk spin and twirl in the water before disappearing beneath the surface.

Lisa looked at her and smiled. "You obviously see great things ahead!" Sharon looked back over at her and laughed quietly. A laugh of almost resigned acceptance. "I don't know," she began. "It just seems like your life, or *a* life, is just kinda dropped onto you. And you keep thinking of all the things you want to do and it just seems less and less likely that you ever will. Like they make a plan and I'm just there to carry it out. That's it, that's what your life is going to be. And you're just supposed to shove everything else away and forget about it and be happy. -Or maybe being happy's not important? Doesn't seem like it. Maybe I'm just here to do what they couldn't. And that's it. Breed some more slaves to finish the job."

Lisa laughed. "What do you want to do?" she asked. "I don't know," Sharon continued now laughing gently herself.

"Travel, I guess. See the world. Just…" She paused and heaved another sigh. "I don't know…"

Lisa had now joined Sharon in picking the daisies and throwing them on the slow moving water. "I'd like to go to Spain and see real Flamenco," she said after a moment of silently watching the stream glide past. "I was readin' an article in a magazine once about how the stuff we always see is like the tourist version; sanitized an' all but you can find the proper stuff that's like, raw and organic and dark and like, rooted in the suffering and persecution of the gypsies." "Sounds pretty cool," Sharon nodded, feeling a sudden spark of intrigue.

The two of them sat on the bank for a while and chatted about random things they'd like to do and see. "How's Michelle these days?" Lisa asked after a while. "She's okay," Sharon replied. "I was talkin' to her earlier. I think she's goin' to stay with her dad for a few days before we go back. A bit of a break from the place." "You'd need that alright," Lisa said gazing up at the clouds which were slowly growing darker. "Where's her da?" "Galway somewhere," Sharon replied, now following Lisa's gaze upwards. "She really likes her dad but doesn't really get to see him that often. Her and her mam don't really get on that well I don't think."

Lisa, beginning to feel a cramp in her knee, rolled over a little and stood up. She brushed the grass off her bum and legs and took out her phone to check the time. It was half six, James would definitely be finished by now.

"I'm headin' over to James', she began. "A couple of the lads are comin' over we're probably gonna stick on a film or something, you fancy comin' over?" Sharon considered for a moment. "Yeah okay," she agreed getting up to her feet. Lisa waited as she brushed the grass off her dress and they set off towards the house.

When they got to the house the door was open. They walked in and were met by James coming in from the kitchen with two glasses of squash. "Hey," he greeted the girls and shook his head as if to indicate something was not quite right, as he continued over to the couch where Piotr and Harry were sat in a terrible state. They both had bloodied noses and were covered in small scratches and marks. Harry had a purple lump on his cheek and Piotr's mouth was covered in blood. He appeared to be missing a tooth. The girls rushed in horrified. "What happened?" Lisa asked. "They were mugged," James answered as he set the glasses down on the table in front of them. "We were coming uph under the wailway bridghe," Harry started, his words hampered by a swollen bottom lip, "And two ladths jumped out an' kicked the cwap out of us." "Then they took our wallets," Piotr continued. "Jokesh on dem though," he said, raising an eyebrow. "I had no money anyway." He started to laugh then winced in pain, holding his side which was heavily bruised.

CHAPTER 17

"People walk all over ya if you let em'," The guy Daniel grimaced at Keehan. Keehan was sitting in a quiet park on a bench. He had been sitting there for some hours in his misery when this stranger with short greasy hair, wearing a grey t-shirt and stonewashed jeans that were not quite the right fit had approached him in the twilight.

Daniel worked for an IT company in the city, repairing computers. He enjoyed the job as it required him only to sit in an office for most of the day tinkering with his devices and asked for a minimum of human interaction, which was preferable to him. He could tolerate the company of machines. Machines were straightforward. You learned the system and followed it and it worked, most of the time. Human beings were where things got messy. Where the beautiful symmetry and safety of logical thought appeared to fall apart and become something pointless and confused. He didn't leave his flat often now or any more than he could avoid; except to go to his job or to take a short drunken walk every few evenings or so through the park next door, generally waiting until it was getting dark so as to ensure the park would be deserted.

Daniel for all he knew had been a relatively happy boy in

the formative years of his life. He'd had a nice, safe childhood and parents that though quite overbearing at times, were generally good, caring people. He'd had occasional slight problems with angry and aggressive behaviour but nothing that his parents and teachers thought he wouldn't grow out of.

The timbre of his life had changed for the worse when he got to secondary school. Unleashed into the maelstrom of human society and put among the crowds on his own for the first time Daniel found it difficult to adapt. In fact there was a growing part of him that wanted nothing more than to rebel against the frivolousness and self-centredness and the games and nonsense that surrounded him. It wasn't helped by the revelation of a new hierarchical structure to existence of which he hadn't really been aware of before but in which he now found himself no-where near the top.

His school before had been small enough that everyone had been a big fish in their own way: everyone had their own talent or gift and they were all different. It had been Daniel's intelligence and cleverness that had marked him out as special. Here that seemed to almost be to his detriment. It was something that had seemed to attract nothing but hostility and ostracisation. He had managed to play it down, slot in, make a few friends, even join a few clubs. At the same time as he'd been carrying off the role of an average, inconspicuous student; an anger and bitterness had been slowly growing inside him and his behaviour had subtly been becoming increasingly aggressive and disruptive. He wanted to be at the top and knowing that he wasn't and never would be made him feel like he was nothing. It didn't help that he seemed to be physically smaller and more frail than the other boys around him.

It wasn't that he was unpopular or outcast, he just wasn't held in such a superior light as he felt he perhaps should have been. Not like the bigger, tougher guys who played sports and were fawned over by the girls and could push the little guys around.

He found a way of overcoming his own feelings of inadequacy by picking on others. By singling out those he perceived as having some weakness. This led to an incident where he himself had been on the receiving end of a beating, due to pushing around the wrong boy at the wrong time. The boy's brother who was in the year above Daniel, happened to witness the incident. He waited for Daniel after school and had gave him a hiding in front of a crowd waiting to catch their buses home. Daniel had left school that day with a bruised face and ribs and a further bruised ego.

True, many of the people that had been abused, including those he himself had picked on, had managed to recover over time, to get on and lead happy, normal lives: but Daniel, for whatever reason, was simply unable to let things go. He was unable to forget, much less forgive. And what had initially become an embarrassed self hatred and resentment at his lack of power over his own destiny; gradually over time had turned to a violent hatred of people, of the human animal.

He had gotten by, kept his head down and finished school relatively well and without much further incident, got a job and got on with his work; making sure to keep his real feelings about the world around him as much as he could under wraps. It had all been going relatively smoothly up until a month ago, when an incident with a fellow employee with whom he'd had some previous quarrels had ultimately led to him receiving a suspension from his job. Embarrassed, angry and alienated and without the anchor of somewhere to be every day he'd been drifting aimlessly and had spent most of his time since then drinking, logging onto forums where people shared his bleak world views and generally digging himself deeper and deeper into a hole. He stayed alone now in his small flat while his troubled mind fed on itself, and on the occasions when he did go out was overcome by disgust and hatred, seen with eyes that had been trained to see nothing else.

He had stumbled on Keehan sitting in the fading half-light and where on most occasions he would have immediately turned back; sensing something of a kindred spirit -and also a little buzzed from the few shots of Jack Daniels that had been remaining in the bottle, he had wandered over to share in Keehan's toxic stew.

Keehan passed him the bottle of vodka and Coke he had been swigging from and they got to talking. It was a conversation moulded by years of misanthrope. They had both known the pain of feeling like an underdog, and their resentment at feeling small was a burden on both their lives and something that was a relief to share at last; although Daniel's mind had seemed to have descended further and more rapidly into nightmare. His outlook complemented Keehan's mood at the time; a mood which had been becoming more prevalent as his own dreams had become more frantic and desperate as they had begun to rot and stink.

"Life used to be fun," Keehan growled, staring virulently at nothing in particular and taking a swig from the bottle as the distant street-lights became more vivid against the darkening sky. "How do ya keep goin' when ya just can't be bothered anymore? He took another swig. "What's the fucking point?" he muttered wearily to himself.

"Payback!" Daniel turned to him and sharpened up suddenly as he stared intensely into Keehan's face.

Keehan turned from his gazing at nothing to meet Daniel's eyes and was met with a steely resolution and sense of purpose that was almost inspiring. "Payback?" he queried. Daniel nodded slowly and resolutely, his focus unwavering as his eyes remained fixed and determined; sparkling with the reflection of the increasingly luminescent moon. "It's time to take the power back from all the assholes."

Keehan, though slightly unnerved at times by the level of Daniel's vitriol had felt a definite buzz at the sense of power in his words. It was what he'd always wanted though he'd never known exactly how to go about it. He felt it now already. The intoxication of control. Daniel seemed to have a vision and was clearly ready to begin making it a reality.

Though still slightly wary of Daniel, and on some level a little worried about what exactly this taking back of power would actually consist of in its execution; Keehan was in thrall to the dream of power and was now at least curious as to what Daniel was planning. "Yeah so how'd ya actually go about it," he asked. Daniel paused, his eyes glazed as he stared at the ground which had been starting to shake and wobble since he'd taken his last large gulp of vodka. Somewhat regaining himself his eyes darted upwards with a sharp jerk.

"See that flat over there," he pointed towards a blind covered window in a block of flats just beyond the trees. "Yeah," Keehan replied twisting his head around to see. "That's my flat. Drop over tomorrow and I'll show ya something..."

With that Daniel got up off the bench and stumbled off up the path, a wry, drunken smile on his face.

Keehan woke up the next morning in Gary's spare room. Gary had been in bed by the time he'd gotten back from the park the night before and had since been up and gone to work. Keehan stretched and rubbed his temples. There was a slight pain but he'd had worse. He thought back to the events of the previous night and tried to remember the guy's name. *Daniel -that was his name. He'd made some good points,* Keehan thought, *even if he was a bit intense...* He remembered that he had been invited over to Daniel's to see something. He was slightly intrigued but knew he wouldn't be going over today. He figured he'd drop over tomorrow.

He didn't feel like going anywhere at that moment and he'd arranged to meet Gary at some festival or other that was on in town. His relationship with Gary had been running less than smoothly since he'd wangled himself a spare room for a couple of days and he figured he'd better put some effort in to ensure he had somewhere to stay for at least another night. He had been in touch with Kevin in the meantime to confirm that he was okay and though they'd generally managed to smooth things over Keehan knew that staying there again was not a viable option and probably wouldn't be for some time.

He got up and made himself some breakfast and sat down to eat it on the couch in front of the telly, staring blankly while he ran through the previous night's conversation in his mind. Daniels resolution to "Take the power back from the assholes," had sparked something inside of Keehan. It had deflected the downward trajectory he had been on and sent it in an exciting new direction. He thought what a coincidence it was that they'd happened to meet and he decided it was destiny.

Although Keehan in practise didn't believe in God, he liked to think about destiny a lot. It seemed to him necessarily obvious that he was set on some path to a higher calling; less by way of actually believing in anything, than in not wanting to believe that it was he who was actually responsible for what happened. It seemed that destiny always popped up just when he needed it to remind him of his importance and the needlessness of actually doing anything that might be difficult or painful.

He wasn't meeting Gary until three so he sat for a while watching TV. At about half two he got up, took a gulp of vodka to lubricate the afternoon and headed into town. He got to the restaurant at three on the dot, and peering in through the window he could see Gary inside still working. There was a girl in there with him, also waiting the tables. She had long shiny hair that reached halfway down her back which was dyed electric orange with fluorescent pink streaks. *She looks pretty hot*, Keehan thought. *Hair's a bit mental though...*

He went in and walked over to Gary who was collecting some plates from a table. "Alright," he said. "Hey," said Gary, turning around cautiously so as not to upset the balance of glasses and plates he'd just collected in his arms. He smiled. "I'll be out wit ya there in a couple of minutes, I just have to finish clearin' these tables." "Cool," Keehan replied and headed out to a bench that was on the path outside, taking an inconspicuous look at the orange-haired girl as he walked past.

After about twenty minutes Gary came out with the

orange-haired girl. They said their goodbyes and the girl waved to Keehan and smiled before heading off in the opposite direction as Gary came over to where Kehan was sitting. "Sorry about the wait," Gary said as he got over to Keehan. "Ya can never really have a definite time for getting out." "That's grand," Keehan said. "Who's yer one?" He nodded towards the girl who was walking off up the street. "Oh, Laura," said Gary turning around to look after her. "She's pretty cool. She works in here three or four days a week. She's an artist. A painter." "Keehan nodded and pursed his lips. "Some hair on 'er." "Yeah, it's pretty cool," said Gary. "Shall we head in?"

Keehan got up and they started to stroll up the street. "So what've ya been up to all day?" Gary asked Keehan. "Ah nothing really, I was knackered when I got up and didn't really feel like doin' anythin'." "Yeah I noticed you were out late last night," Gary remarked. "Whatcha get up to?" Keehan was about to tell Gary about Daniel but he decided not to. He wasn't sure exactly why. They had only talked. But explaining the content of their conversation to someone like Gary felt like something that would only cause an unnecessary need for justification. There was something of their meeting that reeked of a guilty pleasure. Like they were a secret order that knew the truth about people; the truth that lay simmering beneath the clappy-happy reality that was pasted over everything; the illusion that everyone seemed intent on maintaining. "Ah I just went for a couple of drinks then had a stroll around," Keehan said.

Gary could sense that Keehan was hiding something. He was a little irritated that Keehan had been treating him so impersonally. He'd essentially been treating the house like a hotel since he'd arrived. He'd sat tapping away at his phone most of the time Gary had been there and had barely made any attempt at conversation since he'd shown up; then had turned up at all hours of the night last night with only the barest acknowledgement. At the same time Gary was fairly certain that he had nowhere else to go and so was just hoping to get through the next day or two without any major upset before he sent him on his way.

Pushing away his irritation Gary asked casually a question he'd already asked several times and had not yet gotten a straight answer to, "So what did ya come up here for anyway, just a bit of a break or what?" Keehan's mind was drifting and he called it for an answer, but the one he had prepared, that he had been spinning off thoughtlessly; was no-where to be found. He had pushed the note from his mind the first couple of days he'd been in the city, and had found it easy to forget, but once the novelty of the lights and the noise had begun to wear off, and the dreams he'd brought with him had begun to crumble in the face of reality; the spectre of the folded, lined sheet of yellowing paper had returned to permeate his thoughts and was now the only real answer he had.

He'd been spending the days since hiding it in distraction and hiding himself from the people that surrounded him in case they sensed its presence in him. His night with Daniel had been a brief respite and had provided some possibility of escape and although right now he wasn't sure what the cost would be; he knew the part of him that really gave a shit was slowly dying away.

"Uh, yeah," he finally managed to stutter. "Yeah just a bit of a break away. Bit of a change of scenery like."

The streets began to get more densely packed as they neared the epicentre of the festivities. They could hear the sounds of horns blowing and the primal beat of drums in the near distance. Keehan looked at the growing excitement beginning to spread across Gary's face with a mixture of bewilderment and revulsion that began to dissipate somewhat as he almost allowed himself to get swept up in the festivities.

They moved in closer and the music got clearer and louder. The people were packed tightly together now as the two of them snaked through the crowd up to where they could now see the procession moving past. They watched as dancers and brass bands passed by, intermingled with huge floats shaped like fish and aeroplanes; all escorted by people walking alongside the parade with giant papier-maché heads that bounced as they moved. The atmosphere was a euphonious hum that enveloped everything like a warming mist.

Keehan was almost beginning to feel that life could be a laugh. Maybe things could be different. Maybe he could actually enjoy the company of people and live a life among the swarming hordes -doing stuff, getting involved, being normal. All of a sudden he felt a solid bump on his left shoulder and would have lost his balance had the density of the crowd not held him up. His left shoulder and all down his back was now soaking wet. He looked up to see a guy looking at him bleary eyed with an almost empty plastic pint cup, the bottom tenth of it holding a foamy beer head. "Ah shite," the guy exclaimed surveying the liquid which was no longer in his cup. He turned to Keehan. "Sorry pal," he muttered and turned off and continued on his path.

"You alright?" Gary asked turning back to see why Keehan

wasn't behind him anymore. Keehan had lost it now. His mind was gone from a brief glimpse of cautious wonder and was careering through immorality and suffering. *He should have shouted at the guy. Maybe hit him. No hitting him was probably a bit much –ah screw it he deserved it...* He'd forgotten what the guy looked like now and was just sifting through the slide-show of other people's recklessness that seemed to lay on constant standby in his head, just waiting for something to flick the switch. He nodded at Gary without saying a word and they began once again to continue up towards the front of the crowd.

The comforting hum had now turned to a deafening clatter as Keehan fought for the concentration to craft his perfect world and now all he saw was idiots, milling around him like slugs.

When they got to the front the parade was still in full force. The bands and floats and dancers were joined by jugglers in colourful costumes and fire-breathers and girls twirling ribbons and people waving flags. Gary with a broad smile on his face turned around to Keehan, who had his head down and was looking into his phone.

That evening they got back to Gary's flat and Keehan slumped straight down on the couch, while Gary, energized by the day's events; went to stick some music on the stereo.

Gary, while initially feeling quite sceptical of Keehan, was beginning to feel a little warmer towards him. The initial sheen of arrogance and disregard that seemed to constantly pre-empt Keehan's every interaction with the world had given way in Gary's eyes to an almost pitiful helplessness. He had noticed the change in Keehan during the parade after the incident with the spilled drink. How he had so easily faltered at the most innocuous and mundane of human interactions. Granted, everyone had to deal with the rough and tumble of life but it just seemed so sad to see someone have such a negligible grasp of happiness; a happiness that could be swept away so easily and uncontrollably and so totally.

Gary went to the fridge and opened the door. There was a six-pack left over from the last party. "D'ya wanna beer?" he called in to Keehan who was still sat blank-eyed in front of the television. Slowly registering that he was being called, Keehan turned and mumbled "Whaa," as Gary appeared at the sitting room door holding up two cans of Heineken. "Beer?" he repeated. Keehan perked up a little and nodded, smiling half-heartedly. He said thanks as Gary handed him the ice-cold can and took a seat beside him on the couch.

"The parade was alright wasn't it?" Gary said. "Yeah," Keehan replied. "It was alright." Gary cracked open his can and a small tuft of white foam bubbled up as it hissed open. "So what are ya actually doin' with yourself these days," he turned to Keehan. "Are ya still livin' with the folks or what?" "Nah," Keehan replied swallowing a neckful of cold beer. "I'm livin' with James, ya know James Dunne?" Gary nodded slowly, "Ah yeah I knew James pretty well. Didn't hang out with him a lot or anything but we had a few classes together." "Yeah me 'n him are sharin' a house." "Are ya workin' at all?" "Nah. Not bothered." "Have ya no ambitions or anything ya want to do with your life?"

Keehan sighed and began to formulate an answer. The can of beer was almost half gone and had begun to fizz through his brain and he was starting to feel quite relaxed and strangely candid. "I dunno," he began, looking down into his can. "I don't think I ever really wanted to be anythin'. I think I had vague ideas when I was a kid but... I guess I just never really expected to be anything else than whatever crappy job I happened to fall into."

Gary, laying back sleepily on the couch, tired after a long day, smiled to himself. Then his face brightened as if remembering something and he pulled himself up resolutely. "Did ya see my decks?" he said to Keehan who looked at him slightly bewildered in his tired, alcohol induced stupor. "Hmmm?" "In my bedroom, my decks -come in and have a look." Keehan pulled himself up and followed Gary down the hall to his bedroom.

Peering into the room for the first time since he'd been there he saw two massive speakers occupying a corner of the room, on top of which rested what looked like a panel from the cockpit of a plane. There were knobs and buttons and dials and rows of different coloured LED lights that illuminated as Gary traversed the mass of wires to plug the machine in. "I've had these about a year," Gary said turning to Keehan after flicking some switches and illuminating the desk even more. "I've been writin' and recordin' some stuff myself. Will I play ya a bit?" Keehan nodded. Gary put the headphones on and flicked some switches as a thumping beat began to emanate from the speaker -a beat that almost sounded to Keehan like it came from somewhere ancient. Gary stood, eyes set and lips pursed slightly, rhythmically tapping buttons and twisting knobs as the electronic sounds began to weave in and out of each other creating a pulsing rhythmic soundscape. As different melodies began to enter and intermingle

Keehan found himself getting carried along and swept up in the strange sounds.

As the vocals came in the music began to build and build to an epic crescendo, at which Keehan began to feel overcome by a trembling euphoria that tingled in his chest and continued to do so as he had the realisation thrust upon him that most of the times when life felt really special was when music was playing.

He had memories of the most innocuous and simultaneously most beautiful moments that were stored in his mind, saved somewhere in between the sounds of a particular song -a soundtrack of moments when life just felt strangely beautiful for whatever reason and imprinted its strangeness; to be inextricably and eternally linked with whatever music happened to be drifting through the air. He wasn't sure if it was the music that created the moment or the moment that was merely caught by the music or just one of those inexplicable things that happens when the two of them meet occasionally. But whatever it was he knew these memories were stored in his mind within music and they were among the things he prized truly above anything in the world.

With Keehan swimming in his reverie, the music slowly began to fade out; and the room having once again descended to silence, Gary took off the headphones and left them to hang loosely around his neck. He looked over at Keehan. "Well? What did ya think?" Keehan for once genuinely impressed answered, "Yeah that was really cool."

Gary smiled. Switching off the equipment he climbed out and gesturing Keehan to follow him went into the kitchen to grab another couple of beers. The two of them then headed back into the living room and crashed on the couch to watch some TV.

The momentary glimpse of awe Keehan had gotten when listening to Gary's music had subsided into feelings of inadequacy and his mind slipped off to watch himself in an Ibiza superclub, manning the decks and raising his fist in the air as thousands of sweaty revellers gazed up at him perched high. The vision though began to lose its definition as it dissipated into his growing ambivalence. "How long have ya been playin'?" he asked Gary almost resignedly trying to regain the flicker of his own interest that had glistened momentarily. "Ah I've been playin' music for years," Gary replied. "I've been playin' guitar since I was about ten, then picked up a bit of piano soon after. A lad I know gave me a Daft Punk album in like, third year or something and I knew that was what I wanted to do. So I started workin' and saved up some money and got the decks an all." "Ya must be livin' the high life up here," Keehan said draining his can. "Ah I get a gig here and there," Gary replied. "You're probably well in with the movers and shakers up here," Keehan continued. "I may come up an' start gettin' in with em."

Keehan's ambition for fame or infamy was becoming an all-encompassing and singular pursuit and though he didn't quite consciously realise it; had become for him the only possible cure for the pain of his invisibility. He could feel the path to finding this cure beginning once again to solidify in his mind and the lights began to sparkle more brightly in his eyes.

"So who do ya know?" he asked turning sharply to Gary. Gary, not sensing the renewed intensity of Keehan's interest answered, "What, like, celebrities? Ah no-one really. I see 'em around but I'm usually only doin' the gig. I generally head home straight after." "Who do ya see though?" Keehan continued. Gary was beginning to notice the slight emphatic quality in Keehan's voice and turned to look at him. "Ah the usual crowd ya see in the papers every day," he answered, turning his head away again and scrunching his forehead as he tried to remember specifically. "Yer one Kara Hughes is nearly always out." Keehan sat back in the chair and looked thoughtful. Gary a little puzzled and slightly intrigued continued, "Ya know the artist Robin? He's throwin' a party down at the marina this week sometime. My mate Laura, that ya saw earlier, knows him. We could probably get in if ya want to go?" Keehan felt a rush of excitement bubble up inside him as his dreams began to find substance before his eyes; and he saw the end of misery and the shining life of diamond and prestige that he deserved glistening brightly ahead of him. He nodded sagely. "Yeah, that'd be cool."

CHAPTER 18

Two days later Gary and Keehan were sitting in Gary's flat having some casual drinks as they prepared to head out to the party at the marina.

Keehan's apathy and moroseness had all but disappeared and for the last two days he'd been almost pleasant company. He had met Laura the day before, after Gary told him to come down to meet him after work. The two of them were sat on the bench outside the restaurant chatting when Keehan got there and they looked up and smiled as he approached them, shuffling nervously with the shy reticence that tended to accompany his brief flirtations with sobriety. "Hey guys," he waved. "Hey man," Gary said and smiled up at him. "Hi," Laura greeted him and smiled, her bright eyes sparkling and catching Keehan as to almost make him stumble as he had headed to take a seat on the bench beside Gary. They proceeded to share their stories with each other.

Laura was a painter who'd gone to college with Robin. She was neither a fan of his work nor considered him a close personal friend but she had maintained a polite contact with him. Robin of course had always seen Laura as being perfect for the role of his significant other; although his attempts to extend their relationship beyond the bounds of polite friendship had never met with any reciprocation or the slightest encouragement. After college Robin had gone on to acquire a level of celebrity after a number of well-publicised gallery showings in which he exhibited his post-modern musings accompanied by objects of vague interest. Laura continued to paint and her work drew a small but dedicated group of admirers although received nothing like the fanfare or the sales that accompanied Robin's career. They talked occasionally still and when Laura had enquired about invites for the party, Robin was quick to provide; although he reserved some scepticism for the company she would be bringing. Nevertheless, the three of them had obtained access and now the night had come, and Keehan and Gary awaited Laura's arrival at the flat.

She arrived about half-nine, her hair a more vibrant orange than before and the lids of her eyes painted with lime-green and azure blue. She wore a shining silver dress that cut just above her knees and proved quite a striking figure in many ways. They had a few drinks in the flat before calling a taxi and heading off towards the marina.

It was not a long journey, and from only a few streets away they could hear the music thumping already. They got out of the taxi at the bridge and paid the driver. As they crossed the bridge the water below shimmered and sparkled and Keehan, already getting quite drunk; felt an excitement build in him as he looked around this foreign land of sparkling lights and music and felt as though he were walking through his own dreams. Dreams that were now as real as the cold breeze on his cheeks and the footpath which now pressed against the soles of his feet. They stepped off the bridge onto the wooden boardwalk that held them aloft above the sparkling crystal water; Keehan just remembering in time to maintain his composure and some semblance of sobriety as they neared the glass doors of the club: outside of which a burly looking man with a black jacket and an earpiece was stood staring intensely into the distance.

The man turned and looked at them as they approached. He had a quick glance at Laura and a slightly longer one at Gary and then stared blankly at Keehan. "Invite only," he muttered. "Yeah we're friends of Robin's," Laura stepped forward. "We should be on the list." "What's the names?" the man asked, mechanically reaching for a clipboard. "Laura Baker, Gary Lynch and Keehan Dang." The bouncer's eyebrows furrowed as he scanned through the list before coming to a rest at the three names. "Yeah, there we go." He glanced at them again and looked at the list again, as if wondering if they had just made an extremely fortunate guess; before nodding to himself. "Go ahead," he said and he smiled almost imperceptibly, as he stood aside to let them pass through the door.

In the split second it took for them to push open the door, the muted rumbling instantly became a crystallized cacophony of laughter and chatting that streamed outwards, suffused with thudding bass and some vaguely familiar tune. Keehan looked around with amazement at all the sexy, pouty girls scattered around and his heart began to beat faster. The guys were all dapper and handsome and almost as eye-catching as the girls. There were faces he'd seen hundreds of times before, that now seemed uncanny; that had suddenly lost the veil of opacity that separated them from real things -but in that, had now somehow become more real than everything else that existed. He followed along as Gary led the way towards the bar with Laura behind him.

The three ordered and got their drinks, getting a round of shots in first and having to shout for them over the deafening rumble of the music and chatting. Keehan grimaced momentarily from the fiery burn as the Sambuca hit his stomach, before feeling his head become light and swim nicely. He leaned on the bar and gazed around and felt he was in the right place at last. Somewhere he might be appreciated. Somewhere he belonged. He was surrounded, soothed, by the dense air of immortality that pervaded the night; the immortality bestowed to faces on magazines and newspapers. He was swept up in the importance of the people that surrounded him. Everything seemed to have meaning here. No incident would die away into the perishable abyss of memory but would be recorded to stand above time. Unlike all the other normal moments involving normal people: all the things he'd done before; which slunk away to nothing down the drain of life.

Keehan was suddenly disturbed from his basking by Laura. "Hey!!," she shouted, leaning over towards him and gesturing with a jerk of her head towards Gary who was stood beside her gazing around contentedly. "We're gonna go an' find Robin and say hello. Be rude not to seen' as he got us in. Ya comin'?" Keehan nodded and picked up his drink then followed the other two as they made their way through the crowd again toward the VIP area, where they were certain Robin would be presiding.

Keehan, woken from his merry tipsiness by the sudden movement, was beginning to notice the hidden snarls in some of his companions; was beginning to notice the slithering undercurrent of competition, and his magical world began to feel like school all over again: with the runts thrown to the bottom as usual while the strongest and brightest held court. He began to sense some eyes on him as he made his way through the crowd and felt once again as a stranger -or as he usually felt in life; like he was a gatecrasher at the party. Suddenly distracted by the blinding flash of a camera going off somewhere in front of him, his mind balanced on gossamer strings and dissolving in alcohol fell away, and the room brightened up once again. The overheard smatterings of laughter became mirthful and benevolent once again and the music infused his body with a bouncing lightness.

Laura and Gary had gotten slightly ahead of him as they politely negotiated their way around the groupings and he shuffled forward a little more quickly in order to catch up with them.

Robin was indeed in the VIP area. Laura, on hearing and recognizing his polished, nasal voice cascading across the floor; scanned in the direction it was coming from and easily spotted him. She turned and pointed him out to Keehan.

He was quite an eye-catching figure. His hair on one side was raven black, on the other peroxide blonde. He had a scarf wrapped around his neck and Keehan wondered how he was not dying in the dense heat of the place: but he didn't seem at all perturbed. He was sat in the centre of a semi-circle, on a white leather upholstered couch, with an entourage of blank-eyed, eager faces either side of him.

"Of course there's no such thing as reality anymore," Robin was informing everyone around him. "Everyone creates the reality they want to see. I recently attended a lecture in Trinity on the..." He trailed off as he spotted Laura approaching through the crowd. "One second guys," he turned to the blank faces as they waited in anticipation and raised a finger to pause, before turning back towards Laura, who was approaching the cordoned off platform "Ah you made it," Robin declared as he stood up and smiled in a benevolently regal fashion. "Come sit down," he implored them gesturing to some empty spaces on the outskirts of the little crowd that had gathered. "We don't want to intrude," Laura replied, smiling hesitantly at Robin's companions on the leather couch and receiving only scowls and blank expressions. "Nonsense, come on," Robin bade them sit down. "This is Gary...and Keehan," Laura said gesturing to the other two. "I think we met once before," Gary said holding his hand out, which Robin shook limply as he stared at him blankly without recognition. He turned to Keehan who, initially unimpressed with Robin himself; had been impressed by the awed stares he was receiving from his loyal group of admirers. "Have *we* met before?" Robin offered Keehan his wet-fish hand." "I wouldnt've thought so," Keehan replied shaking his hand. They all sat down and Robin offered the newcomers a glass of champagne.

Keehan who had been drink-less for half an hour and was getting antsy, took the glass with relish. As Laura and Robin exchanged platitudes and politely enquired as to each other's recent activities, he sat back on the couch and sipped from the glass, letting the bubbles fizz on his tongue as he soaked in the glamour and prestige. *I'm sitting in the VIP lounge drinking champagne,* he thought to himself. *At last...*

CHAPTER 19

As the night drew on Keehan began to grow restless. He was getting slightly bored. Laura and Gary had gone to get more drinks at some point, while he had decided to stay put and attempt to ingratiate himself more into Robin's group; which had become more and more estranged from the three of them as time passed.

Keehan didn't know what they were talking about. He wasn't even sure if *they* knew half the time. He didn't know any of the people they were referring to. He started to feel under-qualified. He'd had some time with them now to make some sort of in-ways and yet here he was still, on the outskirts. He began to wonder if he just wasn't made to be one of the special people. This was the thought that troubled him the most. What if after all that dreaming, the absolute certainty he had in his head; he was here now at the point where it was supposed to come true, and could only watch as it all crumbled to nothing before his eyes? He began to feel a slight panic building in himself, and attempting to maintain an exterior of casual restraint, edged even closer to Robin and strained to separate the strand of his dry-treacle voice from the surrounding din. "It's all about creating chaos," Robin was drawling now. "About stirring up the pot… Shaking people out of their staid conformist bourgeoisie lives and showing them how weak the foundations of their lives really are –what a knife-edge we stand on." Keehans attention was piqued as the surrounding noise fell into the background and Robin's words shot laser-like to his ears. "In pure chaos there are no patterns." *Chaos*, Keehan turned the word over in his mind. *Freedom. That's what this is all about. Free from rules. Anarchy. These people answer to no-one. They do what they want…* He sat and continued to listen, agreeing loudly so as to make his presence known, as Robin and his friends regaled their eager disciples with tales of their anarchic exploits and their adventures in mayhem.

With a renewed vigour and taste for spectacle Keehan got up and headed to the bar to get another drink, the shining moment beginning to beckon him. When he got to the bar he checked his wallet. He was getting pretty low on funds. He had just enough to get wasted anyway and was not going to think about getting home right now. *Freedom*, he continued to repeat in his mind like a shimmering mantra as he took a JD and Coke off the barman and slurred a thank you. "*Chaos*." That would be his guide for the night. He would burn the brightest of them all.

Some time later Keehan was up on the dance floor with Laura and Gary, his inhibitions discarded long ago and edging close to recklessness. In his quest for freedom Keehan had thrown off his shackles. He had cut loose completely and abandoned himself to the chaos of hedonism. In his messy state combined with his privileged company, all the rules and restrictions that dogged him daily seemed to have fallen away and excess had become his only guide and vision. "Chaaaaaaaaaooooooooooossssssss," he shouted, bleary-eyed and wobbly, raising his fist in the air.

He turned to see Gary's face looking into his own, his lips moving soundlessly. "Whaat?" Keehan slurred, lost in his wild abandon. Gary leaned in close and shouted hoarsely into Keehan's ear. "I said we're just goin' over to my friend Mike..." He gestured to a guy on the outskirts of the dance floor who looked to Keehan to be at least six and a half feet tall with a bushy but nicely trimmed beard. He was dressed all in black and was holding a brown cowboy hat in one hand and was just taking a seat at a nearby table with a group of people as Gary pointed over at him. Keehan nodded, only barely registering what Gary was saying: and resumed jumping about wildly as Gary and Laura went over and sat down at the table with Mike.

Keehan couldn't sit down now if he tried. It was as if his life had been a slow fuse burning from the beginning and now conditions were ripe for him to explode. The crazier he'd gotten; the more he'd leapt around and shouted; the more people had watched him go, had high-fived him or leaned in for a laugh and a joke. He was riding a wave. *Chaos was what was needed! What everyone secretly wanted!* Before he even realised what he was doing, almost as if led by Robin's words, Keehan was now climbing the steel banisters that led to the upstairs balcony area. He had his eye on a silver bar that was protruding from the upper level and his muddied intention was to swing across and land on an empty couch some way across. A few people nearby noticed him crawling up the banisters and turned to watch with curiosity and puzzlement.

With the recognition of an audience, any meagre doubts that were left in Keehan's mind evaporated completely. He was Keith Moon driving into the swimming pool. He was The Rolling Stones throwing televisions from hotel windows. "We are all fr..." he began to shout, raising his arms in victory, when his balance -which had been none too steady even on the solid ground, now abandoned him completely; and his feet slipped on the sweaty steel banister. A crowd of people who had turned, sensing the commotion, watched him plummet unceremoniously onto a waiting table below; sending glass smashing all around him and flying in all directions, as he rolled over and dropped with a dull thud onto the ground.

He lay looking up at the swirling colours washing across the roof for some moments before his eyes began to come back into focus and the muffled din surrounding him began to clarify again into music combined with overlapping and intermingling snippets of laughter, shouting and chattering, all creating an unsettling morphing soundscape.

The first person he noticed was Robin, his face contorted with rage; who was standing over him jabbing an angry finger directly at his face. "Get him out of here!!!!," he was screaming at two huge guys in pastel polo shirts who were already in motion towards Keehan.

Before Keehan knew what was happening the two guys had each grabbed an arm and were dragging him off somewhere. Everything for him now was a spinning mass of lights and shadows; raised voices and a vague murmur of thumping bass; and then a sudden chill and eerie silence as he realised he was lying on the ground outside. He raised his head just in time to see the sole of a boot crash into his face, then lay back on the cold tarmac as he watched the two guys who had accompanied him to the exit go back inside.

Keehan felt a searing pain course through his face. He didn't even try to get up. He just lay on the cold ground and looked up at the stars. His shock and confusion was beginning to wear off and the pain in his face was getting stronger as it did. Every throb he felt began to stoke his anger like a bellows at the base of a flame. He thought of Daniel. Thought of the surging power in his eyes as he talked of vengeance. He pictured the glory of righting all the wrongs of his life, cutting the chains of karmic oppression that swirled over his head like a law passed down from the strong to the weak, and securing retribution. Yes, *retribution*.

He gritted his teeth and felt the heat begin to rise in him. *Retribution. Retribution, retlibluton, zezlibute, ellyooa, aee-a.* Gradually it just fell away. The words and the anger that spun in his head all day, every day just dissolved and drifted off like a pile of paper slips in a gentle, firm breeze.

He was tired. Tired of being angry. Tired of plotting. Tired of dreaming. He didn't care anymore. Fantasy no longer provided the escape he needed; yet it had always seemed the only alternative to the gaping nothingness and cruel joke that life had turned out to be. Both now seemed to be cumbersome charades sapping his spirit and leaving him empty. He was beginning to realise what he'd felt for a long time; as if no longer existing was the only way he could escape the constant and relentless turmoil. His dreams now had become frantic visions of a widening chasm; pulling him apart like a piece of chewing gum stuck between someone's fingers. Now they drifted away and for the first time he let them go. He just lay and watched. He looked at the wooden door with its veneer of chipped black paint standing solid and impenetrable in front of him, that led to the wall surrounding it; that ran to meet the sky. That held the clouds…That touched the moon…That shone on the ground…That ran underneath his feet, and met the door, and continued; and led to the wall, and the sky, and the clouds, and the moon, and the road, and the feet, doorwallskycloudsmoonroadfeet…dorwwalskyoomrodee… dormskrodee…blurmske…He couldn't remember ever seeing anything so vivid. The silence of the night permeated his mind and seeped into all the spaces left vacant by reflections of himself and he felt a peace he'd never known.

The searing pain in his face had turned now to a gentle, almost soothing throb as he lay almost unaffectedly aware of it. He turned his head slowly towards a skinny brown birch tree that was standing quietly across from him on the vacant street. There on a low hanging branch, he saw a small monkey that was sat peering out through the leaves. The monkey sat staring at Keehan for some moments, his glassy eyes sparkling brightly in the moonlight; then with the ambivalence of something unhampered by ambition, he turned, leapt and scampered up a drainpipe; quietened and dormant in the dry autumn night. He stopped briefly on the smooth roof tiles to glance back once at Keehan before disappearing through the orange lamp-lit glow.

Suddenly with a bang the door flew open and wide-eyed and gasping Gary emerged, followed by Laura and Mike. They crowded around him, crouching down and looking into his face with gasps and expressions of horror.

After going some time without seeing Keehan, Gary and

Laura had taken a walk around to see if they could find him among the crowd. On meeting Robin and enquiring as to whether he'd seen Keehan they were angrily informed of his whereabouts and had immediately rushed out to find him. Keehan sat up as they rushed out and huddled around him.

"Jesus man, are you alright?" Gary said bending down beside him and putting a hand on his shoulder as he looked him over. Keehan nodded. "Yeah I'm okay." "Look at ya," Laura said taking a tissue out of her bag. "Here wipe off yer nose with that." Keehan took the tissue and wiped the bottom of his nose and his top lip which had a small amount of caked, dry blood. "What happened?," asked Mike who was standing over him calmly peering into his eyes. Keehan, now beginning to re-adjust to the world and regaining his conception of time and place, felt a slight rumble of anxiety building again in the pit of his stomach as the events of the night began to return to him. The sense of peace he'd experienced moments ago was still vivid in him and he grasped it before his thoughts ran into panic once more. He took a deep breath and sighed.

"I was acting the eejit," he muttered, looking down at the solid cobble stones surrounding him. "I was messin' around climbin' a banister and I fell down onto a table and smashed a load of glasses. These two lads dragged me out and one of 'em hit me a kick in the face." He looked up at them. "I've just been lyin' here." Laura put a hand on his shoulder. "D'ya wanna go to a doctor?" she asked, her brow knotted as she examined his face for signs of any serious injury. "Nah," Keehan replied. "I'd a bit of a pain in me face but it's pretty much gone now." He smiled half-heartedly then looked down at the ground again as he felt the renewed battle of hope and hopelessness rise inside him again. The open vista of possibility in the wretched hands of painful memory. He sighed deeply again, not entirely sure if he was really happy or really sad but feeling something definite that seemed to transcend both and that he wasn't quite familiar with. "I don't care," he muttered still looking at the ground, "I just don't care anymore."

The others looked at each other, surprised by his erratic change of tone. "I don't want to do anything," Keehan continued, and his voice which had begun sounding as if about to crack into weeping; now became calmer, more resigned and matter-of-fact. "I don't want to be anything. I just don't care. There's no point in anything and I just don't give a fuck anymore." The others watched him silently as he continued, looking forlornly down at the ground beneath him once more. "I keep draggin' meself around, doin' this and doin' that, just fuckin' movin' around and I don't see the point. I'm not goin' anywhere, I'm just movin'."

He paused briefly as he looked up to the moon for inspiration then looked back down as he gathered his thoughts. The others stood expectantly. "Did ya ever just think what's the point?" Keehan continued. "Just no matter what ya do nothing ever goes right. Like what's the point of any of this? Just doin' stuff..."

Just like that Keehan's words floated off in front of him again and he watched them fade away without concern. The thought suddenly popped into his head *-I cant listen to myself anymore:* and as that thought drifted away the wave of peace came to wash over him again; to pour into every crevice and crack of his existence and empty him out like a warm rinse.

Mike walked over to him and gently grabbed his arm to lift him up. "C'mon lad. We'll go sit down an' have a quiet drink to settle ourselves."

Keehan sighed then hauled himself up, his legs wobbling slightly and his head swimming with the change in altitude. He felt better being off the ground; and regaining himself, began to step tenderly forward with the rest of them as they made their way down the side street and out onto the quay. They crossed the bridge where what seemed like a lifetime ago, Keehan had stepped out of the taxi to taste the life he'd been promised. Although his dreams were now gone, the water still shimmered and sparkled as it had before; perhaps even more brightly.

They turned down another street past rows of shadowy shop windows, the only sound the echoing of their footsteps on the deserted road and the receding dull thud of the nightclub in the distance. Laura turned to Keehan, "How ya feelin now, alright?" "Ah alright," Keehan replied attempting to smile. "Where are we goin'?" he asked. Mike who had been walking slightly in front with Gary turned around. "Just round the corner here, there's a nice little quiet pub." Sure enough just as they rounded the next corner, nestled between the sleeping grey buildings was a small pub, providing the only light and life for many streets around. There was a small table outside the door at which was sat two grey haired but not particularly old men, who were smoking cigarettes and sipping from frosty glasses of beer as they chatted in the mild night. The one man who was sitting facing the door nodded and smiled at the four as they headed inside.

CHAPTER 20

The bar wasn't quite crowded but there were a number of tables occupied. Mike ordered four beers and led the way to a secluded corner where there was a semi-circular booth. They sat down and made themselves comfortable as the barman arrived with their beers on a tray. "There ya go," he said as he placed the glasses in front of each of them in turn then nodded and smiled warmly as they thanked him.

"So you're feelin' a bit disillusioned with it all are ya?" Keehan looked up from the beer he was peering at with glazed eyes and turned to look at Mike who was scratching his beard thoughtfully as he eyeballed him from across the table. Keehan sighed. "I used to enjoy life," he began to muse, the barriers to his free expression having melted away slightly. He looked back at his glass and began to trace the path of a bead of condensation with his finger as he gathered his thoughts. "I used to look forward to doing new things," he continued, "and I used to think I could change things; do something good with me life. I was fine and then I stopped to think about life and that's where everything fell to shit."

Mike raised the glass to his lips and took a draught. "Were you fine though really," he asked, as the cold brew bubbled its way into his system. "Or were you just pretending? Were ya just afraid that the pain and misery you tried to ignore might be the truth; might be reality, and that there would be nothing else underneath that?" Keehan stopped playing with his glass for a moment and looked over at Mike, whose upper lip now had a delicate frosting of beer foam. "What do ya mean?" he asked, feeling his heart beat ever so slightly faster. Mike ran his tongue across the tips of his moustache hairs, clearing the foam in a clean sweep. "I mean, idealism is a dangerous thing when it's not tied in with true beliefs. And true beliefs are betrayed by actions. If you don't act every day as if you believe there's something you can do then imagining will never make it so." Keehan looked at him. "Well so what if I don't think there's anything I can do?" Mike smiled. "It's not about thinking," he replied, "it's about *believing*." Keehan scrunched his shoulders up and frowned. "Yeah so what if I don't *belieeeeve* there's anything I can do then?" "Then you've taken the first step," Mike replied resolutely, as if he had been expecting the question. "You've examined your life as you actually live it and not as you want it to be... You've identified your deepest motivation, the beliefs that really guide your life." He paused for a moment. "Remember back at the club when you said you don't care anymore? How did you feel at that moment?" Keehan took a slow sip from his glass. "I don't know," he replied, furrowing his brow as he tried to revisit the memory in his mind as clearly as he could. "Just, fed up I guess... Fed up with everything." "Were you depressed, angry...?" Mike probed. "Ahh... A little, I guess -no, not really," Keehan continued, still focusing on holding onto the memory and trying to interpret it as best he could. "Did you feel *real*?" Mike asked.

Gary smiled as Keehan turned from staring at his glass to look at Mike with an eyebrow raised in slight incredulity. His mouth open to retort he suddenly stopped and his brow furrowed again. Mike continued; "You saw clearly the futility of living in the mind, even if you didn't quite realise what it meant." Keehan took a mouthful of beer and looked at him. "What are you some kinda guru or something?" Mike smiled broadly as Gary and Laura laughed. "No," Mike continued. "But I think I know what you're going through. I started off an idealist –or what I thought was one anyway. Ye know, 'If you dream it you can do it' and that kind of stuff. Then when it was time to act, life turned out to be more complicated. It took work; so I just kept on dreaming and ignoring reality, thinking I was being a romantic or something. As I kept dreaming of how life should be I more and more neglected real life -with the consequences being that my real life more and more turned to shit. It was only later on, as I started to really examine myself that I realised I was actually a complete cynic. That I'd split myself in two and while in the world I believed myself to be in I was a dreamer, a kind of saint, or hero; in actuality I didn't believe a word of it... I made the mistake of confusing words with actions –blind platitudes and fantasies with actual living."

"Yeah but what does that mean, that you shouldn't dream, or whatever?" Keehan asked, his cheeks turning ever so slightly red. Mike smiled. "A dream should be something you make real," he continued. "Without an intention to act then dreaming is worse than useless. It's actually detrimental, to you and the world around you. My point is that realising you just don't believe in what you thought you believed in anymore is the first step to finding what is actually true. Sometimes you have to let a certain view of the world fall apart so that you can replace it with a better one. It's not giving up on life. It's not abandoning higher aspirations; on the contrary -it's the first step to truly seeing the world and your place in it as it is and taking actual tangible steps to make it better."

Mike looked up suddenly as he finished this last sentence and peered over towards the bar. He began to wave at someone who had entered the pub and was ordering a drink. "Ah here's P.," he announced sitting himself back down as Keehan turned to see a guy in a dark blue overcoat standing at the bar.

The guys hair was elegantly and tightly shaved around the sides and back of his head, while on top it jutted up in unruly and messy spikes. Keehan noted he had the most vividly blue eyes he'd ever seen as he came strolling over towards them.

"Good evening," the guy chirped, taking a seat beside them and smiling at each of them in turn as they greeted him. Keehan felt a wave of something like comfort as P.'s eyes rested on him for a moment and he smiled. "This is Keehan," Mike put a hand on Keehan's shoulder. P. nodded and smiled again as he held out a hand to shake Keehan's. "Howya Keehan," he said as he grasped Keehan's hand and shook it firmly and warmly. The barman came over then with P.'s beer and a glass of whiskey and asked the others if they wanted any more. They ordered another round. P. smiled and took a lengthy draught from his beer. "Haaahhhhh," he gasped and put the glass down carefully on the table.

"So whatch'ya been up ta?" Laura asked him as she swirled the remnants of her pint. P. leaned back on his chair. "I did some writin' this mornin', mostly just been hangin' out.

How bout yourselves? How was the party?" Gary and Laura grimaced and Keehan felt his stomach drop slightly. "It was alright," Laura answered. She looked over at Keehan and smiled tenderly. "Keehan had a bit of trouble near the end alright." "Oh yeah?," P. enquired, looking over at Keehan. He had noticed that Keehan had looked a little worse for wear but didn't think it polite to mention just yet. "Yeah," Keehan mumbled sheepishly as he directed his gaze down to the beer mat he had been absent-mindedly crumpling up. "Ah it was me own fault really," he continued still looking down. "I was bein' a bit of a tool." "You've a nice lump on yer nose, I hope ya didn't get in too much trouble," P. continued, taking another mouthful from his glass. "Nah I'm alright," Keehan replied, looking up finally and rubbing his nose; the pain of earlier now nothing but a dull numbness. "I think we may be having a breakthrough," Mike interjected. Keehan looked over at him as P. raised his eyebrows. "Oh yeah?" "He's finally stopped caring," Mike continued. P. smiled again. "That's good. That's the first step."

Keehan was growing a little irritated about being discussed in such vague terms in front of his own face and was almost beginning to forget his shyness. "So how's this a good thing?" he asked pointedly looking around at the four of them. "I've realised how shit everything is…That I don't give a fuck about anything anymore… This is a breakthrough? That nothing means anything?" "No," P. said smiling at Keehan again.

There was a moment of silence as Keehan waited for the continuation of P.'s answer, which evidently wasn't coming.

"No what??" he pressed. P. leaned over towards Keehan. "This is the thing," he began, crossing his arms on the table in front of him. "The so-called *spiritual journey* is not about finding meaning... It's about escaping the need for meaning beyond what is."

Keehan waited again. "What is *what*?" he asked eventually. P. stared back at him, "What *IS*." He raised his arms in a swirling gesture to encompass everything in the room around them. Keehan was feeling the resignation swell over him again and decided to sit back and relax and listen. "P. continued, "The thing is, the present moment, the *now*, is all that's ever real. But you're always thinking about the past, ruminating on something you've done or haven't done or worrying about what will happen. Hoping someday to find something that feels real, a good future. The now contains the future within it -unseen and unpredictable but within your grasp." Keehan perked up again as he felt a spark of intrigue kindle inside him. He took a moment to process what P. had just told him. "But what if now is boring?" he asked, after a thought, "Now is boring as fuck. There's never anything to do." The other four laughed. P. took a swig from his glass. "Boredom is caused really by having *too much* to do," he continued; "Too much you think you *should* be doing." He looked deep into Keehan's eyes. "If you pick the one thing you want to do right now and just do it you'll never be bored."

Keehan rubbed his chin thoughtfully as he tried to digest what P. was saying -or discern whether he was just talking shit. There seemed to be something going on here alright, maybe something important; and it was stuff he'd heard before, but it had just never gelled with him. "Yeaaaah, okay," he stuttered. "Well so how do you know what's the right thing to do like? What if you're doin' somethin' that's never gonna go anywhere, that's a waste of time?" "Good question," Mike interjected and nodded at P. Laura and Gary were listening intently.

"The moment is the key," P. continued raising an index finger defiantly. "Your true self is always in the present moment, waiting for you to become aware of it and aware through it. Awareness. To find yourself, you have to cut through all the voices in your mind that are telling you who you are, how you should be acting -that's all the past you've collected; and based on the future you are attempting to create in your mind. Plots and plans and vain attempts to fit the moments of your life into a coherent narrative. When you find that infinite space that is just the present moment it's an absolute bliss. It's a bliss, but not like seein' visions or trippin'... It's more of a subtle bliss: like you were mentally drowning your whole life and now you've suddenly broken the surface and taken a breath of fresh air. It's a bliss that's less sensational but more deep and profound. Like putting on dry socks after you've been walking around all day with wet feet. And it comes with awareness of what is. Responsibility for where you are in that moment." "Yeah but why?" Keehan interjected, returning to the question that plagued him every day and was the only one he felt really needed answering. "Why bother? What's the point?"

Mike who had been quietly listening now leaned over to Keehan. "No-one can tell you what the point is, the same way you can't tell anyone else what the point is. You just have to have faith." *Oh here we go*, thought Keehan. *Here come the bleedin' angels again.*

A tinge of disappointment crossed his face, which up to

now had been growing ever so slightly brighter. Laura who had been listening quite intently screwed up her face also. Mike sensing their disappointment smiled to himself and took a swig from his glass before continuing. "Faith doesn't have to mean faith in God specifically or *a* god. Have faith in the moment, in existence, whatever it is. Faith is a quality of being *-joie de vivre*. It's something you find in yourself; a sense of being comfortable with the unknown and accepting the reality that exists now, for all it entails. In fact as soon as you maintain to have faith in any specific concept, or any particular god then you no longer have faith. You've left your reality to find comfort in ideas; an empty map of reality. And the act of living, of being, is the only thing that counts. Reality is here." "Why are we here?" P. interjected, again addressing Keehan directly. "To experience this world as fully as possible before returning to source: to realise our own awareness in the world of form."

He looked over at Mike. Mike drained what was left in his glass. "That's basically what I said," he mumbled, placing the empty glass down on the table. P. shrugged, "I like it better the way I said it." Mike smiled at him and looked over again at Keehan who still looked slightly unconvinced. He continued; "One thing we do know is that we're alive now when we could just as easily not be. Our existence has taken precedence over our non-existence –for some reason. And so there's a reason we're alive whether we can define it yet or not. And reality... a meaningful life; is there if you just look for it and look in the right place. There are people who have been everywhere, done everything; got fame and acclaim and prizes -and they're like a zombie. Probably spent most of their time with their face in a damn phone or thinking about more rewards or status; without ever really knowing what was inside themselves. Never knowing what they were truly passionate about. And there's lots of people; Buddhist monks who've spent their whole lives sitting in a monastery, that are more alive than a lot of people. Aliveness is just a state of being; it's not any particular activity or any number of activities. And it's the only thing we should strive for." "Yeah," interjected Laura, "But are ya sayin' that we all have to become monks and sit in a room for the rest of our lives? We can't all do that like, we've stuff to do, we have to live in the world." Mike nodded. "Yeah I agree," he replied, scratching his beard, "That was just like, a stereotypical example. There are plenty of monks I'm sure who are just as caught up in the game of identity and mind; as there are and have been plenty of people in cities, towns, villages across the world that are fully in tune with their existence and just getting on with their lives as they are, working their jobs or doing whatever."

He paused for a moment to attempt to clarify his point in his head before continuing. "I guess all you need to do, as far as I can see anyway, is take the time to look at yourself honestly; to find out who ya really are -beyond what you think you are, or think you should be, and *live it*. We know we're not immortal, or at least not in this manifestation; but we also know we can have a meaningful life without being so. We can experience this reality without ever needing to be anywhere else. So that's it as far as I can see. The reason to live is that you're alive; you don't need to achieve anything or find any system, you don't need to resort to suicide or dreaming. It may take a little time but that's what time is there for... To help you realise its own irrelevance. In the end you can live your life, be real every moment you can, or waste it with suicide and the search for immortality and external justification."

Mike looked directly at Keehan while saying this last sentence and Keehan felt a little spike, with the fear of exposure that had become more transparent but was not anywhere close to disappearing completely.

"Who said anything about suicide?" he asked attempting to sound casual. "Like I said before," Mike continued getting up. "I've been there."

He went to pick up the two empty glasses on the table and then paused a moment before continuing. "I value intelligence and rationality so much that I cant believe this just happened. It can only be some kind of master-plan. We've been given the gift of rationality to understand that universes don't just pop out of no-where for no reason. There is a reason for happiness and for sadness and everything else, and the living is in the learning." He picked up the glasses and smiled. "Who's for another drink?" "Yeah cool," Gary replied and the other three nodded.

"I love Mike," P. said as he watched Mike amble up to the bar scratching his beard, "he sounds awful bloody Christian at times though..." Keehan, Gary and Laura laughed and P. looked at Mike once again and smiled.

He turned back again to Keehan, "So what do ya think?" "About what?" "About everything. What we're sayin'. Is it makin' any sense?" Keehan nodded but then frowned slightly. "So, but... "I still don't quite get like what's the point? The actual way to go about it? *You*'re sayin' it's just awareness." He nodded in Mike's direction. "And *he*'s sayin..." "That ya have to be aware but then livin' is the only thing that counts?" P. who had been tilting back in his chair pre-empted him. He continued to lean dangerously far back on the two hind legs of his chair as he sighed and scratched his chin and looked upwards towards the ceiling as he attempted to formulate an answer. The other three watched on expectantly.

With a sudden slam he dropped the chair back to rest its four legs securely on the ground and leaned in again, re-adjusting himself to the most comfortable spot on the edge of his seat. "This is the thing," he began, holding his hands in front of him as if holding an invisible box. "We have two selves. Our true self is awareness: It is connection with the universe, and is whole and complete in every moment. Our other self, our self in life, consists of our mind, our body, our actions -our whole life. And this self is merely a project whereby we set the parameters ourselves; set the values; set the meaning of this particular life; or set no values if you so choose. Meanwhile you always have access to your true self, which is both eternal and timeless; always whole and pure and will remain so, even after this life ends -even when you do nothing. The only thing you need is your own awareness. The answer is not any particular idea –it's the absence of ideas, pure engagement with what is, as it is. What you're doing right now, where you are. If you want to live life fully, you have to detach from your ideas about life, from your ego –and see the world as it is, in every single moment. The ego is intoxicating. Individuality, the lone self -it's alluring, exciting. But it's not the whole story. While it's true we are here to create this character over a lifetime of experience; the danger comes when you begin to get lost in the character and forget the game. It can happen that as you place more importance on the creation itself you can lose the ability to create. All the sights, sounds, situations, thoughts and ideas, happenings and movement, are the mind dancing as form, while awareness lies silent and eternal."

Just then Mike rejoined them with a tray of drinks which they all happily availed of. P. continued, "When you're thinking of yourself, imagining yourself, you're defining yourself; and you're defining yourself only by that which you already know -taking a type and maybe adjusting it somewhat now and again. When you truly live in the moment you abandon your self image, but you *gain* the realisation that you are not ever truly defined in who you can be. To make choices in every moment without deference to the last ones or the ones to come is to live a life that is truly original and is *you* completely. The character that you leave behind as the sum of your moments will be someone absolutely beyond type and beyond cliché. Breaking down the boundaries of definition for those who follow. The whole universe of possibility opens up. Absolute freedom to express your true self in every moment -the true original, uncontained even by your own mind. The master of infinite possibility. The external forms really make no difference. They're completely empty. Everyone comes from and contains within them pure awareness. Our purpose is to connect with and manifest this awareness in the world of forms."

Keehan looked puzzled. "Yeah but surely ya can't be completely free to do whatever ya want?" He pointed over towards the stained glass window on the opposite side of the room. "I could smash that window couldn't I, but I'd still have to deal with the owner, and the cops or whatever." Mike nodded agreeably and looked over at P. who continued unfazed, "To be aware, is to be aware of the possible consequences of every act. To be truly aware is to realise that you are creating a life; that you have the power to at least question everything that you've been told is real or everything you think is real in every single moment. If you decide then that you should or shouldn't break the window then that's your choice. If you're about to smash it in anger then you have the choice to become aware and say to yourself; is this really me doing this? Or is it my anger? Is it my reputation, or a belief; or someone's comment that pissed me off? The point is that you always have the opportunity to smash the window, even if you're supposedly a 'nice guy' or an 'upstanding citizen.' You have the power to *not* smash it even if you're supposedly a 'thug' or a 'troublemaker.' None of us is anything really; and pure awareness is where we will all meet truthfully, regardless of how your life is; regardless of the body you live in and regardless of the things you have or don't have. The answer is not in any particular idea -It's the absence of ideas. Pure engagement with what is, as it is. What you're doing right now, where you are. It's the fear of being responsible for your own choices that causes people to live in ego -to live in denial and excuses. There are no guidelines in awareness. It's total freedom and total responsibility. That's why absolute awareness is the greatest liberation but can initially be terrifying."

Mike who had been nodding and scratching his beard now joined P. who was polishing off a second Jameson and was beginning to grin drunkenly from ear to ear. "Ego feels safe initially," Mike began. "It's known. It makes you feel concrete, like you're not gonna disappear someday. I used to say to myself when I did something wrong, acted like a dickhead or whatever, that 'It's my personality', 'It's my identity', 'I couldn't help it.' But I know now I was free to act how I acted. Free to say or not say what I did -and that's that. The source of good and evil. Ignorance is our only enemy. And unfortunately ignorance is not so easy to fight. It takes more than swinging a fist or pulling a trigger, firing a missile. It takes strength of character. Only when you are aware of your own freedom can you act authentically and become a real person. A true identity that's fluid and conscious. And live how you want to live. By continually choosing and being aware moment to moment." "And once you realise," P. jumped back in, "How you cannot carry anything with you -not memories, not dreams, not identity, then all there is is experience. To be and then not." They all laughed at P's increasing exuberance as he raised his fist to the ceiling in exclamation. "True enough," Mike agreed, still chuckling as the laughter died down and the pub regained its atmosphere of almost mystical solemnity in the midst of the urban sprawl.

Keehan leaned on the table still smiling to himself as he watched his own finger trace its way down the droplets of condensation on the outside of his glass. After a moment of silent contemplation he looked up. The other four also were sat silently and peacefully, sipping from their glasses.

"Why are ya's tellin me all this?" he asked, and the four of them all looked over at him, still half-lost in their contemplation. Mike took a mouthful of his pint and wiped the foam off the bristles on his upper lip with the back of his sleeve before clearing his throat and leaning in across the table. He looked into Keehan's face and smiled. Hope radiated from his eyes and Keehan felt a warm glow as he began to speak in a whisper that held so much weight it was almost breaking.

"Isn't every persons ultimate goal underneath it all to feel like they don't have to achieve anything? That they don't have to complete themselves or look for validation? Isn't that what what you would wish for someone if you had the chance to change one thing in their lives?" He paused for a moment as he continued to gaze tranquilly into Keehan's eyes. "Wouldn't the world be a spectacular place if everyone knew that? If everyone could believe that they were already perfect somewhere inside themselves and all they have to do is find it. Your life doesn't lack meaning: it's fucking suffocated by meaning. Everything means something beyond what it is, or requires meaning beyond what it is. So you can never see the true beauty in what just is."

He took another sip from his beer. "You found it tonight," he nodded at Keehan, "The start of your real life. The true self that lives inside you. The process of awakening is not something that just happens in a few days -not for everyone at least, but all I want to say is that it is possible for anyone and everyone to start the journey right now no matter what your circumstances. Sometimes you think like if I make that choice, find that answer; then everything will just be normal, whatever that is; and there'll be no more struggle. I can just relax and let life happen. The fact is there will always be struggle. There will be heartbreak. There will be a constant stream of awkward and embarrassing moments. That's what life is. The only answer is to accept that fact and then focus on being able to deal with it -on being the best *you* you can be." P. leaned in and smiled, looking first at Mike and then at Keehan. "It's about seeing where you can go; rather than figuring out which path you need to take or how daunting the journey may be. And so the destination is always nothingness -absolute possibility; and the death of the physical body the only ever certainty in this life. Purpose is not a thing to do it's a state of being, a constant discovery. Life doesn't come with an instruction manual, it's not a puzzle to be completed...It's poem that you write every day." P. drained his glass. "And we, my friend," he concluded, "are all beings of light, hidden under veils of confusion."

CHAPTER 21

Mike came back empty handed. "The bar's closed," he informed them. "I'm gonna head over to a mates for a couple if ya's fancy it?" Laura and Gary agreed to head over for one anyway. It had been a long night and tiredness was starting to creep in on them.

Keehan, who'd had an especially exhausting and revelatory night was feeling like he needed some space to process everything and decided against going with them. "I'm just gonna go for a bit of a walk and head back," he told them.

The night had felt like a conclusion and having suddenly remembered the note once again -the reason he had come in the first place: he decided now would be as good time as any to finally find the source and put his adventure to rest; feeling ready to return to real life once again. "Ya sure you're alright?" Gary asked getting up and nodding at Keehan's nose which still had the tiniest flecks of dried blood speckled around his septum and nostrils. "Yeah I'm grand now," Keehan replied and genuinely meant it for the first time in a long time. "I just fancy a bit of a stroll to get a bit of air and clear my head." Gary was sceptical about sending him wandering the streets alone but decided to let him go. "Grand," he replied. "Sure give me a text when ya get back to the house and we'll see you back there." P., Laura and Mike smiled and waved goodbye. "See ya's in a bit," Keehan waved back. He walked out behind them into the cold night. Stopping for a moment to inhale a mouthful of the fresh, crisp harbour air, he reached into his pocket and took out his wallet in which he had tucked the slip of paper with the address written on it.

Looking at the map he saw that it was not far from where he was and so he set off confidently in that direction. He walked swiftly, having gained a second wind and a new jolt of energy as soon as he had left the pub and gotten out in the fresh air.

The city sounds grew fainter and the lights became sparse as he entered the residential areas. The occasional bike lay cold and abandoned on the footpath, and along with several footballs scattered here and there, were the only obvious signs of human presence. Only the occasional window was still illuminated by someone keeping the night alive.

Keehan stopped in front of a sign on the corner of what appeareded to be the entrance to a cul-de-sac. The words on the sign read *Hillview Drive*. It was indeed the street he had been looking for.

He swallowed and began to walk slowly up the footpath with a slight growing trepidation. For the first time since he'd left the others it occurred to him that he had no idea why he was even there, especially at this time of night. Even if someone had been there he couldn't disturb them at this time. He would have to come back in the morning regardless. And in fact, he wasn't quite sure he even wanted to meet them at all. The honest truth was that something beyond rational thought had sent him on this mission, and although he couldn't explain it, he'd felt all along that it was something of vital importance. He checked the address on the piece of paper once more to confirm the number. *86 Hillview Drive.* He looked at the house to his left. There was a brass number five in cursive script on the door. Beside it number seven. He would have to go much further in.

He walked casually through the empty street, looking around as he went. The houses were older; from the eighties maybe. Solid. A little weather-beaten and worse for wear but generally in quite good shape. He was feeling a little tense still but had resigned to his need for some sort of closure and willed himself on despite the fluttering in his stomach.

Getting deeper in now he began to check the numbers again looking back and forth from one side of the street to the other. He was nearly there. *Eighty-three... eighty-four... eighty-five...* and then a gap. He moved across to the next house. *Eighty-eight.* He stood and looked around. There were no more houses on the opposite side of the street, just a fence which continued down the road for a few metres, turned left and then turned again up along his side of the street; enclosing the road in its final destination. Keehan took a deep breath and walked cautiously into the gap between the two houses which was enveloped in a deep black shadow, to see if the row continued down the side. His eyes adjusting to the darkness he began to make out a small patch of grass leading to a tall fence, which appeared to run the whole way up behind the rows of houses. On either side of him, behind the houses, were small gardens; both containing washing lines and various scattered toys. Keehan stood in the gap between the two houses and looked around bemusedly as though hoping to find some clue or explanation for why there wasn't a house there where there should have been. All of a sudden a jolt of laughter burst out from deep inside him, catching him by surprise; and he let out a sharp, loud guffaw almost before he could stop himself.

Instantly aware that he was standing in someone's back garden in the middle of the night he managed to stifle his laugh and retained his composure, and had a quick look around to ensure that all was still asleep. Seeing no lights come on and hearing nothing but silence he shrugged and walked over to the fence to peer over, still grinning quietly to himself.

He could see nothing on the other side of the fence but an expanse of green grass with small groupings of trees on either side. Squinting in the darkness he began to make out a path running around the outside in front of the trees. He noticed for the first time the towering rugby posts that had been hidden behind the trees and speculated it must be the park near Gary's flat. Grabbing the top of the fence he hauled himself up and over as stealthily as he possibly could, trying to avoid making too much noise; and dropped down on the other side.

He looked around trying to orientate himself and realised he was at the direct opposite end to where he had been before. He turned to have one more conclusive look at the backs of the houses of Hillview Drive before turning and heading off across the park back towards the main entrance and Gary's flat.

Hearing muffled voices as he passed a clump of bushes Keehan peered over and saw a group of about eight what looked to him to be sixteen or seventeen year olds, who were sitting on the grass drinking cans of cheap cider. A sharp spike of fear fired inside him and he felt his body tense up and become tight and rigid. But just as quickly as it appeared, the feeling disappeared and he relaxed again into his casual stroll. He nodded and smiled at the group of adolescents and walked on as they nodded back and looked at him curiously before resuming their chatting and laughing. *A bunch of kids,* he thought to himself *-each with their own lives and problems, just looking for something to connect with like everyone else...*

He felt a little ashamed as he examined his own initial reaction to them. How he almost dismissed as thugs or probably would have before -would have looked at them and treated them as extensions of his own fear and shuffled past them tensely avoiding eye contact: made them into criminals or delinquents just by always treating them as if they were. Of course the prejudice had still leapt to his mind, the same way it always had –at least he knew now that it wasn't real. That he could dismiss it. *And maybe,* he thought, *one of those kids looking at themselves with the same prejudice might also realise that it's not real; that they could be more than how the fearful looked at them.*

Keehan was beginning to gain a sense of responsibility and he liked how it felt. It had none of the connotations of responsibility the way he'd been taught. Of obligation and punishment and laws handed down from above: of churches and policemen and stoic repression of horrid impulses –of towing the line. On the contrary, he felt a light growing inside of him, however tentative; and felt responsible –no, *privileged,* to ensure he brought this light into the world as much as he could. He felt a sense of lawlessness and freedom that came from absolute compassion. A guide that was coming from within himself and cared for nothing but truth. He was suddenly aware of how the act of accepting responsibility for himself had opened up an expansive vista of freedom. Taking full control of his own thoughts and beliefs he had never felt so free. He also realised how seeing the good in human beings made him feel good himself.

He was almost across the park now, basking in his own sense of hope for the future as he approached the bench he had been sitting on the night before. As he got closer he noticed a figure stepping out of the shadow of the trees. Despite it being no more than a silhouette in the darkness, Keehan recognised almost immediately that it was Daniel.

He approached still further and the silhouette's empty form began to clarify into specific features and details: the thin, greasy hair which lay flat and stylessly on his forehead. The beady eyes staring from beneath the line of his fringe. He was wearing a baggy Umbro sweatshirt and the same badly fitting stonewashed jeans. Keehan remembered the night he had looked so powerful, so in control. Now he just looked weak and fragile and confused. Like a lost little boy. Keehan knew that Daniel was the same now as he had been then. The change had been his own, and he was once again almost overcome with gratitude for his newfound perspective. He looked at Daniel now like a mirror of his former self; trapped in anger and fear and just frantically looking for some reprieve.

Daniel, from his apartment window had noticed Keehan crossing the park and had headed down to meet him. Keehan, after recovering quickly from the slight shock of his sudden appearance, greeted him warmly. "Hey man hows it goin'?" he asked. Daniel smiled meekly. "Ah you know. Not too bad" Keehan sensed a reticence in him and it worried him slightly. "What've ya been up to?" he enquired further as he took a seat on the bench and gestured to Daniel to join him. "Ah not much," Daniel replied, taking a seat on the bench beside him. He appeared to warm slightly and relax a little more after the initial ambiguity of their meeting for a second time. Keehan waited for a moment for some elaboration but nothing came. A moment of awkward silence passed between them. Keehan detected the sickly sweet banana scent of Jack Daniels as it wafted through the air.

"How've you been doing?" Daniel asked finally. "Ah grand," Keehan replied and began to tell the story of his last few days –about staying with Gary, the parade, the nightclub, Laura and Mike, and the bar by the quay. "How's your nose?" Daniel asked after all that, his eyebrows now lowering and his lips slightly pursed in the beginning of a frown. "My nose, ahh…" Keehan stuttered. "Yeah it's grand now. The pain is gone." He was slightly disappointed by the question, having himself considered it a minor, almost inconsequential detail in a tale of such nuance, drama and mind-blowing liberation; but he conceded that it was a legitimate question to ask even if dishearteningly off his own track. "Who were the lads?" Daniel persisted. "Ah I dunno," Keehan replied, attempting to recall to memory some specific details of his assailants but coming up with nothing remarkable. "Some guys. I'm not really bothered. I was bein' a bit of a tool." He looked over at Daniel who was looking down at the ground, his cheeks beginning to redden. "Yeah but still," Daniel muttered, "Ya didn't deserve a kick in the face." Keehan shrugged his shoulders. "Ah probably not. But sure... It's done now anyway." Daniel lifted his head up and looked at Keehan. "D'ya wanna come up to the flat for a bit?" he asked, nodding in the direction of the nearby building.

Keehan thought for a second. He was exhausted and wanted nothing more than to go back to Gary's and sleep. On the other hand he was still feeling quite merry and pleased with himself and thought Daniel looked like someone in need of a friend. "Yeah okay, I'll head up for a minute," he agreed and got up to join Daniel as they headed up the path towards the shortcut that led to his apartment.

CHAPTER 22

In about five minutes the two were standing outside Daniel's door as he wiggled the key in the lock until it clicked and he pushed it open. Keehan followed Daniel into the apartment and looked around. The place was a complete mess. Worse even than his own room back home. There were clothes scattered in random piles on the floor and the coffee table and draped over chairs. Keehan could see microwave dinner trays with the remnants of meals still in them and knives and forks that obviously hadn't been washed for weeks. Scattered among the piles of clothes were empty crisp packets, Coke cans and other assorted rubbish. "Sit down there," Daniel said as he went through to another room while gesturing towards a couch that was pushed up against the back wall. The couch like the rest of the room was covered in clothes and rubbish. Keehan grimaced. He stepped reluctantly across the room and stopped for a moment to contemplate the huge mound on the couch, before tentatively pushing it to the side; careful to avoid its collapse. Having made a gap just big enough for him to fit he examined it quickly to make sure he wouldn't be sitting in or on anything he would regret. Deeming it sufficiently hygienic he took a seat. Just then he heard

Daniel call in from the other room. "D'ya remember before, I told you I had something I wanted to show you." Keehan's chest tightened. He could picture the scene as vividly as if it had been happening right before his eyes. He remembered how upon hearing the phrase that night; though on the face of it a rather innocuous phrase -something about the intensity of Daniel's eyes and the context that surrounded it had left it sitting uneasily in his mind to be pushed out of his awareness in the time since. As if he needed to pretend he hadn't heard it. As though if he ignored it defiantly enough it would disappear forever. And now it all came flooding back. Of course he didn't know for sure to what Daniel was referring, and hadn't been given any specific clues, but he knew it wouldn't be anything good. "Ummm, yeah I think so," Keehan called back in.

His voice was trembling slightly but he was just managing a somewhat resolute hold on the inner peace he'd finally found. It had fallen away at Daniels beckon but had begun to hum again weakly. It was growing stronger and medicating his panic somewhat as he focused on it with all the concentration he could muster to keep his mind from spiralling, as he waited hopefully but with trepidation to find out for sure what Daniel wanted to show him. His worst fear was realised when Daniel entered the room swigging from a bottle of Jack Daniels in one hand, and with his other holding a sleek, shiny, black handgun. *Oh fucking bullshit,* Keehan thought to himself. Just as his life had seemed to be coming back together now he was straight back into another mess.

"People are worms," Daniel was exclaiming, finding boldness and conviction in the bottle. "Fucking spineless worms.

Like them pricks that kicked you in the face." With the hand which was holding the gun he scooped the pile of rubbish which Keehan had edged aside and swept it onto the ground. He sat down on the couch beside Keehan and looked at him as though waiting for validation.

Keehan's mind was attempting to spin off again as it did into fantasy, as various heroic scenarios and happy endings to this situation began to flash in front of him. Luckily though now his ability to accept reality was growing stronger and he realised that nothing good was likely to come if he didn't focus on what was actually happening. Each time he glanced from Daniel's face and caught sight of the gun on his lap however the panic jumped up inside him, leaving him hovering between focused clarity and a catatonic stare.

"I dunno…," Keehan began tentatively as his voice, though cracking slightly, finally came to him and his mind all of a sudden became a barrage of faces. Of Mike and Gary and Laura who had been so good to him and taken care of him without question. Of Kevin and Melissa and baby Jake –and Lisa and James; who he'd hardly thought of in the swirl of the last few days. Of his mother and Alan. He coughed to clear his throat. "I dunno, he stuttered, "I guess everyone's just confused and like… tryin' to deal with their shit…" He picked up a chocolate bar wrapper that was lying on the couch beside him and began to fold it and crease it nervously. "Like it's hard…It's hard to know what to do… He looked over at Daniel who was turned facing away from him now and was taking another mouthful from the bottle. Keehan continued, "Ya know I'm pretty angry sometimes, and confused, but I dunno…I guess it's just pointless. Like all your doin' is makin' more misery."

He was beginning to build up steam in his argument and he realised that while trying to convince Daniel he was as much attempting to elucidate the answer he'd been looking for himself. "Life seems pretty shit sometimes," he continued. "But I guess the fact that we're here at all is pretty cool. So it must mean something… just bein' alive… There must be some answer -even if we don't know it yet. I guess ya just have to wake up at some point… Because we're gonna die… and death gives meaning to life -so *life* gives meaning to death! So only to die in the middle of life; in the process of experiencing life to the fullest, is the only meaningful way to die…"

"What the fuck are you goin' on about?" interrupted Daniel, who had barely been listening but had been steadily getting drunker and more mired in his own misanthropy. As if Keehan's newfound joy and hope for the future was surrounding him, cutting him off, and pushing him more inside his own misery. Having been certain he'd found someone finally to share his nihilistic vision: someone who would support his yearning for the apocalyptic; he now found himself feeling more alone than ever. His jaw clenched tightly and his hands beginning to tremble, he suddenly jumped up onto his feet, brandishing the gun.

Keehan instinctively ducked and held his hands up in front of his face as Daniel swung towards him and stood over him, pointing the gun directly at him. He screwed his eyes closed tightly, not believing that Daniel would actually shoot him but finding instinct hard to fight.

After a few seconds when the shot hadn't come, Keehan tentatively opened his eyes and peeked out from between his arms. Daniel was still stood over him with the gun pointed directly at him. Keehan winced. Daniel's face was contorted with rage, but Keehan knew that it was not directed at him. He could see Daniel's eyes had become glassy as though his attention had left the room and returned into memory as he stood impotently but defiantly holding the gun pointed towards Keehan.

Keehan was just about to attempt to slowly get up when Daniel's attention returned. He froze as Daniel fixed him with an apathetic stare. For a moment the two stared at each other, neither saying a word. All of a sudden, Daniel spun and bounded towards the front door.

He wobbled slightly as he reached for the door handle and missed it on the first attempt. Managing to catch it on the second attempt he flung the door open and rushed down the stairs with a furious conviction that was offset somewhat by his wavering balance.

Keehan sat frozen to the spot gaping at the open door. Although he wasn't sure exactly what to do he knew he had to act. In fact all possible outcomes in which he could do nothing and still maintain this sense of peace –this sense of being *real:* floated in the ethereal distance and dissolved as he refused to give them form. The situation was before his eyes; he knew he was in it. All possible futures disappeared, as he pushed past his momentary hesitation and leapt up to follow Daniel where he was headed, out onto the street. He realised in that moment that this wasn't an abstract theory or idea but a direct call for action in some form. A decision to live and fight for life, or flounder in a world of passivity and hopelessness.

He flew down the stairs, the adrenaline now pumping through his veins compensating for his almost absolute exhaustion. He knew Daniel was not too far ahead of him. He could hear his drunken clambering just below; and he had almost caught up with him just as Daniel reached the buildings front door and almost fell out through it. Keehan, not far behind him, grabbed the door just before it swung closed.

The sun was almost rising as he stepped out onto the street and he squinted in the early morning twilight. Partially blinded for a moment, he paused and shaded his eyes with his hand while they re-adjusted. He looked around to see which direction Daniel had gone in.

Looking to his left he immediately spotted him less than ten yards away, lying face down on the ground. He had obviously fallen and appeared to be attempting with difficulty to push himself back onto his feet with the pistol still in his hand. Seeing a perfect opportunity and without stopping to think, Keehan sprinted over to him. Before Daniel had a chance to recuperate and get back on his feet, Keehan jumped on his back to hold him down.

Laying on top of him in order to pin him to the ground with his full body weight, Keehan reached for Daniel's right hand which was still clasping the gun and began to squeeze it, digging his thumb into the side of his knuckle. With a yelp and a jerk, Daniel loosened his grip and the gun skidded across the smooth, cold tarmac. Keehan, almost completely sober now, and his reactions considerably faster than Daniel's, leapt to grab the gun, stumbling awkwardly in an attempt to get back on his feet as he scooped the pistol off the ground.

Seeing the shimmering sparkle of the canal in the near distance as he recovered his footing, Keehan began to run towards it. He was pretty sure that Daniel wouldn't be chasing him but all the same he didn't look back and he didn't slow down. Reaching the bank of the smooth, glassy water he swung the gun behind him and launched it into the canal with all the strength he could muster. It sailed through the air for what seemed to him like an unnaturally long time before finally dropping with a distant plop; then began to sink slowly down through the surface of the water, sending ripples radiating to break neatly and hurriedly against the far bank.

He stood looking out over the water for a moment trying to catch his breath. The slow but consistent diminishing of the ripples soothed him as the surface of the water once again turned to glass, like the last layer of topsoil on a grave in which a terrible secret was buried. His breath slowed down to normal as he waited and watched for the evidence of the horror he'd potentially just witnessed to disappear completely. He turned to look back at Daniel. He could see him in the distance, still in the same spot he'd left him but sat upright now, clutching his knees to his chest. Keehan began to walk back over towards him, approaching him cautiously at first for fear of a reprisal.

As he got closer he could see clearly the wet tracks of tears running down Daniels cheeks and down his chin. Daniel raised his face up mournfully from the ground as Keehan approached. Keehan stopped. Looking into Daniel's eyes he read, as clearly as if it had been written in plain English; the same sense of absolute futility and sad resignation he'd felt himself just days before. He could see Daniel without the conviction for hatred he had previously held. Without it, the illusory power that it had seemed to bring had proved to be as substantial as candyfloss in the rain. It had vanished completely, to be replaced ironically with something solid and real; even if that something was sat now on the road, clutching its scratched bony knees, with tear stains tracing their way down its face. "I was only going to scare 'em," Daniel mumbled. "I didn't really want to hurt anyone." His voice was trembling as his gaze returned to the ground he was sat on. Keehan looked down at Daniel and saw him consumed by his true being completely for the first time since they'd met and was heartened and more than a little relieved. Somehow he knew in that moment that there was a real chance for both of them now to move on at last and to finally reach something resembling happiness. That despite having written himself off only days ago he had found reason to believe that he wasn't a lost cause and he could see the potential now in Daniel to have the same kind of realisation. He smiled tiredly at him and offered him his hand to pull him up. Daniel looked up at him hesitantly for a moment then extended his arm as he began to push himself up off the ground. Keehan grabbed his arm and pulled him up and they headed back inside.

As they trudged their way back up the stairs to Daniel's apartment, Keehan attempted to impart some of the wisdom he had gleaned along the way. "I feel like I woke up," he was saying wearily but happily as they neared the top of the stairs where Daniel's open door swung slowly and heavily in the slight draught. "Like I finally saw things as they truly are." Keehan despite everything was still quite jazzed about his experience and feeling genuinely excited about the future for the first time in quite a while. His courageous act this night of preventing Daniel making a life-altering and potentially ruinous mistake felt like a confirmation of everything P. and Mike had said to him and confirmation that what he'd had that evening had been a truly positive, life-changing experience. Something that would send his life in an entirely new direction he could never have foreseen. "Like I was tellin' ya about before," he continued, "When I just stopped tryin' to control everything and my mind emptied, everythin' felt good; really peaceful." "Yeah I guess I kinda get that," Daniel replied haggardly. He was more than anything now just relieved and grateful that that episode had come to an end without him doing something that he would have regretted for the rest of his life. Beginning to sober up now he could see the reality of how close he'd come to the edge. And what had been inspiring as a fantasy; in its near actualisation in the cold light of morning had horrified him. The potential damage he could have been responsible for had suddenly become a tangible reality and he was scared. Scared of losing himself to hatred and delusion. Scared of his own mind. The pressure of the need for power, for greatness; had almost crushed him completely and had led him to a place he could now see he never wanted to be. But for now all the bitterness and anger and the plans for revenge had been replaced by true humility and relief at being able to return to his own bed, away from the world: free to start again in the morning.

They stopped for a moment outside his door. "Well, I'm

gonna head back and get some sleep before I collapse," Keehan smiled, after offering to stay the rest of the night but being reassured by Daniel that it was not necessary with a subtle but appreciative smile. He was confident that Daniel was safe to leave alone and that he would in fact be happier in that moment to be left alone; and he was more than a little relieved to get back to his own bed. "I'll drop over before I head back home," he added. Daniel smiled back wearily. "Yeah, okay," he muttered and shuffled back inside, closing the door gently and preciously behind him. Keehan turned and headed back down the stairs to the front door.

As he reached the bottom of the stairs he suddenly felt the weight of the whole night crash down on him. He opened the front door of the apartment block and headed out into the street to begin the walk back towards Gary's, feeling as though his legs might not have the strength to carry him the whole way. At the same time he was happy. His exhaustion was the exhaustion of a full night. The weight of life rather than the weight of apathy: which would enrich his sleep and awaken him in the morning with a new freshness.

Just as he finally reached Gary's front door he met Gary rushing out. "There you are," Gary exclaimed, a wave of relief washing over his face. "Where were ya? I got home and you weren't there. I tried to call you and it wouldn't go through." Keehan took out his phone. The screen was blank. He pressed the button on the side a couple of times but got no response. The battery had obviously run out at some point over the course of the night. "I was just gonna go back lookin' for ya," Gary continued. "Uhh shit. Sorry," Keehan replied, putting the phone back in his pocket, "My battery must have died.

I..." He sighed as he attempted to find a simple explanation for where he had been over the course of the last couple of hours but was struggling to find an adequately concise summation. Gary could see that he was struggling. "Come on, let's go inside," he said gesturing towards the door.

They headed back inside and Keehan slumped on the couch. He groaned with pleasure as he felt his aching muscles drift into its plush softness until there was almost no separation between it and himself. "Tea?" Gary asked. "Yeahhhhh." Keehan panted. "A small one please." Gary disappeared into the kitchen and returned moments later with two piping hot cups of tea. He handed one to Keehan and took a seat on the couch, and Keehan proceeded to give a relatively concise review of the events of the night as best he could, as his body and mind began to shut down completely.

"Jesus,' Gary exclaimed as Keehan arrived at the moment of their meeting at the front door. He necked the last draught of tea in his cup and set it on the coffee table. Keehan's eyelids were beginning to droop heavily. "Go on and get yourself to bed," Gary said, flabbergasted at the drama that had unfolded and not quite sure what to make of it all. He had a hundred questions but he could see that Keehan was dead on his feet and knew they'd have to wait until morning. He picked up the two cups and dropped them in the sink and they both said goodnight and retired to their respective rooms to go to bed.

Keehan pulled off his clothes and lay down happily in the dark, and within seconds he had fallen into a deep sleep such as he hadn't had for years. He dreamed deeply and pleasantly, completely oblivious as the city outside gradually began to awaken into the new day.

CHAPTER 23

The previous day's events swirled in Keehan's mind and morphed and shifted and blended into each other. Their form lay drifting in and out of clarity and their meaning lay fizzling brightly in his consciousness as he yawned and stretched and sat up in the bed. It was half past eleven and the sun was bursting into the room through the thick cream poly-cotton blind, imbuing the white walls with a golden lustre.

He rolled over on the bed far enough that he could stretch across and pull the cord of the blind, which rolled up with a slap exposing the full glory of the day. He lay for a moment gazing up at the turquoise-blue sky, then rolled slowly to the other side of the bed and off the edge onto his feet.

Pulling on his jeans and his shoes, he stumbled groggily into the kitchen listening for Gary, but the flat appeared to be deserted. There was a note on the kitchen table. Keehan went over and picked it up. He felt a slight jolt of shock mixed with excitement as he read that James and Lisa had called while he was asleep. They had come to look for him and apparently were now with Gary down on the strand. Keehan checked his phone to see if there had been any missed calls or messages from them. There didn't appear to be any which he found strange. He shrugged and smiled to himself as he readied to head down and join them. Unable to ignore the rumbling in his stomach he decided first to fix himself a bowl of cereal.

He sat down at the table and began to eat his bowl of corn-flakes slowly and carefully, feeling each mouthful slide down his neck. He thought he must have never enjoyed a meal so much, as he felt the rumbling in his stomach gradually cease with each swallow and be replaced by a feeling of fullness. After finishing he gave his bowl a quick rinse, grabbed his sunglasses and headed out to meet the others.

As he walked, feeling his cheeks flush in the unseason-ably warm sunshine, he considered his place in the universe. Not much had changed. Not in the case of his overall life. He was still in the same world with the same obstacles. But he felt better than he ever had before. Something was vastly different. Something like clarity. He felt like a fog had lifted, and for the first time he could see clearly, and he realised that that was all he ever really wanted. The ability to choose his direction -to trust his own clarity uncluttered by the noise of voices in his head.

As he reached the edge of the strand he immediately spot-ted Gary with Lisa and James sat on the sand looking out over the sea. The three turned as he approached and he smiled at them and raised his hand in an almost-wave. They smiled and watched him as he took a seat beside them on the dry golden-grey sand.

"Well," James greeted him merrily. "I hear you had quite a busy night?" Keehan rolled his eyes. "God, don't get me started," he muttered wryly and the others laughed. They leaned in to listen eagerly as he began once again to recount his tale thoroughly from the time he had left Gary and the others in the marina bar the previous night to the time he arrived back at the flat. He made sure to de-emphasise the role of the note in motivating him to begin his journey in the first place and pass it off as a fairly inconsequential diversion; a curious thing that he happened to remember. He felt that it would raise more questions than he was really ready himself to answer yet, and luckily the others were happy to accept it as having no particular meaning or relevance, for now at least. Considering the drama that followed, it was reasonable enough that it would be relegated in importance behind the details of his relationship with Daniel and the events that had transpired between them.

"So quite an eventful night after all," Lisa commented as Keehan, in his element, finally reached the culmination of his saga. "Mmmm," he agreed, nodding. "Quite eventful."

They all took a moment to allow it all to sink in and sat basking in the sun watching the waves roll over each other and sink and roll again in a hypnotic perpetual movement.

After a few moments Gary turned to Keehan, his eyes narrowed and the corners of his mouth sunk down solemnly. "Did ya hear about yer one Kara Hughes?" he asked. Keehan shook his head. "No." "She died this morning." Keehan's eyes opened wide in shock. "No way," he muttered, and stared dumbfounded at Gary. "I'm sure I seen her at the party last night," he said as lines of disbelief furrowed his brow. "Yeah," Gary continued. "It was after we left. I heard she was doin' coke and had an overdose or a reaction to it or something. Dunno if its true, that's what they're sayin'." "Fuck," Keehan muttered and turned to look out over the water.

For a moment they sat in silence again and just watched the sunshine that pierced through the azure blue sky glittering off the rippled waves below. Keehan thought about the girl he had seen with his own eyes only hours before. The flesh and blood epitome of glamour and good times; and how she would never get old: would never see another moment of this existence, and how sad that was. In a sense he was thinking about himself also and all the time that he had spent living inside his own daydreams; giving importance to ideas of status and prestige and his own superiority; and feelings of bitterness and hate; that all faded to nothing when faced with a moment of actual true existence. He listened to the other three chattering and his mind emptied again as he turned around to look at them, feeling a fluttering in his chest as he watched an inimitable miracle happen in front of his eyes. As though the three ephemeral, recognizable faces in front of him and the eternity of all existence were both existing simultaneously, different but the same.

They sat and chatted for some time before Gary got up to leave, having work that evening. Keehan got to his feet also. "Thanks a lot man," he mumbled bashfully, squinting at Gary in the sun. "I really appreciate ya letting me stay an' all." "Ah no bother," Gary replied and smiled and they shook hands. "Drop up again sometime," he added, "the three of ya's," he nodded at James and Lisa. "Yeah we will," Lisa answered. "Definitely," added James and smiled back at Gary. The three of them waved as he turned and began to make his way back up the strand.

"So what's happenin' wit you's? Any craic?" Keehan asked as he sat back down on the sand and turned to James and Lisa.

"Ah no nothing really," James said as he scraped circles in the sand with a stick. "Bits and pieces. We're thinkin' of movin'. Not sure where yet. Probably won't be for another while. We have to try and save some money. But yeah, gonna start doin' something." "We're at least gonna go somewhere for the summer next year," Lisa continued. "I'm pretty sure Sharon is comin' with us too." "Sharon Davies?" Keehan interjected, his heart leaping. His imagined life, with her ever-present, had almost faded over the course of the last day or two, although she had in some form never been far from his thoughts. Now with the sudden shock of her appearance in his life again he felt her suffuse his mind once more. It was different this time though. He had lived. He had survived on his own. He felt good about himself and his place in the world. And he felt a deep caring for her that for the first time seemed like it might actually be genuine. An appreciation that he had to give to her for the first time without any thought of recompense and without requiring ownership of her or her image. "Yeah," Lisa continued, smiling at Keehan's stupefaction. "We started hangin' out a bit since ya left. She's really cool."

Keehan felt a tightness building in his chest as he remembered the last time he saw her. He took a deep breath and allowed the emotions of the memory to settle and dissolve. After a moment the feeling of tightness in his chest dissipated somewhat and he relaxed again. "God, I was a real dick to her," he said, smiling bashfully as he looked out at the sky and resolved to never be so careless again. "Yeah you were a bit," Lisa said and James laughed. "So is that it now for your celebrity career?" she asked, an affectionate smirk spreading across her face. Keehan laughed. "Ah I dunno. I'm not really bothered anymore. I suppose I'll just see what happens." "Any plans at all?" Lisa asked. "Ah nothing in particular yet," Keehan answered, rubbing his chin thoughtfully. "But I feel like gettin' up in the morning, I guess that's a start."